BORN TO BE WILDE

IMMORTAL VEGAS, BOOK 3

JENN STARK

D1519553

For Geoffrey

THE STAR.   VII   ACE ♣ CUPS.

CHAPTER ONE

Tonight's assignment had everything a girl could ask for: fairy-tale palaces, mad kings, Victorian decorators with a serious case of the swans.

I tucked my Tarot cards back into my clutch. The limo rolled to a stop in front of Castle Neuschwanstein and I fixed my expression into polite indifference as I was helped out of the limo and into the cool Bavarian evening. So what if I was walking into the original Disneyland castle? My daydreams of princesses and dashing knights had long since detoured into far darker territory.

The line through security at the palace's main entrance was short. Only the crème de la crème of the international art community had been invited for tonight's exclusive art auction, and my own letter of introduction was accepted without comment. Given that I'd been sent by one of the richest collectors in America, it should be. Hotelier Armaeus Bertrand had money, power, and a known weakness for *objets d'art* — the older and the more arcane the better. Granted, the leader of the ultrasecret, ultramagical Arcana Council had also seemed a touch too earnest about the piece he'd wanted me to grab tonight...but his finder's fee had been all the incentive I'd needed. Given my extracurricular interests, money was always in short supply.

BORN TO BE WILDE

"Your bag, miss?" The burly security officer held out his hand and hesitated the barest moment as he discovered the silk-wrapped Tarot deck tucked in with my lipstick and credit cards. He glanced up at me.

"For luck," I said. "Check them if you'd like. They're only cards." The top three had been turned back into the deck already, their message clear. The Star, the Seven of Swords, and the Ace of Cups were waiting for me within these walls, and I wanted to get on with it.

After a perfunctory scan, the guard did his German best not to look at me like I was a loon. I gave him my standard "eccentric American" look, then I was through.

A line of auction officials herded us quickly through the courtyard and a half-dozen chambers before we all stepped into the dazzling throne room of King Ludwig II. Fantastically lush paintings, gilded scrollwork, and ornate tapestries lined the walls above the draped auction exhibits. My gaze moved up, up, up…and I stilled.

Stars. A virtual constellation of stars spun out in all directions from the throne room. As the general horde moved forward toward the musicians and hors d'oeuvres, I picked one branch of the celestial trail and followed it into one side antechamber, then another.

Each of the small rooms contained more art—these pieces uncovered. They did not, however, contain the piece I was looking for.

According to Armaeus, Ludwig II didn't just harbor an extreme affection for elegant waterfowl. He'd hidden a cup of great renown somewhere amid those feathered friends. And I was supposed to find it.

The third chamber held no interest for me, but the fourth seemed more promising. I nodded to the docent at the door and moved into the small room. At least the shadows here were long and quiet, in sharp contrast to the crash of Wagnerian music that had begun swelling from the next chamber. I relaxed my tension a notch. Any place that allowed me to avoid over-the-top opera music was okay by me.

I stepped deeper into the shadows, and squinted into the gloom toward the dimly lit jewelry display—

My head cracked against the wall.

Pain blossomed above my right ear as stars of an entirely different universe exploded in front of my eyes.

"Sara Wilde. What a lovely surprise."

I flipped around, but Nigel Friedman's hand was at my throat, and my attempted cry of outrage sounded alarmingly gopher-like. The best I could do, given my lack of oxygen. The fist of the ex-UK Special Forces all-star tightened around my esophagus as he shoved me farther up against the wall.

"Who sent you here?" Nigel's polite British accent complemented perfect features, a well-cut suit, and expensive cologne, and his lips twitched with satisfaction as I clawed at his manicured fingers.

"Client," I managed, attempting to triangulate the precise location of the man's groin despite my blurring vision. *Seven of Swords*, my brain pounded as I struggled for air. Seven of Swords. Deception, surprise, and time for a change of strategy. Sometimes my cards could be painfully on the nose.

"Which one?" Nigel flexed his fingers against my windpipe as he waited for my answer.

There really was no reason to lie to him, even if he was my most irritating artifact-finding competitor.

I couldn't resist, though. Habits.

"Mercault," I gasped as Nigel's gaze sharpened. He

abruptly relaxed his grip, allowing me to slide back down the richly painted wall. As expected, the name of the French kingpin of the arcane black market served as a universal "open sesame" for Nigel's choke hold. The Brit always was too curious for his own good.

Unfortunately, however, said Brit continued to stare at me with renewed interest. Renewed interest from Nigel Friedman was always bad.

"There were rumors he'd escaped the massacre," he murmured, tilting his head. "Were you part of the reason why?" In the shadowed chamber, he seemed much larger than when I'd seen him last. Then again, when I'd seen him last, we'd both been completely naked. The two of us knocking over the same Amazonian orgy for the same ancient fertility idol. So my perspective was a little off.

"Maybe I was." I lifted a hand to my neck. "Maybe I wasn't. What are you doing here anyway? Because we'd better not be looking for the same thing. I'd hate to see you miss out twice."

"We're not." Nigel curled his upper lip in disdain. He was really good at that. "We should return to the main hall, however." He turned slightly at a noise in the hallway, then uttered an impressively impolite word that still sounded refined, coming from him. "Too late."

I scowled, palpating my crushed thyroid. "Too late for —"

Nigel didn't give me time to finish the question. He turned back and pushed me up against the wall once more, only this time his mouth found mine in a brutal, teeth-rattling kiss while his hand snaked behind my neck. His lips were surprisingly soft, his body rock solid, but the look in Nigel's eyes as they bored into mine wasn't amorous, exactly, despite the intensity of his gaze.

Play along, those eyes seemed to say.

I could work with that.

I'd never kissed Nigel Friedman before, and I found the experience far more enjoyable than I would've expected. I was beginning to wonder if he'd feel me up as part of the charade when newcomers breached the doorway and light flooded the room.

"Nigel!" The man at the door burst into a flood of embarrassed German, but I appreciated the distraction, if only to get a good look at the room around me with the benefit of light. As expected, there were more swans, but none of the Parsifal imagery that dominated the throne room. That meant the secret cubby hiding the cup I was searching for wasn't here...but it couldn't *actually* be in the throne room, right? That place was way too crowded.

Nigel's answering explanation to our interrupters was polite, perfunctory, and apparently satisfactory, despite all those harsh German consonants. Peeling me off the wall, he draped his arm over my shoulder. He wasn't a big man, but he was well built, and I knew from experience he was both quick and strong. I knew from very *recent* experience he had a mean choke hold too. So, I allowed myself to be pulled forward, smiling and blushing credibly. Then I slipped off as soon as we entered the main room.

I attempted to slip off, anyway.

"Not so fast." Nigel was at my ear, his hand resting lightly on the small of my back. The sleek material fit me tightly, so I could feel the weight of the Brit's hand—and would have felt its warmth if he wasn't such a cold-blooded bastard. "What does Mercault have you looking for? I thought the French art had been completely recovered from this site."

"There's always more French art to be recovered." Not untrue. Castle Neuschwanstein, original home of Mad King Ludwig, had served as one of the de facto Nazi hiding places for gold, artifacts, and precious art, much of it stolen from France during the occupation. A great deal of that art had been reclaimed immediately after the war, but there remained rumors of more treasures to be found in the endless castles dotting the lush German countryside. "Mercault heard of the Nazi gold getting dumped at the Rarity show last month. He thinks it's a good time to grab the rest of the Third Reich's goodies before they find their way into less discerning hands." I turned to him. "Who's *your* client, since we're on the subject? I didn't think MI6 went in for lost art."

"They don't. There's new blood in the game, Viktor Dal. And trust me, he's not looking for art." He peered at me. "You know him?"

"Viktor Dal?" I blinked at him, weathering an eerie flash of déjà vu. I *had* heard the name before, but the guy I'd met ten years ago hadn't had the kind of money it took to hire Nigel Friedman. He hadn't had the money to pay for a decent shave. He'd been a shrink for the Memphis city school district, and a pretty mediocre one at that. Definitely a different Dal.

"Never heard of him," I said. "More to the point, now seems an odd time for a new client to break into the arcane black market. What's he—"

Before Nigel could respond, a tapering of music recalled our attention to the front of the room, and the crush of people shuffled forward. Nigel let go of me a little too easily this time. I didn't trust the guy, sure, but tonight in particular he rubbed me the wrong way, setting aside his unexpected and frankly unnecessary kiss. What had that been about?

6

I brushed my hand against my mouth, then scrutinized my fingers. Nope, no skin-eating poison. A quick shake of my hair—nothing there either. But when I slid my hand along the back of my collar, my finger pads connected with a tiny ridge.

Very cute, Nigel. I left the bug where it was for the time being. Nigel was dangerous, and he was nosy. But if he thought I was handled for the moment, he'd relax. Mulling over my next move, I focused on the room around me as our host spoke first in German and then English, welcoming us to Neuschwanstein. I didn't have much time now. I needed to find the cup before the art auction ended, then exit stage right.

My gaze drifted up to the ceiling again. Yep, stars. Got that part.

Still, I forced myself to study the ceiling more carefully this time, trying to utilize all my senses, including the extrasensory ones. This was newish territory for me, but I didn't have time for more dead ends. Up until a short while ago, my work as an artifact hunter for the Arcana Council and other paying clients had relied almost exclusively on my ability to read and interpret Tarot cards. It was a skill that proved very handy when it came to ferreting out the kind of magical trinkets that went for top dollar among the rich, powerful, and occasionally psychic.

After I'd started working with the Council about a year ago, however, things had gotten a little weirder. I'd begun to be able to find things with psychic abilities that didn't rely on the turn of a card. Even now, as I peered at the ceiling, something shifted in my gaze, some of the stars appearing…different. Brighter. Bolder in a highly defined line that arced down the room. I lifted a hand to my eyes and waved it, but the brightness remained.

Armaeus had activated my third eye a few weeks ago as sort of a gift with purchase while helping me recover from a particularly painful run-in with enemies of the psychic community. He was big into healing. I had an impressive skill for getting injured. So it worked out.

Since then, however, anything remotely supernatural lit up like a glow stick if I focused hard enough. And as I looked up again, I could definitely see a trail of magic arrowing down the ceiling of the throne room toward a far door.

An excited buzz in the room indicated that the auction was about to begin, and the fabric covers were pulled away from the art displays. While everyone else surged forward, I edged back. This was my cue to leave.

My backward progress was stopped as I came back to chest against a large, solid mass: Nigel again.

"Going somewhere?" he murmured in his impossibly civilized British accent.

I turned toward him, taking in his easy smile. Too easy. Every one of my nerves prickled, and the Seven of Swords mocked me in my mind. Something sneaky was going on here, I knew it. But I gave him a wide grin anyway.

"Thought I'd take some air."

"I wouldn't advise it. The castle has trained attack wolfhounds on the grounds, and they're out in force tonight."

I'd been worried about machine guns, not wolfhounds, but I appreciated the heads-up. Especially since I didn't plan to leave this place by the front door. "Good to know." I shrugged. "You find what he had you looking for?"

Nigel fairly hummed with satisfaction. "I did."

8

His move was so fast, I almost missed it, but I instinctively jumped back as the flash of bright metal cuffs streaked across my vision. Blocking Nigel's hand with an elbow jab, I yanked out my Arcana Council-provided hairpin and clipped him in the neck. The voltage from the tiny device lifted Nigel off his feet. I sent a cheer out to the council's tech wizard as the Brit staggered back — stunned but upright, gaping at me in confusion and clearly unable to speak.

Worked for me.

Sliding my hairpin back in place, I turned on my heel and strode quickly down the long throne room, keeping the trail of stars in my peripheral vision. The entire third floor of the castle was open for the event, with docents in every room and additional artwork on display beyond the main hall. No one batted an eye as I turned sharply into the king's bedroom.

More neo-Gothic magnificence greeted me, but I kept my gaze fixed to the ceiling with its swirl of stars. According to Armaeus, Ludwig had gushed to the famed composer Richard Wagner about an esteemed guest he was looking forward to housing at Neuschwanstein. Scholars had assumed that guest was Wagner, the object of Ludwig's massive crush. Armaeus believed that the guest was something far more precious than a king's potential lover, however. He believed it was a famed cup of antiquity, a cup that had come to be represented as the Holy Grail.

I stepped into another antechamber. Here there was only one docent, and only one piece of art on display, a lovely Moorish vase. More to the point, the stars suddenly stopped. I whirled, ignoring the startled look of the docent, who was distracted by a rather wobbly Nigel stumbling into the room.

"Stop her!" Nigel shouted, or tried to shout. The

vocal cords nearest to the impact site of the electrical shock would take a while to recover. I'd been warned not to use the zapper anywhere close to my target's vital organs, if I wanted to stay discreet. Based on the fact that Nigel was starting to twitch violently, his hand slapped to his neck, that'd been a good call. The docent, confused, looked back to me—and then I saw it, right over her shoulder.

A gilded, swan-festooned panel engraved with a silver cup. Silver, not gold.

I turned away from the panel and dashed back to Nigel. "Oh no!" I cried to the docent at the door. "He's having a stroke. A stroke!"

His eyes burning with fury, Nigel lunged at me as the woman gasped. I blocked him easily and swiped my leg behind his knees, dropping him to the floor. I fell down on top of him. Heavily. "Get help!"

As the woman rushed out, I leaned down close to Nigel, not letting up on the pressure I had on his throat. Or on his solar plexus. He gurgled for air, and I growled at him. "Why did this Viktor person send you after me?"

His eyes focused finally, a hint of amusement leeching in. "I always—did like you, Sara," he managed. "Job was—to find—not take you down. Figured I could collect the fee *and* warn you. Win…win."

"But why—" My eyes flared wide as reality dawned. Someone *else* was supposed to collect me. Probably lots of someone elses. I glared at Nigel. "Cutting that warning a little close, aren't you?"

His smile was sardonic, despite the pain. "You'll manage."

The sound of pounding feet barely penetrated through the thick castle walls. I ripped off Nigel's surveillance bug and dropped it on him, then delivered a roundhouse punch for good measure, cracking the man's head against the tile floor. When he went slack, I moved quickly to the cup-engraved panel and shoved all my weight against it.

It sank immediately into the wall, and a second panel beside it popped open, as if the lever had been set yesterday, not generations ago. I dove inside. A quick backward push against the door popped it closed again, but I didn't bet on it staying closed. I sucked in a deep breath and pulled out my hairpin, which was proving to be way more useful than a Swiss Army knife. It crackled to life to illuminate the empty space around me.

The shallow, completely empty space.

The room was a narrow-paneled closet, airtight, but there was nothing in here—no cup, no altar, no easy chair. Nothing to indicate where to go next either, other than back the way I'd come. My card reading could offer no more help—the Seven of Swords and Star had played out, and the Ace of Cups too.

But I still didn't have my prize.

Crap.

Voices erupted on the other side of the panel, and a sudden tattoo of fists pounded on the door. I didn't speak German, but I suspected I wasn't gaining any friends. I swept the light around the room again, struggling to see past its crackling glare. Then I heard the sickening sound of the panel triggering the mechanism in the wall behind me...

Exactly as the wall in front of me spun.

I clicked off the hairpin and burst forward, plastering myself against the wall as it completed its semicircle—carrying me safely around until the wall clicked once more into place. I didn't have time to congratulate myself, though, because in front of me — there was nothing. Not even a floor.

With a sickening lurch, I half bounced, half slid down a sharp stone slope, banging off no fewer than three concrete abutments before landing in a heap atop the remains of a ladder and one particularly creepy set of bones.

I didn't generally have a problem with bones, truth be told. They usually meant their owner was dead. Didn't mean I liked to land on them, though.

Rolling to the side, I flicked my crackling hairpin to life again, instant Zippo. The bones were shrouded in a simple woolen robe, the whole mess a sad puddle at the edge of the floor, as if the deceased had been doubled over when he'd shuffled off this mortal coil, lost in prayer next to the shattered ladder.

In…prayer?

Cautiously edging forward, I poked at the bones. First gently, then with more force. At the second shove, the robed skeleton sprawled over to the side, and from its center rolled a long silver-embossed cup. Not the famed "cup of a carpenter" at all, nor the goblet of a king, but a long Nordic drinking horn rimmed in hammered silver, a thin silver and leather braid attached to it in two places.

Armaeus had given me no indication of what the cup would look like. I'd completely assumed it would look more holy grail than ox horn, but who was I to judge?

More shouting sounded above me, along with some ominous pounding on the wall. I scrambled up, draping the horn around my neck by its braid, and swung my minilight in a wide arc.

The room immediately opened out into a cavern that appeared to have been hewn out of the very rock of Neuschwanstein. I vaguely recalled that there had been two older castles on the site before King Ludwig's getaway had been built.

Whether or not this room dated back to those original castles, there was no question about what it had been used for since then.

"Sweet Christmas." Every avaricious nerve ending in my body snapped to attention, reveling in the bounty spread out before me.

Dozens of crates were stacked in neat rows, many of them lined with neatly stenciled German words, exactly none of which I could read. Piled on the boxes, leaning up and scattered around, were statues and what looked to be covered paintings, as well as huge bowls and jars of pottery and friezes tumbled on top of each other like a Jenga game gone terribly wrong. Some of the boxes had other words scrawled on them—Cyrillic, Egyptian, French, Japanese. A hidden horde of artifacts moldering in the bowels of the Disneyland castle.

More of the famed Nazi stores? Had to be.

But how had it stayed secret so long?

Something rustled in the far shadows, and I swung around, stifling my urge to call out. A whirring flutter, the sound of a flock of birds hopping to a new ledge, whispered through the gloom. My third eye flicked open, and I staggered back.

Magic arced through the chamber in a kaleidoscope of crazy lines running over and under and through the items gathered within. These weren't simply artifacts, they were magical treasures, a virtual cornucopia of the kind of items my clients would spend fortunes on. And I was *here…alone…*with only two hands!

I scanned the room wildly, forcing myself to concentrate on whatever glowed most brightly that

13

was small enough to carry. In the Neuschwanstein Art Grab video game, I'd clearly made it to the bonus round. I was *not* leaving without some sort of prize.

Time, sadly, was not on my side. The sound of the panel cracking open high above me sent me fleeing deeper into the room, toward the far door I could barely see ahead. I scooped up one of the smallest boxes as I rushed past. It shimmered with such a white-hot frenzy that I assumed I'd singe my fingers, but I was happily surprised to find it cool to the touch. I tucked it against my body like a football and bent into my run.

I reached the far end of the room and dived for an arched doorway as the first of the men chasing me shouted out in surprise and wonder. I knew their discovery of the room full of spoils would delay some of them, but from the sound of boots crunching on stone that continued to get nearer, clearly not all. I charged into the doorway — only to practically face-plant into a wall. The corridor beyond teed sharply. I swung right, then left, desperately shoving my crackling pin light into the darkness to see which direction was the better option.

A whistle was the only warning I had.

I flattened to the ground as the men burst through the doorway as well, their cries indicating they'd taken the brunt of the arrow blast I'd triggered. Clicking off my light, I scrambled down the corridor, away from where the arrows of death had emerged, keeping low, racing blindly.

Well, not quite blindly.

As I rushed forward, I felt a keen pressure in the center of my head. Then light pulsed above, around, and through me, illuminating the corridor with a glittering green glow.

14

My third eye apparently had a night vision mode. I vastly preferred relying on my Tarot cards, but any port in a storm.

A path lay dead ahead. As I gained confidence, I gained speed. The tunnel dropped precipitously, carrying me farther into the mountain. I twisted and turned and chose direction after direction, split after split, all following the pulse of energy. Exhaustion weighed on me, the drag of the energy expenditure tapping stores I didn't know I had.

I'd pay for this later, I suspected. But I had to keep moving.

I wasn't sure when the men behind me stopped following, but when the tunnel finally spit me out onto the rocky valley below Neuschwanstein's sister castle, Hohenschwangau, I didn't stop scrambling. Nigel and a posse of hired goons remained at the main castle. And unless he'd been lying to me—there were attack dogs up there too. Attack dogs were never good.

I swung around, squinting in the darkness, using my real eyes to lock down my position. I could see the glow of Hohenschwangau on the next rise. The auction's overflow of parking would be in the village between the two castles, farther down the mountain. There'd be cars there. Motorcycles.

I sucked in a deep breath, preparing to launch myself forward. I could totally do this. With speed and luck and a decided lack of Fido, I could seriously—

"Halt."

The absolute authority in the voice caught me up short. I looked up, then up farther. Ordinarily, I wasn't much on following direct commands. Then again, ordinarily, I wasn't being ordered around by people whose voices made my bones vibrate...and who were sporting honest-to-God wings on their backs.

15

I stopped.

Surrounding me were a half-dozen women, easily topping seven feet tall, their wings adding another few feet to their height and quite a bit to their width as well. They were beautiful in the way an ice storm was beautiful: cold, austere, and hard-angled, their eyes a brilliant light blue, their skin fair to the point of snow. Three were blonde, two brunette, one a deep auburn. They were dressed in long robes cut open over thick breeches, and they did not look happy.

Valkyries. Had to be. Except…were Valkyries a thing? Why hadn't I known they were a thing?

I squared my shoulders as the nearest one gestured to me. When she spoke, her voice sounded of wind and rain, chilling me to my toes. "Mim's horn is sacred to the swan king. It is death to those who drink from it. Are you so ready to die, Sara Wilde?"

I frowned down at the horn slung around my neck. *Mim's horn?* I wasn't up on my Norse mythology, but I vaguely recalled Mim and his compact between heaven and earth, a compact sealed with…a drinking horn. Because that's how the Vikings rolled.

The Valkyrie appeared to be waiting for an answer, however, so I gave the only one I had. "It's not for me. But the person who asked for it isn't big on dying either. It's kind of a thing with him."

The woman's smile was wintry. "Death finds all, eventually, whether they seek it or not." She tilted her head. "We know you."

Given the mythological Valkyries' penchant for identifying who would live and die, this wasn't particularly good news, but her gaze next fell to the box I held clutched in my hand, her white-blonde brows lifting in surprise. She nodded. "Gather your weapons, then, mortal. Your battle is upon you." She stared at me for a long moment, her lips curving into a ghost of a smile. "Tell Armaeus he owes us."

She disappeared. A moment later, so did the other five silent women. I peered into the darkness, trying to process what I'd seen...

As the sound of baying wolfhounds cut through the brittle night sky.

Crap!

I turned down the mountain and ran.

CHAPTER TWO

I spent the flight back to Vegas alternating between catnaps and attempts to pry open the ornate blue-and-green inlaid box I'd snagged on the way out of the Mad King's castle. Neither proved very effective. A quick check of my accounts showed that the Council had wired me the cash, and I forwarded it to Father Jerome's account.

Jerome, the French priest I'd met more than five years ago when I'd started my work in the arcane black market, wasn't your average holy father. His vocation might have been the Church, but his crusade was the Connected children of the world—children now at deadly risk as the war on magic took progressively more sinister turns. I helped as I could, usually with cash. And though I was quickly coming to realize that money wouldn't solve all my problems, it sure did solve a pile of them. Especially with the reports Father Jerome was feeding me from France: More psychic children were being targeted by the dark practitioners of the Connected community, which meant more money was needed to house and protect them.

The transfer done, I waited for Armaeus to contact me. He didn't. Not via phone nor via his annoying habit of crawling around in my head until I noticed him. It was weird to have my brain all to myself, even though most of the time I was trying to shut him out of it. I should have been happy he was leaving me alone.

Oddly, I wasn't.

To distract myself, I shuffled the Tarot cards yet again, though I knew just by touching them there'd be no answers from that quarter. I'd been casting cards on Viktor Dal off and on the whole trip, to try to figure out who he was, and why he'd picked Nigel for the job against me. Nigel, who I'd not particularly counted as an enemy, though if you were on the outside looking in, you might think he was. We'd been set at odds on enough jobs, after all.

Then again, Nigel hadn't delivered me to the bad guys exactly. He'd located me, but he hadn't incapacitated me, and he easily could have. So what game was he truly playing?

As they had all day, the cards once again came up Sixes and Sevens, Moons and Swords and I put the deck away in disgust. Sometimes, it really did hurt to ask.

Google was no help either. There was no way Viktor Dal could be the same Viktor from Memphis, but there was nothing on the Internet or the Darkweb about the guy, and nothing about his line of work. Had Nigel given me a false name? And if so, why? I wasn't in the mood to play "guess the allegiance," but something about Nigel's involvement in tracking me down for Viktor was unsettling. It felt too...intimate. Too personal.

I thought about the Seven of Swords again. Something was going on I didn't know about. That was a good way to end up dead.

I landed at McCarran International Airport as night draped Sin City. The box remained resolutely shut. The drinking horn remained about as generic as a horn could be. I remained surly and on edge. As we taxied toward the terminal, I swung my gaze out at the Vegas night and rubbed my face with my hands. Sleep hadn't come easily, not even on Armaeus's private jet. I needed to sleep in a real bed.

When we were finally cleared, I disembarked, leaving Mim's horn and the blue-and-green inlaid case aboard the plane. Armaeus would know where to find them.

He'd know where to find me too. Whenever he got around to looking.

"Passport?" The bored woman at the immigration kiosk flicked me a dead-eyed glance as I reached her, and I obligingly handed over my documents. Las Vegas's primary airport looked the same way it always did in the middle of the night—filled with tourists and wired for sound. The new rush of Vegas hopefuls spilled out of terminals and converged on the baggage claim area like ants swarming a honeypot.

I shouldered my own carry-on and glanced up at the TV screens as I pushed toward the exit. Stark missing persons announcements cycled across the screens in between flight listings, a blur of grainy images and clinical details. My mood soured further. How many of those notices had I seen over the years, long after I'd stopped officially assisting the police in the search for missing children?

Too many.

Made sense, though, to advertise at an airport, especially in a city that billed itself as the crossroads of corruption. I'd only recently started thinking of Vegas as home, but even that was a bit of a stretch. There were many faces to this city, and I truly knew only a few of them: the Strip, a few blocks off Strip, and the old casino district downtown. Who knew what other secrets the city held?

I moved with increasing fatigue past baggage claim, toward the constantly churning taxi line beyond the plate-glass doors of the airport. Flying the Arcana Council skies meant I could avoid the luggage carousels that I could see were already clogged with bags despite the fact it was two in the morning. A few more steps and I'd make a clean getaway from the airport. No muss, no fuss.

So why wasn't I feeling better about the world?

"Yo, dollface! Sorry I'm late."

I jerked to a stop as I focused on Nikki Dawes coming toward me fast. She was wearing a perfectly crisp chauffeur's outfit despite the hour—smart cap set atop her lush auburn curls, a black tuxedo and bright white blouse open at the collar to display the barest hint of her impressive assets. The only concession she'd made to the cool desert night were the long, sleek leggings that stretched down her mile-long legs instead of her typical skin-tight miniskirt, and her platform heels had been replaced by knee-high stiletto boots. As usual, she turned heads in a long line of appreciative admirers, men and women alike.

She grinned as she reached me, eyeing me with approval. "Glad to find you in one piece. But Armaeus needs to learn the difference between 'cell phone lot' and 'my apartment' next time he thinks it only takes me three minutes to show up at the airport."

"He contacted you?" I frowned. "He's been radio silent for me. I was beginning to think I'd pissed him off somehow."

"Pretty sure you'd know if that was the case. He's not exactly the shy and retiring type." Nikki cocked her head. "And, to be fair, maybe it wasn't Armaeus with the wake-up call. Maybe it was just me shooting bolt upright in bed with an urgent freak-out that you

21

were at the airport."

I snorted. "Well, I appreciate it, no matter what." Nikki wasn't the most powerful Connected I'd ever encountered, but her abilities as a member of the psychic community were impressive and very focused. She could see what others saw either with their eyes or their minds, whether those people were in front of her or halfway across the world, as long as she was keyed into that person. The more she got to know you, the sharper her visions. It'd made her previous career as a cop a successful one, and her current career as a Strip-based psychic and occasional Council gopher lucrative as well.

"I gotta say, I assumed the Council had made plans for your safe return." She grinned. "Then again, I'm here, and you're here. So maybe I *was* the plan all along."

"Maybe." However it had come to pass, I was glad. Nikki had attached herself to me over the past several months that I'd been working in Vegas, and I'd grown used to having her by my side when I was in the city. Especially given how crazy the city had gotten of late.

I breathed more easily as the doors spit us out into the cool Vegas night. Rubbing the worst of the grit out of my eyes, I fell into step with Nikki as we picked our way across the lanes of traffic, heading for the short-term parking garage.

Minutes later we angled alongside an ungainly construction site that jutted out from the wall of the main parking ramp, skirting tarp-draped plywood. The temporary walls were already showing signs of wear, yellow caution tape and orange hard hat stickers warring with graffiti and random flyers. We'd almost reached the main opening when a line of blue-and-white signs caught my eye. The same blue-and-white missing persons posters I'd seen on the airport's interior screens, only here the images marched down the plywood barrier in lockstep, each more heartbreaking than the last. It was always the kids that were the worst.

Gritting my teeth, I forced myself to look at the first face, because—you never knew. Especially in a city like Vegas.

My focus wavered as I considered the reality of the city I was walking back into. A city I'd helped change recently, and not necessarily for the better. "How are the other Connecteds on the Strip?" I asked. "They recovering?"

"Nope. Still jacked and loving it." Nikki grinned as I stopped and turned toward her. Several days earlier, Vegas had served as the latest site for the war on magic, and Magic hadn't taken it lying down. The resulting energy spike—which I had helped channel— had left everyone riding a psychic high that had nowhere to go but down. Only that high was lasting a lot longer than I would have thought it could. "Fortune-tellers are raking it in," Nikki continued. "Card readings have been off the charts, and there's rumors of excluding psychics from the casino VIP suites for fear they can predict the outcomes of hands. Everyone's walking around with a chip on their shoulders. If this wears off, *when* this wears off, there are going to be some disappointed Connecteds out there. Dixie's already bracing for the technoceutical market to jump when that happens. If the Connected can't get amped by natural means, she figures they'll do it by artificial."

"Oh, geez." Dixie Quinn, the horoscope-reading director of Vegas's Chapel of Everlasting Love in the Stars, had her finger on the pulse of all the city's

psychics. And if that pulse was currently hammering...
"That'd be bad."

"Real bad," Nikki agreed.

We started walking again, my gaze hitting image
after image of the depressing posters. "Have you seen
me?" each of them asked. The pictured kids had that
eerily familiar look that all kids on missing persons
flyers had, the kid you might have seen anywhere,
around the corner or in the grocery or playing on a
subdivision sidewalk. Their hair and smiles school-
picture perfect, and their age-progressed pictures
achingly innocent, cheerful gazes reflecting nothing of
what must have happened to them...

Suddenly, I stopped short. It took Nikki a few steps
to realize I wasn't right behind her.

"What is it, dollface?" she asked, coming back to
stand by me as I stared at the fourth flyer in the series
of posters.

The *fourth*.

"I know that girl," I said, lifting a hand to the
child's face. The curly hair, the bright smile, the
laughing eyes. "I know that girl. I—she was one of
the..." I shook my head. The age-progressed image
showed the same girl, the same smile, the same eyes.
Her face was fuller yet more heartbreakingly beautiful,
and her hair was long, only a hint of the riot of curls
from her childhood hairstyle remaining.

"What's this *doing* here?" I muttered as I glared at
the copy beneath the pictures, but I couldn't make out
the words at first. "She disappeared nowhere near
here."

"Says here she's from Memphis," Nikki supplied.
She looked at the picture to the right. "This one too."

"What?" I glanced at the flyers to the left and the
right of the girl I'd recognized. The one to the left was a

24

stranger to me. The one to the right, however…

"No." I scanned the copy rapidly, but it had only bare-bones information. Date of disappearance, age at the time of disappearance and present age, number to call in case of sighting. Not a Memphis area code number either, but a number I already knew all too well. Brody Rooks. The LVMPD detective I'd first worked with ten years ago in Memphis, with me as a fledgling psychic and him as a rookie cop. And what we'd done…was search for kids.

"What's Brody doing digging this up?" I snapped. "What angle is he working?" I glared at Nikki. "Did you know about this?"

"Nope." She shook her head, confused. "All these kids — these were the ones you guys were searching for when you were a teenager?"

"*No,*" I said decisively. "Not all of them. That's what makes this even weirder."

I went back to the first poster, racking my brain. I'd never seen that child. I couldn't have forgotten him. When I'd worked with Brody, there'd been only three kids we'd been tracking. Two from inner-city Memphis, one from the burbs. Three had been enough. These other three… I didn't know. I pulled the flyer from the wall, staring at it. "I don't know this boy, this Jimmy Green. I swear he wasn't one of ours. And these age-progressed images… There's something off about this."

Nikki pulled another poster free. "They look like photographs, you ask me. Not computer renderings."

I nodded sharply. That was exactly what was off about them. "And there are three new ones. If Brody somehow has linked more kids to the same crime…I can't imagine it." Outrage rippled through me as Nikki moved along the line of posters to the end. "What is

Brody *doing*? And why are these *here*?"

"Sara." Nikki's voice was a whip crack, and I looked up. She was standing at the end of the line of posters, her diamond-hard nails already peeling away the flyer from the wall. I moved toward her as I pulled more posters down, memorizing the names, the photographs, especially when I once again got to the ones I knew. Hayley Adams. Corey Kuznof. Mary Degnan. Children whose faces I'd seen in my sleep years after I'd left Memphis. Children whose faces I could never forget if I'd wanted to. And there'd been many times when I'd wanted to.

I got to the end as Nikki freed the last flyer from the wall. She turned it toward me.

The face staring at me had been one I'd seen all too often as well.

MISSING: SARIAH PELTER

There was an image of me at seventeen—not a school photo either. A snapshot at a moment I hadn't been looking at the camera, not intentionally. I'd been staring beyond it, eyes intent, expression hard. There was an age progression too, but instead of it being a generic recreated image, it was a blown-up digital photo of me standing by a brick wall. I could have been anywhere in the world, but I knew exactly where I'd been when that photo had been taken. It was barely four weeks ago. I'd been next to Nikki on a sidewalk in downtown Vegas, about to head inside Binion's Casino.

Which meant someone had been *following* me. Someone who knew who I'd been. What I'd been. Before I'd gone to ground. Before I'd changed my name. Before I'd stopped finding children myself and instead used my skills to finance *other* people doing that work. People who could do it better. Who wouldn't fail when it mattered most.

I took the sheet from her, then turned sharply away, ripping down the last two posters on the wall. "What is this about? What is Brody *thinking*?"

Nikki didn't have time to answer.

Without warning, a shot rang out in the night. Nikki grabbed me and thrust me forward toward the closest protective line of cars and roared, "Gun!"

The lights came around the corner of the parking garage so quickly, it took me a moment to understand what was happening, blinded as I was against the plywood wall. Another peal of gunfire helped clarify the situation. Nikki and I scrambled away from each other, splitting the focus of the shooter as we dashed into the lines of cars. As I ran, I heard Nikki's bellow into her phone, demanding the police, the National Guard, the pope if he was handy. I watched the swing of headlights bounce around to me and realized the truth of it quickly.

They were following me, not Nikki.

And Nigel had warned me about this, warned me they were coming.

My spinning thoughts kept time with my pounding feet. Of course they were following me. I'd been the one in the pictures. I'd been the one back in Memphis. I'd been the one who'd lost the trail of those kids, who hadn't found them, who'd—

A second blast of gunfire peppered the concrete, and I cursed, stumbling to my knees, then race-crawled between two cars. I could hear Nikki yelling for me, and I popped up in time to see her jumping over a guardrail onto the hood of a car on the next level down. She spat curses as she slid across the roof, then she disappeared from view. I heard the slam of a door. She'd found her car—but there was no way she could catch up to me, not with the shooter between us. Even now, a big sedan barreled into the row where I was hiding, and I risked a glance up. Were there other cars? Snipers somewhere?

Nikki gunned her engine and backed out of her spot, her horn blaring as she roared around the corner at the far end of the row. She was driving toward me, technically, but I wasn't her primary goal, I knew in an instant. The gunners were. She wanted to find some way to distract them.

She succeeded.

I heard the first smash as I rounded the corner, arms pumping. I turned to see Nikki sideswipe the vehicle, then bounce back, and a new sound of gunshots blasted along with the sound of broken glass.

Crap! She was taking a chance there, but I'd seen the gun she kept stowed in her limo. It was about the size of my head. Another strafing round of gunfire opened up, this time aiming away from me, and Nikki's car roared backwards, her own gun firing. She was drawing their attention, at least for the moment, which meant I needed to move.

I wheeled around another turn in the parking garage, and a new flare of lights kicked up, the car barreling down on me fast. There *was* a second shooter—this one a heck of a lot closer than the one accosting Nikki. I reached for my own gun, which wasn't there. I hadn't packed for firepower in Germany. I'd packed for brains and magic. Stupid not to be prepared, though. *Stupid!*

Another round of gunfire kicked across the pavement, and I jerked back as a *third* set of lights squealed around the turn, the two cars trapping me.

Then the third vehicle started whirling in a frenzy of blues and reds.

"Sara!"

I turned instinctively at the sound of Detective Brody Rooks's voice, diving between two other cars as he shot past me toward the other vehicle, which promptly squealed and backed around as Brody angled his car sideways. The passenger door popped open. "Get in, dammit!"

I raced toward the vehicle and piled in, shoving my papers at him. "Posters!" I gasped, as if this was far more important than the shooters, as if he needed most of all to understand that someone had hung up pictures that shouldn't be here, not in Vegas, not now. "Brody, there were posters—"

"Later—close the damned door!" He reached across me to haul the door shut, then hit his siren. The two vehicles sped for the exit. Brody took off after them, bouncing his sedan through the parking garage as I hugged the side of the vehicle.

"What the fuck was that about?" he gritted out as we took another curve. "Dispatch patched Nikki through screaming at the top of her lungs. What were you doing out there? Who's shooting at you?"

"No idea. But there were these—we were looking at these." I uncrumpled one of the flyers and waved it at him again, though he was smart enough not to take his eyes off the road. "Six missing kids flyers, Brody, posted bigger than life, exactly where I'd see them."

"Missing kids?" He scowled at me, raking his gaze over the flyers I held in my hands, though the one on top wasn't a missing kid at all, not really. "Christ, that's you!"

"That's me, yeah." I sank back in my seat. His shock was plain and that…relieved me. A lot. "So you weren't the one who hung those up?"

"Are you fucking nuts? No." Brody cut the wheel

29

again and grabbed for the sheet, splitting his time between the tight turns and the flyer with my seventeen-year-old face on it. "That's my goddamned number at the bottom there. I didn't authorize this." He tossed the flyer back at me. "That particular picture of you was police property, never released to the public."

"So, what, Memphis PD is putting this out? That's what's happening here?" I gripped the console and the door as we slammed over the speed bump at the garage exit.

"No goddamned idea." He glowered at me, then jerked his gaze up as a police cruiser bounced in front of us, lights roiling and sirens screaming. The car tore off toward the shooters, down the airport's main drag. Brody turned his vehicle sharply at the next intersection, sending us onto a maintenance road.

"What are you doing?"

"I'm not focusing. They'll go faster," Brody said. He double-parked the car and turned on me.

"Give me those."

I handed over all the flyers, watching him as he scowled. Brody Rooks wore his thirty-something years more comfortably than most men, for all that they'd been really hard years. Six feet tall, with a hard, functionally strong body that he dressed in rumpled suits and attitude, he was a grimmer, rougher-edged version of the man I'd known and massively crushed on as a teenager, when the two of us had worked missing children's cases through the Memphis police department. But his scowl was the same, and he leveled it now at the posters, lingering over the kids' images we both knew all too well. Without looking up at me, he kept talking. "Why were you in the airport? Where are you coming from?"

30

I stiffened at the accusation in his tone. "Not really your business."

"You getting shot at makes it my business." He lifted his head and speared me with his glare. "Where?"

"Germany. Pleasure trip."

Brody's snort spoke volumes, but I didn't care about his delicate sensibilities. Nevertheless, it marked the second time this week that I'd been targeted, and even for me that was a lot.

"Um, you remember Viktor Dal?"

He hesitated a second too long, then handed me back the flyers. "Why? We're going to the station. Why do you mention Dal? What the hell does he have to do with anything?"

"Nothing. It doesn't matter. Why are we going to the station?" I tried the door, but he'd locked it. Figured. "I don't want to go to the station. I want to go to my hotel."

"Tough." We drove in silence until we reached the familiar building, and he turned into a parking space, popping the locks on the door as he picked up the flyers. "Nikki'll be here within the next ten minutes anyway, the way she was ramming her limo into anything with wheels. If she isn't arrested, she'll be making a statement as well." He glanced at me when I didn't move. "Why, you got someplace else you need to be?"

I tensed, waiting for Armaeus to speak in my head. He didn't. I shrugged.

"I guess not."

We went inside, and the rounds of paperwork and reports commenced. Night turned into morning, Brody growing surlier by the minute over the posters. He placed a lot of calls, but we weren't getting any

31

information back. To make matters worse, the police cruisers had lost the fleeing shooters.

Nikki never showed either. I had a feeling there'd be no official record of any cars slammed into by the Arcana Council's town car.

Through it all, Armaeus remained radio silent. Frankly, this was starting to piss me off. Not that I particularly enjoyed his typical babysitting routine, but I'd left two major artifacts for him. He knew I was in town. He sure as hell probably knew that I'd been shot at—yet he couldn't be bothered to make contact? Who was he with that was distracting him so much?

A completely unexpected curl of rage unfurled within me at that thought. I tried to stuff it back into the hole it seeped out of. Rage wasn't helpful. No matter how good it felt.

Neither a Council car nor Armaeus's private limo awaited me when Brody finally let me out of the police station, however. It wasn't as if I expected special service, but up until now it had been Armaeus's habit to fetch me back to him after certain incidents. Tonight had definitely qualified as an "incident."

So where was he?

I hailed a cab. Miles rolled past with the chatty driver, yet still no peep from Armaeus during my ride over to the Luxor or on the way up to his rooms. By the time the elevator doors finally slid open into his opulent penthouse office, I'd worked up an impressive head of steam, which I fully intended to unload on the pompous, presumptuous, totally *preoccupied* Magician.

Right up until I saw him sprawled out on the floor.

CHAPTER THREE

"Armaeus!"

I swept the room with my gaze as I raced forward. I saw the drinking horn on the table, the beautiful box I'd pilfered from the caverns knocked to the floor. I reached Armaeus's side and pushed him over, checking for vitals. I'd never seen him so pale, but he was breathing, and his heart rate was steady.

"What the hell happened to you?" I demanded as his eyes flickered open.

"Horn — drinking horn," he managed, and I scrambled back to the table, picking up the Nordic horn. It was empty, but there was wine and bourbon at the sidebar, and I grabbed both bottles before returning. I dropped back to the floor, eyeing the drinking horn and the booze. Maybe water would be better. Or maybe…

I scowled at him. "I don't need to fill this with the blood of innocents, do I?"

He smiled weakly and shook his head. "Wine," he breathed.

I uncorked the wine and filled the cup, never mind that it was an ancient artifact and probably had serious skeletal cooties on it. If it was what the Magician wanted, it was what he'd get.

I set the wine bottle back on the table, turned to Armaeus, horn in hand — then froze.

"Whoa, whoa, whoa. Wait a minute," I said, my fingers spasming on the artifact. This was Mim's horn. And the Valkyries had said... "Won't drinking from this kill you?"

"Not death." He winced, his eyes almost glassy as his gaze found mine. "Life. Mortality."

"But you're *immortal* —"

"Now, Miss...Wilde. I don't have much time."

Crap. Armaeus really did look bad, and he'd been kicking around since the twelfth century, so he arguably knew how to take care of himself. As I struggled with the idea of feeding him *poison*, however, his eyes slid shut. In case I wasn't paying attention, he uttered a sort of death-rattley groan.

"Dammit, fine." My stomach twisted, and I dropped beside him, gripping the horn with a hand now clammy with sweat. Cradling Armaeus's head in one arm, I disregarded the usual zing of electricity between us as he allowed his weight to sink into my body. "What in God's name is wrong with you?" I muttered as I lifted the cup to his mouth. "Why didn't you call me?"

"Had to be this way," he murmured, but his eyes drifted closed as he accepted the rim of the drinking horn to his lips and drew in the wine like he was receiving a benediction.

I felt the shift in him almost immediately...and not merely him. As the wine from the horn of Mim seeped into his bloodstream, an answering wave of power flowed through me, steady and sure. I hadn't signed up for a psychic oil change, however. And I'd already learned that gifts handed down by the Arcana Council rarely came without a price.

"What is this, exactly?" I asked warily. "What's happening here? This is a thing, isn't it. I'm not a fan of things."

Armaeus ignored me, and as he drank, I glanced around again. "And why are you alone? Isn't there some kind of Arcana Council phone tree that should have been activated?"

"I can block the Council's awareness when I choose."

"Right," I scoffed. "You can block their awareness, but you can't keep upright. That makes sense." I tipped more of the wine into his mouth, mesmerized by the process as he submitted to my embrace and let me feed him. No one would ever accuse me of being nurturing, but holding Armaeus felt different. It felt right in a way I didn't want to explore too closely. And it felt dangerous in a way I knew all too well.

He opened his eyes, and I noted the irises were stained a dark, smoky gold. The same psychic infusion Nikki was tracking through the Connecteds — a psychic infusion I'd helped create — had affected the Magician too, though I didn't know exactly how. That power had called to me as well, but I knew I should protect myself against it, knew I should wait until I understood more.

"Are you really hurt bad?" I murmured as he drained the last of the cup, his hungry gaze finding mine again, a gaze that was finally clearing, refocusing. "And don't lie to me, because my third eye is watching you, and it has a special sensitivity to bullshit."

Armaeus sighed, the pure unaffected beauty of his expression arrowing through me as he allowed his eyelids to drift shut. "What did the Valkyries tell you about the cup?"

Of course he knew about the Valkyries.

Which meant he'd been keeping tabs on me after all.

I shifted uneasily. "They said that it grants life but also death. Death seems kind of like the important part, by the way. And they said you owed them." I went still, my heart clutching with a sudden fear. "Please explain exactly what's going on, Armaeus. Right now. In small words. Because in the past thirty-six hours, I've been chased by dogs and shooters and a cockroach in the women's bathroom at the police station, and I'm super jet-lagged and I won't be responsible for my actions if I seriously just screwed up here."

Armaeus's laugh sounded stronger. So that was promising. "The healing elixir moves through me, repairing the muscle and sinew torn apart. The silver-headed arrows were meant for gods, not men."

I frowned down at him. In the subbasement of an Egyptian temple several days earlier, Armaeus had taken those four arrows to the chest and torso. The wounds had been fairly vicious, but they'd also been healed once already. At least, he'd looked like he'd been healed. When it came to magic, though, I was never really sure.

"Um, exactly how many times do we need to put you back together again before you can let that particular hit go? Because I thought we'd covered this."

"Not all of it." His breathing had evened out, and color returned to his deeply bronzed skin. Lying there in my arms, he was quite possibly the most beautiful man I'd ever seen. Rich sable hair parted to either side of his face, a face that was further marked by sharply winged brows, sculpted cheekbones, lush lips, and a strong jaw. With his eyes open, he was unsettling...but when he rested, Armaeus was perfect.

Now he spoke again. "The weapons were effective

specifically because of my immortality." He brushed a spot on his chest where an arrow had pierced him. "Remove that barrier, and true healing becomes possible."

"Well, okay." I tucked an errant lock of hair behind his ear. "But you *can* get your immortality back, right? 'Cause that's kind of an impressive perk."

Armaeus was spared from responding as the door to his penthouse office opened and the Devil walked in, complete with his own manifested breeze. "I do hope I'm interrupting."

I glared at him. "You could have warned me."

"Yet this is far more satisfying, no?" Aleksander Kreios took in the scene with one lazy glance, then turned his attention to the empty cup lying on the carpet. "The Horn of Mim. Good." He crossed the room, then leaned down to pick up the green-and-blue inlaid box. "But what is this, I wonder?"

Kreios weighed the box in one hand as he swiveled back toward us. Today the Devil of the Arcana Council had adopted the full-on Adonis look—long, wavy blond hair that curled at his shoulders, his lightly bronzed face model perfect, down to the naturally jade eyes, sculpted cheekbones, and firm mouth. He wore a white linen shirt, barely fastened with toggle buttons, and frayed khakis. He could have been a tour guide for a Greek island tour instead of one of the most powerful Connecteds on the planet. He fixed me with an unreadable glance, and I sensed the shift in the undercurrents of energy swirling through the room.

I wasn't quite up to speed on my Arcana Sign Language, however. I sent him back a glance that could clearly be interpreted as *WTF* in multiple tongues.

He seemed unfazed. "Armaeus is quite correct in

what he's done," he said. "The Horn of Mim gives life and death, and he needed both to occur. He also needed you, a mortal, to be the one to give it to him, willingly and without coercion, which is why he waited until you found your way here." He frowned down at Armaeus, who stirred, his color almost completely restored. "And given that he is mortal again, he has a certain latitude that he did not have before, in so many things."

A smile played over his lips. It wasn't a good smile, exactly. The Devil kept his cards close to his impressively muscled chest. "No one will know this, of course, unless he chooses for them to know."

"But he's *mortal*," I confirmed. Armaeus pulled himself to a sitting position but appeared to be in no particular hurry to stand. Instead, he leaned heavily on me, which was kind of nice in a totally forbidden sort of way. "That's bad, right? Isn't immortality a prerequisite of the Council?" When neither of them spoke, I persisted. "How do we change him *back*?"

Kreios placed the box on the table, drawing his finger along the edge. He shrugged. "That's a very good question."

I stared at him. "You don't know? Are you insane?" I swung my gaze to Armaeus. "Are both of you insane?"

Before they could answer that one, I waved my hands. "Do you, or do you *not* need to be immortal to remain on the Council?"

Kreios tilted his head, his gaze unreadable. "You do."

"Does immortality allow you do things that you can't do as a mortal?"

"Kreios—" Armaeus began, but Kreios cut him off. He had a thing with honesty. I liked that about him.

38

"It does. Armaeus is at risk from many factions now, should they learn of his...altered state. Which of course, they won't."

"But how do you know that?" I demanded. "It's not like you people don't have enemies. How hard is it for someone to figure out that one of you has put yourself in Time-Out?"

Kreios smirked. "Time On, more appropriately."

"You know what I mean!" I snapped, but my heart gave a hard lurch. Armaeus was mortal. Would he age faster for some reason? Faster than regular mortals? Would all his years catch up with him at once? And would he fall prey to any stray illness or disease, with so many lifetimes of immunity he hadn't built up? "He can't stay like this, right? I'm right, aren't I. Staying like this would be very bad."

Kreios's lips firmed into a tight line. Then he nodded. "Eventually. Yes."

"Then how—"

"There is plenty of time to consider the problem," Armaeus interrupted me. He stood in one graceful movement, pulling me up alongside him. He squeezed my hand, then dropped it, and I fought the urge to blush. What was wrong with me? "Thank you, Miss Wilde." He turned to Kreios. "I assume there's a reason why you're here, beyond oversharing?" he asked, his voice both fully restored and plainly exasperated.

I blinked back and forth between them, then focused on Kreios as he pulled a long slender blade out of his jacket pocket. He brandished it at me. "Would you prefer to do the honors?"

"Um...what's that for?"

Kreios clearly picked up on my concern, and his grin turned a shade darker. "I assure you, I'm not asking you to knife Armaeus in the throat while he has been weakened." He pointed to the box. "Merely to open the treasure you provided us."

"With a kitchen knife? Do you have any idea the kind of knives and picks and levers I've already used on this thing?"

"You'll find this more effective."

I glanced at Armaeus, who gestured me on. "I'm quite recovered for the moment, Miss Wilde. Open it."

Kreios spun the box toward me as I approached, then handed me a pair of white cloth gloves. "To allow you to handle whatever is inside without concern," he said when I looked at him questioningly. I donned the gloves and took his offered knife. "It appears to be held together only with nails, no locking mechanism. I can sense no magical ward on it either."

I frowned, tracing my gloved fingers along the box. My enhanced sensitivities weren't triggered by it anymore, which frankly bummed me out a bit. Kreios might get excited about artifacts that didn't have magical overtones, but I wasn't so sanguine. My stock-in-trade was the procurement and sale of *magical* artifacts. And I wanted to stay paid for this job.

Beside me, Armaeus coughed a short laugh. "You seem disappointed. Can you sense nothing there?"

"Nope. It might as well be a cigar box." I looked at him. "Why, can you?"

He gave a brief nod, and I caught sight of his eyes again. They'd gone completely black. "Umm..."

"Open the box, Miss Wilde."

The command sounded in my head, the first evidence of Armaeus's strength that I'd experienced in what seemed far too long. And clearly, being mortal didn't dim his magic too much. That was reassuring. Without hesitation then, I slipped the blade beneath the lid of the enameled box and pried up against the cover. The nails held on for all of three seconds, then popped up like daisies in springtime. Pulling the lid away, I peered inside.

But it was Kreios, not Armaeus, who put a steadying hand on my arm. "Proceed very, very carefully, Sara Wilde. What you have here is rarer than diamonds."

I frowned, looking down at the deck of cards. "They're cards, right?" I squinted up at them both. "Since when are cards rare?" I reached inside and pulled out the deck. Or chunk, better said. The cards—if they were cards—had adhered together over time, the entire mess shellacked together in a block.

Oddly, neither one of the Council members moved. "Could be the Marseille deck," Armaeus murmured. "Intact. That would do it, would it not?"

Kreios snorted. "It would, but it's unlikely," he said. "The Church seemed quite proud of themselves for eradicating the last of the Devil cards well in advance of any Marseille decks finding their way to the salons of Italy and Paris. None of those decks remained intact."

"Well, good luck prying these babies apart." I flipped over the deck and froze.

A single eye stared back.

The one card visible in the deck was definitely not a Tarot card. It showed an eye drawn in the heavily kohled outline favored by the Egyptians, but it wasn't the eye of Horus, exactly. It didn't have the sharp lines extending down and at an angle. Rather, full rays extended outward from the center eye, beginning at a point and ending wider, eight pie wedges circling the eye and stretching to the edges of the card.

The image practically ached with age, and I remained still, staring back at the flat black center of the eye. "What the hell is this?"

"Different mythology," Kreios said. He made no move to take the deck from me. "You may place them back in the box. We'll separate the deck later."

Resisting the urge to tell the Devil to put the cards back himself, I did as he asked. When I handed him the box, he didn't move to take it. "Close the lid," he instructed instead.

"Are you weirding me out on purpose?" I asked as I shut the lid. I gave him back the box. "Because if so, you're doing a really great job of it. Just saying."

Kreios bowed with a slight smile. "My thanks as always." He hefted the box and looked entirely too pleased with himself, then slid his glance to the Magician and smirked. "Told you so."

"I look forward to your report," Armaeus replied, refusing to rise to whatever bait Kreios was dangling.

I, however, was not so restrained. "Told you what?" Ignoring Kreios as he strolled out of the room, I turned to the Magician, trying to figure out what the hell was wrong with him. He looked as he ever did, his color was back, but something was seriously off about his energy. He seemed more approachable, but also...darker. More dangerous, but in a new and undefined way. "What was that box all about? Those weren't Tarot cards, so what were they? And from where?"

The Magician's gaze swept over my face, and I got that bug feeling again. Good to know some things didn't change. "Stop looking at me like that."

His brows drifted up, but he continued to regard me with curiosity. His eyes glittered. "Explain where you found the box again?"

"It was in my report. There was a room of artifacts, but I was on the run. I grabbed the closest thing that looked good. And small. Small was important."

He nodded. "And how did you choose it? Why did it stand out to you?"

"Well, it glowed. I mean, all the crap was glowing, but this was the brightest thing that was small. I figured it was probably important." I tried to see deeper into his flat black gaze. "Is it?"

He nodded. "It would appear to be Atlantean in origin."

"Oh, right. Atlantis." *Not this again.* Over the past several months, I'd gotten used to Armaeus's quests for artifacts from the ancient, mythological civilization. I'd brought back bowls, plates, and a shiny bronze shield he'd been convinced were from the sunken island. But never had he acted so weird with the artifacts, so mysterious. "Well, fine, then. Isn't that good?"

He flicked his gaze away, considering. "If it shone so brightly, perhaps it wanted to be taken."

"Maybe. But so what? If I'd been down inside that hole, I'd want to be taken too."

"Perhaps," he allowed with a ghost of a smile. "Yet it interests me that of all the pieces, a card deck from a cursed civilization called to you. It bears study."

"It's not the only thing." I didn't want to talk about Atlantis, about the cards. Even if the lost civilization had actually existed, it didn't trump the fact that Armaeus had been *collapsed on the floor* when I'd found him. "You mind explaining why you were making out with the carpet when I got here? I thought you were all fixed."

"I wasn't." He waved dismissively. "The weapons used against me were calibrated specifically to attack the part of me that was not mortal. I suspected that, but couldn't confirm it until I'd ruled out all other

43

possibilities. And now it's confirmed."

"So now you're okay."

"Now I can heal, yes."

"Because you're mortal."

"Yes."

Armaeus turned away, but I reached out and caught his arm. There was something about that that was important. Very important, but I couldn't seem to get past the idea of touching him, my hand on his smooth silk shirt, my fingers wrapped around—

Focus. "You can't stay this way, though, right? How long until you have to turn yourself immortal again? Is there some sort of—" I stopped short of saying "expiration date," but it was a near thing.

Armaeus didn't seem to notice. Instead, he covered my hand with his, squeezed it. I sensed the blood draining out of my head again, and suddenly I felt dizzy.

"Despite the dangers, there are advantages to the mortal state," he murmured. He was watching me again. "I need to explore them more fully."

Before I could speak, however, he tilted his head. "There is a name in your mind, battering at you. I can sense it past your wards."

Everything from the past day came back in a rush, and I tightened my hold on Armaeus, my gaze finding his. "Viktor Dal," I blurted. "He hired a mercenary I know to find me in Germany."

"Nigel Friedman."

"If you know everything, is there a reason why I'm talking?"

Armaeus's brows lifted, his gold-and-black eyes trained on me still, unsettling in their intensity. "Should you wish to allow me full access to your mind, it would make the process quicker."

"Yeah, no. Anyway, Nigel found me but didn't quite give me up. And he said Viktor Dal had hired him. Then there were these posters of kids, Armaeus, kids I haven't seen in years — missing kids."

There was no inflection in Armaeus's voice. "From when you worked with Detective Rooks in Memphis."

"And there *had* been a Viktor Dal back then. It's just — I mean…no way. That guy couldn't have been — he couldn't."

Without realizing it, I'd edged closer to Armaeus. He was close enough to kiss me, and I sensed his power snake around me like a whisper. "You want to see him, don't you, Miss Wilde," he said. "To travel."

I swallowed, my throat constricting. All of me constricted, actually, caught in the trap of Armaeus's magic. But I couldn't deny what he asked. I wanted to know — needed it. "What if those kids are still alive?" I whispered. "I have to find them, Armaeus, I have to."

He spoke the words.

I sagged against Armaeus as the familiar lurch of astral travel swept through my system. The ability to mentally project yourself into a different location somewhere in the world, astral travel was a skill I'd recently acquired like a bad sinus infection, and it was proving equally hard to shake. But I'd never tried to travel wrapped in the Magician's embrace before. Mortal or no, his abilities sped up the process remarkably.

Instead of the usual sense of flinging myself across the planet, I was suddenly, simply…somewhere else. A house. A room. A vault.

"Where am I?" I managed.

"Describe it." Armaeus's words were sharp and clear, compelling me to speak with an urgency I didn't expect.

45

"Room — white walls, marble floor. Like a bank. Brass drawers in the wall, brass..." I moved forward, confused. I'd been fixated on Viktor. Viktor Dal. The tall, slender, blond-haired man with the kind eyes and the scruffy beard, sensible shoes and faded clothes... Not this cold place of stone and metal. I reached the drawers — there were dozens of them, each the size of a shoebox, all of them numbered.

No. Not all. I scanned up and to the left. The first six had shiny new labels, etched in plates of —

I reared back as I recognized the last of the labels: MARY.

"No!"

As if triggered by the word, the drawers jolted open — all of them, not just the labeled ones — and suddenly the room was filled with flying ash. Ash and small bits of twisted metal and bone. I ducked and crouched away from the onslaught, but it seemed to follow me to the corner of the room, a room without a door, a room without an escape. And a voice pounded through my head, soft and kind and riveting and familiar, so achingly familiar, a voice I hadn't heard for ten years and then only briefly, as a man with kind eyes and a scruffy beard and thick-soled shoes sighed and looked down at me and smiled and said:

"If anyone can save them, it'll probably be you."

"Miss Wilde!"

Armaeus's shout was a slap across the face, and I lurched awake again, still in his embrace, my arms flailing, my legs churning. Only the solid mass of his body kept me from running right through the enormous glass windows of his penthouse and out into the far open sky.

"There were drawers, it was a mausoleum!" I blurted. "He killed those kids, Armaeus. He did it!"

46

Certainty sank like a lodestone, drawing me down, back into the past and the nightmare of that job. The job that had taken everything from me. The job that had ruined my life. The job that had...

"What did you see, Miss Wilde?" Armaeus prompted, pulling me back from the edge of hysteria. "Specifically, what did you see?" He paused. "Was Viktor Dal there?"

"He...yes." I drew in a deep, shuddery breath. "Well, his voice was there. But he said—he said something he'd said to me before, when I was a kid."

Armaeus relaxed his hold marginally. "And what was that, can you remember?"

"That I..." All the adrenaline drained out of me, leaving behind a shell.

Because Viktor had been taunting me all those years ago. And I hadn't even known it. I *hadn't* been able to save those kids. I *hadn't* been able to stop...him. I shook my head again, clamping down hard on my thoughts.

"It doesn't matter," I said woodenly. "The kids are dead." *If anyone can save...* "He murdered them."

I looked up, my gaze clearing. Armaeus's face was impassive, and he looked at me without speaking. "I'm going to kill him," I said into the silence. "Viktor Dal. If he's still alive. I'm going to find him, and I'm going to kill him."

"And if the children whose names you saw are not dead?" He studied me. His lids flickered, and I sensed his touch on my mind. "Mary, Sharon, Jimmy. Harrison, Corey, Hayley. If they are still alive? If you can yet save them? What would you do then, Miss Wilde?"

The sheer cruelty of his question took the breath from me. To hear the names of the children in his aristocratic, foreign inflection seemed to call them sharply to life once more — laughing, smiling videos of three kids I had watched over and over again, puzzling, obsessing, jumping at every thread of hope. And now there were three new kids in the same cheerful flat images, three kids I'd never seen before in my life. They had all simply…disappeared. And I had failed them.

I jumped as my phone rang, the raucous sound battering my nerves. I pulled out the device, and my stomach cramped at the name on the screen. *Brody.* He'd need to know. He'd need to know what I saw, what I knew. I sensed the touch of Armaeus's mind on mine. Resolutely, I pushed him out.

"I have to go." I pulled back from him, regaining my bearings. I refocused on the drinking horn, now empty on the table, then glanced back to Armaeus. "Are you — you going to be okay until I get back?"

The Magician nodded, his gaze steady on me. His irises were now completely black.

"I will," he said. "And I'll be waiting for you, Miss Wilde."

CHAPTER FOUR

Brody was double-parked in the emergency vehicle space in front of the Luxor. He barely looked up from his phone as I got into his car.

"Are you going to make a habit of this?" I asked gruffly, my head still too stuffed with pain to let it all out yet. "I'm not going to jump every time you call."

"I think you will for this." Brody fired up the sedan and turned us back onto the Strip, but instead of heading toward the heart of the city, he turned south, driving toward the Mandalay Bay Casino and then past it, into an area that looked like a whole lot of nothing.

"Where are we going?"

"We have to talk."

"We're already talking," I snapped. "That's what people do when they speak to each other, they talk. Usually in coffee shops, not in cars heading out into the Nevada desert."

He slanted me a glance. "Do I make you nervous?"

"Presidential politics make me nervous, Brody. You just piss me off." I turned toward him, settling against the side of the door, putting as much physical distance between us as possible. The images crowding my mind pressed outward, but I couldn't speak of them yet. Those six brass labels...

"So what do you have?" I asked when Brody didn't

speak first. "You've found something out about the flyers? The ones from the Memphis PD."

"Not from the Memphis PD, actually." Brody grimaced. "I called, and they had no idea what I was talking about. They had a record of the case, sure. But it's long since gone cold. Ancient history. And no one has been sniffing around, demanding it be opened again."

"Right." My throat suddenly seemed a little tight. Probably choking on chemicals from the archaic air-conditioning in the vehicle. But no way was I going to drop the windows, no matter how fast Brody was driving. Which... I shifted in my seat, forcing myself to focus on what my eyes saw, not my brain. "You working out some issues with the speedometer there?"

Brody growled something indistinguishable but didn't lay off the gas pedal. He left the main road without speaking, and we bumped through two subdivisions, each more depressing than the last: short, square, stucco-covered homes, hunkered down in the heat. When he pulled into the driveway of one particularly nondescript tract home, I knew where we were. No way could anyone live on purpose in such a pitiful little house unless he was a cop. There was no landscaping except for a few scrubby cactus plants, and the sunbaked concrete of the driveway was bleached white. The garage door, also bleached white, looked like it hadn't been opened since the Cold War.

"Please tell me you don't have your dead grandmother in there."

He didn't grace me with a response to that, and we exited the vehicle in silence. The heat was a wall of oppression that we had to fight through to get to his front door, but the moment we stepped inside his house, I relaxed. The house might be one sad sack of ugly, but Brody kept the place on arctic. Clearly, he was my kind of guy.

Living up to the exterior's promise, the house was spare to the point of Spartan, but as he led me into his office, I refined my reaction. Brody had toys, all right. They were just highly specialized. "Nice."

The entire space had been converted into a crime lab, with a map of Vegas taking up most of the far wall, pins assembled in clusters to denote gangs, white-collar criminals, popular targets of tourist violence. Stacks of reports and no less than three laptops lined the wall beneath the map, but the material showed signs of being pushed to the side recently, making space for the new crime that had occupied the detective's interest.

Six tattered flyers lined a table that had been shoved up against another wall, and the large-screen computer behind it blinked to life as Brody touched a panel.

Unjustified panic surged anew in my throat. I hoped this wasn't going to become a constant issue, or breathing might become a problem. "What is this, Brody?" I still couldn't tell him what I'd seen. Six brass labels on drawers full of ash and bone. Six kids.

If anyone can save them, it'll probably be you.

"This is how I spent the first few years after your disappearance." Brody's harsh voice cut across my reverie. "I'm not happy to be back at it. Trust me, you're only going to get the abridged version."

The screen flared to life, and three school-picture photos identical to the ones on the flyers flickered in front of us. "Hayley Adams, Corey Kuznof, and Mary Degnan," he said grimly. "As they appeared ten years ago. We didn't have age progressions then because the pictures were current. But these..." He tapped the flyers. "They hold up. We ran the images through our system at the LVMPD, and the pictures are solid."

"Except they have backgrounds. Real backgrounds, I mean. Those actually look like photographs."

Brody's lips tightened. "Except they have backgrounds. So someone is messing with us, or these kids are alive."

I winced. "I don't think so, Brody."

He didn't seem to hear me, though. He brought up another set of images. "These three kids weren't part of our original search. Harrison Banks, Jimmy Green, Sharon Graham. Taken from different small towns in Tennessee and Alabama. They weren't reported right away, didn't make it into the system when our case blew up. And there were other differences too. No reason to connect them to our case."

"They were never found either, I'm guessing."

He blew out a long breath. "They weren't. And of course, we had you to add to that list after you left town." He stabbed the flyer. "But I didn't make flyers for you, Sara. It was considered an inside investigation, because we didn't know the circumstances of your abduction or disappearance or whatever the hell it was." His jaw was tight, a vein pulsing in his temple. "And we certainly didn't know you were alive and kicking back in someone's RV somewhere."

I grimaced. "It was a long time ago, Brody."

"And a long time where you could have reached out, contacted me. At least let me know that you were goddamned alive." His voice cracked a little, and I winced again. He wasn't wrong.

"At the time, it seemed better to let the past be the past. I didn't know what had happened to my mom. You were the only one who was left standing. I wasn't going to risk that."

"And now?"

I shrugged. "I still don't want to risk it."

Something in my tone tipped him off, and he turned sharply to me, his eyes narrowed. "You said you didn't know who was shooting at you."

"I don't. But I seem to be pretty unpopular this week." I blew out a long breath. I had to tell him. "I think—what are the odds, Brody that, um, Viktor Dal had something to do with the kids?"

"Sara." Brody's voice sounded tortured.

I turned back to the computer. "Seriously, hear me out. I mean, we knew back then that he was a shrink in my school district, but we had no reason to suspect Mr. Congeniality. Everybody loved him, he was super helpful. But what if... What is that?"

I stared at the screen as Brody pounded on the keys. A new image came up. Then a second. Then a third. All of them of Viktor, all of them in places I'd never seen before, except one.

"Brody." My breath stalled in my throat. "What's...that?"

Viktor Dal stood smirking in front of a wall lined with brass drawers.

"About three weeks after you disappeared, Viktor Dal became a person of interest in the kidnapping case. He was outraged, then obstructive. He would send us pictures of himself standing next to grave sites and funeral homes. Places like that." Brody tapped the screen. "This one, he'd bought an entire mausoleum wall, filled six of the drawers with ash and bones from a local pet crematorium, and sent us the keys."

I stared at him. "A *pet* crematorium? You've got to be joking me."

"All of it was fake. We had to investigate it anyway. By then, of course, Viktor was well and truly

53

in the wind." He punched up more screens. "We dug deeper and eventually learned that he'd been a German money launderer, drug dealer, and sex trafficker. He'd only been at the school district one semester before the children went missing. We were certain that he'd expanded his market to child trafficking, but nothing ever came of that. We couldn't pin anything on him. Eventually, he drifted away. Back then, we hadn't thought beyond the few missing kids. Back then, I hadn't known about the international Connected community, or that something called 'Connecteds' existed. Other than you, anyway."

I let that go. "And now?" I gestured to the screen, still unable to get past the image of Viktor smirking in front of those brass drawers. They'd held animal ashes. *Animal.* Had Armaeus known they were fake? If so, why hadn't he told me?

"Hasn't been active for years, at least not at the level that would gain attention from Interpol. If he's been a bad boy, he's covered his tracks well." Brody glanced at me. "No other kids were taken from Memphis with the same unique characteristics after that job either. And believe me, there were plenty of psychic kids in the city, or kids who fit the profile in other ways. I'd thought he'd moved on, but maybe he did simply...stop."

"What about these other kids?" I asked sharply. "You said they were different. Different how? And were any of them found?" I stared at the children's faces.

"Different in that they hadn't shown any psychic ability. But hell, they were six and seven years old." He pulled up a new screen. These recent posters list them as Memphis being the site of their abduction," Brody said. "The original posters are these. Notice the

54

differences."

"The cities, the numbers," I murmured, scanning the images. "What am I missing?"

Brody sighed. "The dates. They're all the same date, Sara, in the revised posters you found yesterday. The day of the explosion. The day you left Memphis."

I blanched. I hadn't noticed that.

"What the hell is this about?" I reached out and touched the age-progressed image of Mary Degnan. She'd be seventeen years old this year, her wide smile and sunny eyes somehow making it worse. "You think he has these kids stashed somewhere? These pictures..." Hope shot through me again, despite my best efforts to shut it down. "They look so healthy. So real."

"They could be alive, Sara. But probably not. Not after all this time." Brody's words were gentle, but I couldn't look at him. Could only look at the tattered posters he had lined up on the table. "The kids weren't abducted in scenes of violence. They simply were — gone. Disappeared from parks, school playgrounds, the mall. Parents not three feet away in some cases. That's why you got involved in the first place."

I nodded, forcing myself to recall the details of the abductions. I didn't have to work too hard. The memories were baked into my brain. The cards had represented the abductor as the King of Swords — cunning, intelligent, cold. His positioning card had him being all about power. It had been the Emperor, which showed that his command base had been sound and his financial support robust. His focus had been children, as evidenced by the Six of Cups.

Back then, I hadn't mastered using the cards to pinpoint locations. I could get close, though, and that was why Brody and I had made such a great team. I'd narrow down the search area, and Brody would go door-to-door gathering details. But we never got close enough for those three kids. The best I could get was the Two of Wands. That had indicated a long journey.

Once Brody's captain had heard the words "long journey," they'd rolled up the case to the FBI.

Neither Memphis PD nor the FBI had ever found the abductor.

I thought of the Valkyries choosing who would live and die. The three Memphis kids had been chosen too, in their way: marked for death because of their psychic abilities. But the appetites of child traffickers were not easily assuaged, not then, not now. I knew that all too well from my work with Father Jerome.

Something didn't fit.

"You mean to tell me *no one* was isolating psychic kids after that? I find that hard to believe."

"Not in Memphis. And not in any other major city for the next few years, at least in a way that the pattern was easily definable. And believe me, I looked. I spent half a decade searching for anything that could help explain what went down that day."

"It's not all that complicated." My tone turned flat. I'd relived that day so many times, I finally had most of the answers. Or at least the answers as I knew them. "I upset...well, this Viktor Dal, apparently." After all this time, I had a name, a face. My pulse slowed, my body stilled, every sense pricking as I focused on the grinning image of Viktor Dal. "Mom paid for it. My house was blown up, and I ran." The curling anger shifted deep inside me, turning my stomach sour. "After I ran, the kidnappings stopped, the killing stopped. The explosions stopped." At least outside of my own head, anyway.

"We've never discussed it, you know. Not in

depth." Brody was staring at the screen too. The images of the kids scrolling through, the parents, the data. But I could tell he wasn't really paying attention to the flow of images. He was slave to the same kind of internal picture show I'd been feeding myself for the past ten years. Except he had more pictures to fill out his catalog. Many more. "There's never been a good time to discuss it. But if Viktor Dal is out there, targeting you again…"

"What do you mean, again?" I jerked out of my reverie. "I wasn't his target back then. I was a roadblock. A roadblock he effectively removed."

"So why is he back?"

I thought about that. My campaign to save the Connected children was laudable, I supposed, but I was only one woman. Despite the assistance of Father Jerome and the network he was building in France, we could save only so many from the dark practitioners. It added up to not so many that someone would want to knock me out of the game, I was sure of it.

"There's been no evidence that he's currently an active child trafficker, right? Connected or Unconnected, if he's still moving children, he'd be on someone's list."

"True." Brody blew out a long breath. "Okay, so he's not trafficking children. He's definitely trying to get your attention, though." He jabbed his thumb at the posters. "Those were a plant. The shooters were expecting you — you, not Nikki. Why? Why now?

"I don't know." I stared at the posters as well. "I'm not a big enough deal, and my acquisitions work isn't that exciting. I'm thinking Viktor isn't a Connected, at least not anyone I've ever heard of. And I would have heard of him."

A small, niggling doubt cropped up, even as I said

the words. I'd been surprised when I'd learned about the Arcana Council a year ago. So maybe Viktor had slipped through the cracks as well, and yet...how? Especially if he was targeting children.

My adrenaline ratcheted down another notch, my heart rate slowing, my fingers beginning to tingle. The fog of anger lifted as a cold, hard truth assaulted me.

I knew that Armaeus could hide himself from the Council. Was Viktor so strong a Connected that he could hide himself from the entire Connected community?

Worse...did the Council know about him?

Brody's voice pulled me back from that dangerous thought. "Six children missing, maybe all of them psychic, all under the age of ten, and he never goes after another kid? Why?"

I shrugged, looking at the screen, mesmerized by the double set of faces. "Maybe he needed those particular kids." I discarded that thought as quickly as it formed. "Except some of their psychic abilities hadn't manifested yet, you said. And the arcane black market had its basis in Europe, not the US. Ten years ago, I don't think there was much of a US market for kids." I didn't need Brody's glance to take my mind down the next path. "And of course, I was in Memphis. But they didn't target me. They targeted Mom."

Brody tapped the last poster, the one with my face on it. I swallowed again. "Fine. Maybe they knew about me."

"Viktor did, anyway." He rocked back on his heels. "The woman who picked you up, the RVer. You'd never met her before? She didn't know you or your family?"

"Hardly." I smiled, thinking about the old woman, her hair flying, her sun-roughened skin transformed by

58

her easy grin. "She was a retiree with a soft spot for runaways, nothing more."

"Maybe." He nodded, and the tone of his voice made me glance at him.

"What? You don't buy I'd get picked up that fast?"

"Oh, I buy it, but to be picked up by someone who managed to hide you not only from the police but from what seems like a very bad man with a penchant for psychic kids and the money to track them down? That takes some skill. Some would say some intervention."

"Wrong tree." I shrugged. "You'd have to have met her. She was an ordinary woman. A nice woman, yeah. But I wasn't the first orphaned runaway she ran into. I doubt I was the last."

"And you never thought to go to your mother's relatives?" Brody's voice was eerily cop calm, but I was too strung out to figure out why.

"Um, that would be negative, Brody. Since my mom had no relatives." I glanced at him. His face was as placid as his voice, which didn't seem good either. "I told you that. My mom was an orphan by the time she was sixteen. Runaway by seventeen, working in Memphis as a waitress by eighteen. She was lucky." I grimaced. "At least until I came along."

Brody stared at me for a long minute.

"What?" I finally asked.

He released a deep sigh that sounded more like a groan. "That's…not exactly true, Sara."

With another wave of his hand, the screen changed, and the obituary for my mother appeared, next to a picture of her that brought a pang to my heart, her disheveled good looks and big smile going straight through me. She looked young—too young, but I recognized her, of course.

"Oh, man," I muttered, plunging into the usual

wave of emotion where my mother was involved. "She looks good there. When was that taken? Before I was born?"

"We think so. It was a dating site profile picture, the last photo she allowed to be taken of her until you started to become famous as Psychic Teen Sariah. By then she was drinking a fair amount. Her tox screen showed a complement of recreational drug use as well, so she probably wasn't thinking too straight."

"She didn't like having her picture taken. It was a thing with her." I couldn't help moving closer to the screen, trying to imprint my mother's memory on my brain. How long had it been since I'd seen any picture of her? I couldn't remember. "To me she always looked good, at least till the end. And then, she didn't look bad, just—tired."

Brody started to say something, then appeared to change tack. He went for a question instead. "Did anything else specifically change in the weeks leading up to her death? Did you have money problems, anything like that?"

"No." I shook my head. "Money, for whatever reason, was never a problem. We didn't live well, far from it. But there was always food, and there was always enough money for Mom to go out, for clothing and whatever. I didn't know where she got it, but she had a job."

Brody hesitated. "She did have a job, yes," he said at length. "Taking care of you."

I smiled. "I mean beyond that, Brody. She had a job, job. She made money waitressing. I don't know how we did it, but we managed."

"You more than managed." Brody looked a little queasy, and I stared at him more sharply. "Your mom's bank account had money in it," he said. "A fair

60

amount of money. In the months prior to her death and your disappearance, at least thirty thousand was added. The house you lived in was paid for. Same for your car."

"Well, neither of those were impressive examples of high living." Something about Brody's tone bothered me on a soul-deep level, like dirt being shoveled off a long-buried axe. "But thirty thousand dollars? No way. We definitely didn't have that kind of cash."

"At the time of her death, her account had five hundred and twenty-four thousand dollars in it."

I stared at him. He was still talking, but the words coming out of his mouth weren't making any sense anymore. "Five hundred and—no." I barked a short laugh. "No. That's not possible."

Brody continued inexorably. "Sara, the woman in that picture wasn't your mother. She was a paid caretaker, as best we can identify."

"A what?" I wheeled around. "What are you talking about? That was my mother! My—"

Brody rocked back on his heels, but his face was set. "No," he said. "Sheila Rose Pelter ran away from home at age seventeen and started waitressing in Springfield, Tennessee directly after. About a year later, she moved to Memphis, purchased a home, a modest car, a new wardrobe...and baby supplies. She began waitressing again as soon as you were old enough to leave with a sitter, but most of her first few years, she spent at home. About five years after you were born, she began corresponding with family back in Alabama, though she never once mentioned you and she resisted all suggestions that her relatives visit Memphis. From what we were able to piece together in the months after her death, Sheila visited her hometown twice, giving large cash gifts both times. Her mother had no idea where the money had come from, and refused to spend it until after Sheila died. Her visits home stopped when you began working with the Memphis Police Department, and the family lost contact with her again."

I stared at him, my voice suddenly not working right. "I had a grandmother?"

Brody's lips tightened. "*No*, Sara. That's what I'm trying to get across to you. When we recovered Sheila Rose Pelter's body from the Mississippi River, we performed a DNA check to verify her identity. It came back with more information than we planned. You don't share the same genetic markers. You're not Sheila Pelter's biological daughter."

Everything had started to spin. "And you think..."

"It's the only explanation," Brody finished my words for me. "Someone paid a stranger to take care of you, from the moment you were born."

CHAPTER FIVE

It's not every day you find out your whole life has been a lie.

I was handling it as well as could be expected.

"Hey, doll—whoa, what the hell happened to you?" Nikki slid into the booth opposite me, eyeing Brody while I focused on my bourbon. The Magician hadn't reached out to touch my mind again, but that was okay. It was well on its way to being pickled.

Beside me, Brody nodded to Nikki, the two of them exchanging cop glances without actually admitting to doing so. I'd stopped counting the drinks after about four, and Brody had done his level best to leaven each of my bourbons with a tumbler of water. I'd stopped counting those too, but at least I was well hydrated.

When I didn't answer Nikki right away, Brody waded into the breach. "This new attack on Sara brought up some old history that needed to be aired. Timing wasn't great, but necessary."

"Old history?"

"My mom," I said, looking up at Nikki. I blinked, but it wasn't the booze. Today Nikki had ditched her usual auburn coif and was going full '60s starlet, complete with blonde wig, yellow minidress, and white go-go boots. She looked…exceptionally bright. "She wasn't my mom, turns out. She was paid to take care of me. Paid well."

"Another round," Nikki said to the waitress I hadn't noticed beside us. I returned my gaze to my glass, and Nikki leaned forward, elbows on the table. "You had to have known this for a while," she said, her attention on Brody. "Why bring it up now?"

"Those posters you two found." Brody rubbed his two-day beard. "I'm not sure how much you know about Sara's last job in Memphis, but three of those kids were ours to track down. We couldn't find anything on them, not even with Sara's cards. Then all of a sudden, the woman we believed was her mother is killed, Sara's house is blown up, Sara goes off the grid. If the man behind those attacks is back, she needed to know the full story."

"Three of the kids were ones you searched for," Nikki repeated, tilting her head. "What about the others?"

"They weren't connected to our case at the time, but I've got inquiries out." Brody sat back as the waitress arrived with more drinks. "They're clearly connected now. No question in my mind that we're dealing with the same guy."

"Viktor Dal," I supplied. I slumped lower in the booth, willing the liquor to kick in. So far, it hadn't done more than take the barest edge off the pain. "Some stuff on him has finally come through Brody's people. Dal's a Turkish black market dealer. Traffics in drugs and sex, but not Connecteds, not that anyone's ever heard. His tastes run older by a fair margin for the sex trade too. Kids don't make sense for his business. Psychic kids make less sense."

"You ever heard of him?" Brody asked Nikki.

"No, which isn't to say I would have," she said thoughtfully. "Dixie might, if he's mucking around in the Connected community."

"She doesn't need to be a part of this," Brody snapped back, and Nikki patted his arm.

"Not saying she does, love chop. But she knows a hell of a lot of people, and she has for a long time. Wouldn't hurt to ask."

Brody shrugged, but his tension had definitely tightened a few notches. He and Dixie had sort of a thing going. I hadn't really begun to deal with said thing, and this didn't seem a good time to start.

Nikki kept going. "But probably not unless he's been active in the US." She turned to me. "This Viktor guy is the one who put up those flyers?"

"Maybe." I twirled my bourbon. "No way to know."

"There aren't any more of them, at least nowhere near the Strip," Nikki said. "The construction people also report that they don't allow posting, so the flyers couldn't have been up for more than a few hours at the outside. Considering you were coming in from Germany…"

"He had to know my schedule."

"Down to the minute, dollface. That car was waiting for you."

"I notice you never reported your involvement as a concerned citizen, including your banged-up limo." It was Brody's turn to scowl at Nikki. "You see anything that could be helpful?"

"Two cars, out-of-state plates, rentals. Late-model sedans, nothing special. The damaged one's either been dumped or retooled, I'm thinking. Two men in car number one, or two very big females. You see anything in yours?"

"Two occupants, not large, could go either way."

"So four hitmen to one Sara." Nikki raised her glass. "You're coming up in the world." She eyed me over the rim. "You want to tell me what happened in Germany, since we're all being chatty like?"

I stiffened. "What do you mean?"

"I mean, you weren't surprised, dollface. The posters threw you, but not the shooters. Job go south?"

I suddenly didn't care about keeping confidences. Nothing really mattered anymore. "Viktor hired an old friend to track me down. My friend did, but he also gave me enough breathing room to split."

Nikki nodded. "Who else knew your location?"

"What old friend?" asked Brody. I didn't bother answering that one.

"Client. No one else." I shrugged. "I wasn't trying to keep it secret, though. Private jet into Germany, but public transport from there. The art auction was well-known in the right circles."

"Art auction," Brody said flatly. "Is this another job for that Kreios character? No wonder you got shot at."

"No shooting in Germany. And let's face it, they could have shot me last night if they'd really wanted to."

"Definitely. We were sitting ducks." Nikki tilted her head, her blonde hair bouncing. "Of course, if they shot to separate us, that certainly worked."

At that moment, I hit critical mass on both the conversation and my liquid intake, and batted at Brody until he let me slide out of the booth to hit the bathroom. Walking through the bar was surreal. My head was buzzing from the alcohol, but not nearly enough. It was buzzing more from the bomb Brody had dropped at his house. He'd held that information back from me for weeks. Why? Had he ever been planning to tell me? Did he not think I had a right to know?

In the bathroom, I stared at my reflection in the

mirror, the eyes of a stranger. Not Sariah Pelter. Not Sara Wilde. Not anyone I knew anymore.

It wasn't an uncomfortable feeling, though. It felt almost...right.

And that really *did* make me nervous.

When I finally wheeled out of the bathroom and back into the bar, I heard a familiar Southern drawl exclaim with delight at finding "Duh-TECT-ive Ruhks" and Nikki.

Dixie Quinn. Astrologer and owner of the Chapel of Everlasting Love in the Stars. Mother hen to all the Connecteds in Vegas.

And...Brody's current arm candy.

The biggest part of me, the childish part, wanted to do nothing but waltz right out of the bar and into the relative freedom of the Vegas street...possibly into an oncoming car. If only to put a new spin on the day.

But as I watched Brody's face as he gazed up at Dixie, something twisted inside me. Not a bad twist, I was surprised to note. It was more similar to the detached sensation I'd experienced looking at my own reflection. Brody wasn't mine to want, not anymore. Not ever, really. The Sariah Pelter who'd known him was a girl who had never existed. As Sara Wilde, I had things to do where I couldn't take a cop along for the ride. Not unless I wanted to put him literally in the line of fire of Viktor.

Viktor Dal.

Images lined up in tight formation. This, I could focus on. This, I could claim as my own. Viktor had stolen six children from their parents, their families. He'd also stolen the only family I'd ever known from me. Sheila Rose Pelter might have been a drunk and a borderline addict, and might simply have been doing her job *acting* as my mother, but she'd kept a roof over my head for seventeen years before Viktor had come along. She hadn't known her life was in danger from some maniac she'd never met. And Viktor had killed her in cold blood.

I didn't know much of who I was anymore, but one thing I did know. Viktor needed to pay for that crime.

And Brody couldn't be any part of that. He needed to stay the hell out of the way. If Dixie helped that happen, great.

Even knowing all that, forcing myself to walk over to the table was harder than I would have expected. Smiling brightly, I slid in next to Nikki, inviting Dixie to join us. Brody's smile tensed but got easier as more drinks arrived and food was discussed. It took only a few minutes for me to realize that I was relaxing too, no more bourbon required. This was...easier, I realized, thinking of Brody and Dixie together. This felt right.

I had enough problems to manage without adding Brody to the mix.

It didn't take long for Nikki to steer the conversation back to the problem at hand, but when she asked about Viktor Dal, Dixie's response surprised us all. "Viktor! Well, bless my stars. I haven't heard that name in an age and a half." She blinked her big eyes at our startled faces. "Why are you asking? Do *not* tell me he's dead. He was the sweetest man."

"Sweet, huh?" Nikki grinned, leaning back, her face wreathed in "I told you so" smugness. "How'd you know him?"

"Well, he was one of Roxie's friends, at least for a while, back when she was entertaining and all. The last party, gosh, maybe would have been fifteen years ago?" She chuckled with a blush that only added to her charm. "I swear, time passes far too quickly when

68

you're not paying attention."

Brody reached out and squeezed her hand, the move so unselfconscious that my new-found detachment had its chain yanked. But I kept my face neutral as he spoke. "You said he was a nice guy?"

"Nice as pie. Handsome, in an austere, chilly sort of way. Light blond hair, light skin. Wispy beard. But it was his eyes that were his best feature. Kind eyes, gentle. The kind of eyes that made you feel you could trust him, you know?"

"Sounds like a likable fellow," Nikki said. "What'd he do for a living?"

"Ran a relief organization in India, maybe? I mean, I don't know that that was his job, job. But it certainly was his passion. He and Roxie were very tight."

I didn't choke on my bourbon, but I should have as all the dots connected with a bang in my head. *Holy Mother of Crow.* Up until a short while ago, Roxie had been the Empress of the Arcana Council. Which meant that Viktor—devious, despicable, disappeared Viktor—had to be linked to the Council as well. Maybe more than linked. Maybe a lot more.

Brody's eyes narrowed on me across the table, but I didn't have time for him. I didn't have time for anyone other than people who could give me answers, and those people were not in this room.

They were, however, in this city.

"Guys, I think I'm going to—"

"No, wait, I wanted to tell you!" Dixie brightened and turned to me with beseeching eyes. She did beseeching very well. Brody didn't stand a chance. "You remember you asked about Jimmy next door?"

I blinked at her. "Who?"

"Next door! Jimmy Shadow. Darkworks Ink? The tattoo parlor?"

"Oh! Sure, right." The tattoo parlor next to Dixie's wedding chapel was every bit as Vegas kitsch as the Chapel of Everlasting Love in the Stars, but with less white stucco. And no costumed plaster geese. "Did he decide to get married or something?"

Dixie snorted daintily, as only she could do. "Hardly. All this time, I thought he was the owner of the store, but today he bursts in asking for flowers. Flowers! His boss is relocating back to the Strip, he said, and he wanted to make the place look nice for her. Not that I think pink and white carnations would do anything to spruce up the décor of a tattoo parlor, but you know, boys." She lifted a shoulder, as if to dismiss the decorating abilities of the entire masculine gender. "He was totally adorable and earnest. It did my heart good to see him that way. He always sort of scowls, you know?"

I nodded, edging her gently toward her point. "So did you meet the boss?"

"And she's a her?" Nikki put in on the heels of my question. "That place totally reeks of guy, I gotta say."

"Hey, hey, hey." Brody held up his hands.

"I didn't meet her, but I *saw* her." Dixie's eyes shone with the gleam of the victorious gossip. "And believe me, she suits the place just fine. She's white as snow with a partially shaved head, piercings that run up her ears and one full sleeve of ink that I could see. She showed up today in a tank top and leather jeans on the back of a motorcycle, and stumbled off, totally drunk, if you ask me. Jimmy comes running out and grabs her, and I caught the barest glimpse of her face." Dixie sniffed delicately. "I suspect she's usually pretty, even with the haircut. But when I saw her, she looked like death."

Every one of my nerve endings pricked to

attention. I slid a glance toward Nikki. "I don't suppose you go in for tattoos? If only to be polite and meet the neighbors?"

"And mar the perfection of my girlish form? Not a chance." Nikki grinned. She eyed Brody. "And you, sir?"

He shook his head. "Tattoos were frowned on when I joined the force, and I joined the force young," he said. "By the time I got to a place where I didn't think it would matter, the urge had passed." He raised a brow at Dixie. "You?"

"Well, none I would reveal in polite company," she simpered.

"Right." I took another hard slug of bourbon, then pushed the glass away from me. "Thanks for the scoop, Dixie—and guys, for the drinks. I think I'm going to head home."

Brody straightened instantly. "I'll drive you."

"No, you won't." I held up a hand, doing my level best to keep it steady. It was easier than it should have been. While the rest of the Strip had had their magical mojo recently enhanced, I'd apparently been given preternatural skills at holding my liquor. Everybody had to have a gift, I suppose. "I need the fresh air, and the Palazzo is right up the street. I'll be fine. I'll call you tomorrow about next steps."

Nikki shifted in her seat. "I gotta bolt anyway. Keep me company, dollface?"

Nikki's tone was absolute, and I didn't try to fight her. As we stood, I watched Brody allow Dixie to cuddle up to him a little more closely, and I allowed myself not to hurl. I nodded to him and Dixie with an "I can't really see you" glance perfected by waitresses and librarians.

We turned and made it out of the bar within thirty

seconds, the sights and sounds of the city surrounding us.

"Where are you really headed?" Nikki asked as she hailed a cab. "Because we both know it ain't the Palazzo." She blinked as she looked at me, then nodded before I could say anything. "Prime Luxe. Good. I'll ride with."

Without another word, she folded me into the taxi and slid in beside me. We eased into traffic, and I looked up past the flashing lights of the casinos to catch the image-on-image reflection of the Council's digs.

As always, the sheer magnificence of their domains took me by surprise — the enormous metal-and-glass fortress of the Magician's Prime Luxe, soaring over the Luxor; the peaked glass foolscap structure over Bellagio, where the Fool now lived; the Devil's glass monolith, Scandal, always pulsing with a Technicolor light show atop the Flamingo. There were three other towers on the Strip, all of them empty: the black tower over Paris, and a grey stone keep above Caesars Palace, the white tower above Treasure Island. These magnificent domains loomed over the Strip in awesome, glittering majesty, though only a few of the strongest Connecteds in the city could see them.

I spent an extra moment longer than I needed, staring at them, trying to decide my course. Despite what I'd said to the others, I had no intention of turning in this early. I wanted to see the Magician, and, more importantly, I wanted answers.

I frowned as we drove toward the Luxor. I hadn't heard a peep from Armaeus all day — same as when I'd come home from Germany. Maybe he couldn't at first because he'd been so ill, but he'd gotten *better*. He was healed, or at least healing. He was temporarily mortal,

72

true, but that shouldn't stop him from connecting to me psychically.

To test the idea, I tried opening up my mind, quietly at first, then with greater urgency, pushing out toward Armaeus, imagining our minds connecting, joining. *Armaeus?* I asked, thinking the word as clearly as I could. *Are you there?*

The response came back immediately. *"I've been expecting you, Miss Wilde."*

CHAPTER SIX

Where Armaeus was expecting me, technically, was not his office. The doors of the elevator opened onto the conference room, a chamber I couldn't help but approach with an entrenched feeling of dread.

"Where is she," I called out, standing in the elevator. I had no problems hitting the down button again if the High Priestess was in residence. Armaeus's conference room had been the site of more than one of my top ten worst experiences as a psychic, and they all could be traced back to one person. "If you're in there waiting for me, Eshe, I'm in no mood to play Around the World today."

"Eshe isn't here." Armaeus's voice sounded against my actual ears instead of my brain, so I stepped into the room. It was dimly lit, exactly the kind of look Eshe favored for her oracular trances, so I wasn't about to let my guard down. "Since the events of recent days, she's gained considerable ground in astral travel without an intermediary. She is in seclusion until she perfects the art."

"Seclusion, huh? Tell her to check in for an extended stay." Nevertheless, I couldn't escape the awkwardness of the moment. The last time I'd seen Armaeus, he'd been in my arms for a good portion of the conversation. I kind of wanted that to happen again, which was a little unsettling. Ordinarily, getting too close to the Magician made me panic. Now it was making me pant. What was going on?

"So, um, how are you feeling?" I asked brightly.

"Much improved. You should sit. We have much to discuss."

Armaeus gestured me forward to the end of the conference table, where a soft blue illumination from the surface keyed me into the fact that he was about to play show-and-tell. I moved forward, grateful for something to focus on to take my attention off his presence.

Because his presence was exceedingly…present.

Armaeus was dressed in a style that I suspected he would call "casual." A creamy linen jacket was unbuttoned to reveal a smooth white shirt, open at the neck. A hint of his bronzed skin showed at his neck. His hair was brushed back away from his face, accentuating his sharp cheekbones and dark, flashing eyes. Eyes that remained way too dark, for those keeping score. Which I definitely was.

I slid into the seat opposite him at the corner of the table. "What have you been doing all day?" I asked, innocent as all hell. "Discovering new vistas to your magic previously unexplored?"

He studied me. "Why? Have you?"

"Only if you count a preternatural ability to hold my liquor." At his raised eyebrows, I shrugged. "It's been a hard day."

As I said the words, the mere act of having to tell him something so basic struck me with its wrongness. "What's the dealio with you lately, anyway?" I pressed. "I haven't felt you in my head once in days. You finally reach the point where I bore you?"

"Never that." He smiled and sat back, eyeing me expectantly. I knew that look. It was classic "professor waiting for the student to figure out the obvious answer herself" look. And he was a big fan of it.

"What?" I sat back as well, swiveling my chair a little for good measure. I could do "stupid student" like nobody's business.

"You have undoubtedly noticed the effects of the influx of magic visited upon Vegas recently in your associates. You have been affected by the same influx, Miss Wilde, regardless of whether or not you choose to accept it."

And then, of course, I got it. "Wait. You can't read my mind—at *all*? You can't track me?" My eyes flared wide. "I have a total cloak of invisibility and didn't know it?"

His expression tightened. "When you choose to allow me to see you, as you did when you were here this morning, my ability to plumb your mind is as it ever was. The difference, as you say, is that I no longer have a foothold. Until you invite me in, you are essentially barred from me."

"And I'm it?" I couldn't help but bounce a little "At least while I'm amped, I'm the only one in the world who can do that? Or...no. The Council members mind-block you too. They have to."

"Only in a situation of extreme duress would I trespass on the Council members' minds."

"Right." I wheeled the chair a little farther back from him. "So, you can't crawl around in my head. I guess that's good. But it seems I should've gotten more jacked up, you know? More on the mystical-power side of the equation. I totally feel swindled here."

"I suspect you're simply not paying attention. Your physical strength has been enhanced, your endurance. Your tolerance for alcohol, as you've noticed."

76

"My strength?" I stretched my hands in front of me, inspecting them for additional meatiness. "I haven't noticed that so much."

"Indeed." He waved his hand over the table, and a schematic came to life. "Approximately how long would you say it took you to move from the tunnels below Neuschwanstein to the valley immediately below Hohenschwangau?"

I shrugged. "I wasn't timing it."

"Your hairpin was chipped. You made the trek in slightly under ten minutes, which explains why you outran your assailants after your initial discovery. Ordinarily the amount of terrain would have required thirty. Do you recall being winded? Stressed?"

"I recall being chased by dogs. Does that count?"

"Where before your body relied on adrenaline to survive, your natural physical reactions have adapted to suit your needs more effectively." Armaeus tapped the screen, and the map changed to a topographical feed, showing the clearing where I'd encountered the Valkyries. "Your chip was scrambled for approximately five minutes here, until you started moving again. What took place, precisely?"

I frowned. "I thought you knew about the Valkyries."

"I knew they were there. Not what they said to you."

I weighed my options carefully. I needed Armaeus's help if I wanted to get the answers I needed regarding Viktor and the missing children. Even if he didn't have a currently active all-brain access pass, he could tell when I was keeping secrets. It wasn't too hard: I was always keeping secrets.

This one I was willing to share. "The Valkyries saw that I'd taken the box and Mim's horn out of the castle.

They let me keep them. They told me it was time for me to gather my weapons. That mean anything to you?"

"Of course. What else?"

"They said you owed them." I eyed him. "Care to explain?"

"The Valkyries are ancient beings, and their speech is twisted with cunning." Armaeus tilted his head, considering. In that moment, he looked almost human, and I shook off the sensation of unease that realization brought. "Did they say anything else?"

"They were kind of big on death—speaking of." And here we were, at question number one. "Is Death in Vegas?"

Armaeus's expression didn't change, which gave me my answer.

"You've got to be kidding me," I said, thinking back to Dixie's description of the new owner of Darkworks Ink. "She works at a *tattoo parlor*? Do you people have no shame?"

"It amuses her, and given how long she has walked this earth, amusement is in short supply."

I managed a tight smile, but I for one, was not amused. Death was here in Vegas.

While Armaeus was mortal.

Somehow, that didn't sound like the best of ideas.

"Why has she come back?" I asked. "You summoned her?"

"The High Priestess has summoned all the Council. Those who can hear the call and choose to assemble, that is."

"She summoned..." I shook my head, my stomach bunching into knots. "But you're *mortal* now. They're going to know that, right? They're going to know that you're not at full strength?" I stared at him. "Does Eshe know?"

"Death's appearance in Vegas will be noted and that will aid our efforts, regardless of her direct involvement with Council activities," he said, ignoring my other questions. "When you visit her, have a care, Miss Wilde. She is not what you might expect."

"Right. Is she new, old? When did she come aboard your merry crew?"

"Before my time, you'll be pleased to know." His lips twitched. "Not before Eshe's."

"So she's a veteran. No wonder she keeps to herself." I steadied my glare at him then, and asked the question burning in my gut. Viktor Dal was Connected. A friend of the Council's. And for the last ten years, he'd been all but invisible to anyone trying to find him.

"When did Viktor Dal become Emperor, exactly?" I asked stonily. "And since when do you willingly accept child-abducting scum into your fold?"

To his credit, Armaeus didn't hesitate.

"Viktor Dal is a newer incarnation to the Council," he said, his voice cold with a hint of disdain. "He has not learned all that he should. He ascended on the eve of World War II. At that time, the Council was based in Munich, and he was very much affiliated with the—"

"Whoa, whoa, whoa. *Munich*?"

"You surely didn't think we were always based in Las Vegas?"

"But…geez. Munich in pre-war Germany." I shook my head, refocusing. "So he came aboard the Council. When did he leave it? When did you lose touch with him?"

It was Armaeus's turn to study me. "You cannot truly kill him, Miss Wilde. You must know that."

"Yeah, well. We'll see." I reinforced my mental

barriers, just in case.

Armaeus knew only what I'd known when I'd allowed him to poke through my mind about the day I left Memphis. Back then, I hadn't even considered Viktor as a person of interest. I hadn't known much of anything about the man who'd stolen the psychic children, other than that he'd been impossible to track, impossible to beat. Impossible…because he was on the freaking *Arcana Council*, a group I hadn't known existed.

"Miss Wilde?" Armaeus prompted.

His aristocratic voice suddenly galled me. "Viktor Dal was the man behind the theft of children in the last case I worked in Memphis, Armaeus. You know that. You've known it all along," I blurted. "Viktor showed me that fake pet mausoleum, but I think the kids are still alive. You do too, I suspect." I stared at him. "How did I miss him back then? He was right there, and I never even thought of him!"

He leaned forward. "If I may…"

He wanted to connect with me mentally. Something strange shifted deep in me, and I nodded once, tightly. If he was Spock, he would have placed his fingers on my temple and done the Vulcan mind-meld. But he wasn't Spock, and he did things his way.

Armaeus moved the rest of the way forward, until his lips brushed mine.

I'd been kissed by Armaeus before. As the Magician, his brand of magic worked best and fastest with physical touch, the more intimate that touch, the better. But this connection still took me by surprise. It was more intense, intimate. Without thinking, I lifted my hands to the side of his face, holding him as I leaned in to deepen the kiss. Something stirred in me, deep and profound.

The moment stretched in crystal purity, then—

Armaeus's hands suddenly lifted to cover mine. He pulled his face away and gazed at me, his eyes glittering a dark gold with the knowledge he'd pulled from my mind, my heart. My past.

Knowledge and...something else.

He pressed my hands together between his palms, the heat from his body warming me when I hadn't realized I was cold.

"Viktor Dal was the man you were hunting all those years ago," he said. "And you knew it then, on some level. You identified him. You drew the Emperor card."

Shock roiled through me. "I didn't know—"

"The King of Swords was his covering personality, but you knew. You merely couldn't accept it," Armaeus continued, his voice flat and detached, as if he was recounting the details of a long-ago mass murder. In a way, I suppose he was. "Your mother—" His gaze flickered, then he seemed to become human again, and he frowned. "Not your mother."

"She died because of me," I snapped, yanking my hands away. "It doesn't matter who she really was." I missed the contact with him, but held on to my focus. "Viktor killed her and blew up my house to frighten me away. And I saw Llyr, aka the Council's ancient dragon enemy of doom, hello, in the midst of that explosion. Is Viktor on the side of that thing? Because if so, shouldn't *that* get him kicked off the Council?"

"Not necessarily," Armaeus said, but his eyes fairly glowed as his mind grappled with the possibilities. "Llyr's magic is primeval and strong, and his ability to enter this world is governed entirely by the veil that exists between the worlds. That veil is attuned to the power of the Connected community."

I frowned. "Good power or bad?"

"Either. Hence the need for balance. If any one being or group becomes too strong, their reach truly would exceed their grasp."

As I tried to understand the ramifications of that little bomb, Armaeus pressed his fingertips together, focusing. "If Viktor used significant psychic ability in the course of hurting you and your caretaker, the veil would have been weakened to the point that Llyr could have seen through, if he was looking. Or if someone else was." He shook his head and turned abruptly to the computer screen, waving his hand over the surface. A full complement of missing persons posters gleamed to life. "These are the children that Viktor took, you believe?"

"Where did you get those?" I narrowed my eyes at him. "You created that from my *mind*?"

"Not necessary. Detective Rooks was gracious enough to take digital photographs of the signage that you recovered from the construction zone. We have direct feeds from all law enforcement agencies around the world. It comes in remarkably handy." He gestured again to the images. "The children?"

"Those three I know for sure," I said, pointing at the last set, then shifting direction to the earlier images. "Those three were taken in the weeks before, from other cities in the general region. I have to assume they were psychic too, but we didn't know about them. I had nothing on them, Armaeus. Nothing."

He shrugged. "Look back at the files. I suspect you had more than you believed, as you did with the Emperor. But you weren't willing to see it."

Irritation knifed through me again. I knew what I'd seen and what I hadn't. "What about this?" I jabbed my finger at the age-progressed shots. "Those don't look like computer simulations. Those look like real people in real settings. If that's the case, it means they're alive, right?"

Armaeus gazed dispassionately at the images. "Alive, possibly. But you have no idea what state they're in. Or what dimension."

I lifted my hand and squeezed the bridge of my nose, feeling the headache coming on. "*Dimension*. You seriously just said dimension. What, a secret island stronghold wouldn't do it? Some supervillain hangout in the Andes, that's not enough for you people?"

Armaeus's smile was arctic. "Every mortal on this plane emits a light energy, Miss Wilde, via the images taken of them, the words written about them, items they have touched, places they have been. Even if I cannot fully identify the source location of that energy, I can sense its existence." He tapped the surface of the table. "There are seven posters, of seven apparently living mortals. But only one of these image pairings emits any light energy. Yours. If those children still exist, it is not in this world."

Before I could respond to that, he sat down next to me, swiveling toward the table. "I'll have Simon look at the poster images and map them against facial identification software. He'll be able to tell if they're computer-generated simulations or actual teenagers."

"Let's assume that they *are* actual teenagers." I drew in a deep breath. "I want them back, Armaeus. If they're alive or if they're dead. As long as Viktor hasn't turned them into something that isn't human, something that would be more horrible than them staying missing would be, I want them back from wherever he stuck them. How do I make that happen?"

His gaze shifted to me. "The purpose of the Council is not to interfere in the actions of man."

"Viktor's *not* a man. He's one of you!" I erupted, smacking the table. The images on the surface started scrolling swiftly. "You weren't policing him ten years ago and he *took those children*. I don't know why, and I also don't know if he's taken anyone else. But he definitely took these six kids and you're going to help me get them back. And then—*only* then—can we talk about your precious balance. Because the Council broke the balance. Not man. The Council has to make it right."

Armaeus's stare didn't waver. "If Viktor has moved them to another dimension, that is a very ancient magic. Not something to be taken lightly."

"I've taken nothing lightly since I've met you." I jabbed my finger at the screen. "How do we get it done?"

He shook his head. "If the children are being held in another plane, you'll need a particular set of weapons to release them. Weapons forged specifically for use in other dimensions, and created by a people who lived when the veil between the worlds did not exist. I don't have those weapons here."

Gather your weapons, the Valkyries had said. Now we were getting somewhere. "Fine." I nodded. "Where can I get them?"

He flashed his hand over the screen once again, and a map of the world appeared. He pointed to an area between two continents, awash in a deep, unrelenting blue.

"For what you seek, Miss Wilde, you must go to Atlantis."

CHAPTER SEVEN

"Atlantis," I echoed flatly. "You say that like you expect me to believe you."

"I do." Armaeus expanded the computerized image, and it still looked like water. A lot of water. He shifted to topographical view, and it changed to water mixed in with a fair amount of mist.

"This isn't really helping me, Armaeus. Is this place under the ocean's surface? That's going to make finding those weapons a little difficult."

"Not exactly, no." He zeroed in further, and there was yet more mist. I scowled at him.

"Is it floating in the air? I saw the city that showed up over China, the one they thought was proof of aliens or secret space technology or some combination of the two. Is that what we're talking here?"

"Also not exactly. You're not looking with your full senses, Miss Wilde." He reached for my hand and covered it again with his, drawing me to my feet. He stood as well, turning me to face the table.

Where his fingers touched me, electricity arced out, making my heart race and stalling the breath in my lungs. I blinked, and my sight snarled up as well, everything around me becoming shooting beams of light instead of table, floor, and walls. I braced myself against the table, dizzy from the glare. "Um, you could simply have explained with your word, words."

"This is far more effective," he murmured, and he dropped his hands over my shoulders and down the length of my arms. Everything on my body that had the capacity to tingle lined up for tingling duty. He lifted my hands, and the surface of the table seemed to lift as well, the image moving off the static map to a three-dimensional whirl of spinning pixels.

"Whoa."

"See and explore, Miss Wilde. This time, with all your senses."

As he spoke the words next to my ear, I could feel the sudden pressure in my forehead, the whirring blink of my third eye awakening. It wasn't a change in view so much as a richness of perspective, and I drew in a startled gasp as the scene before me filled in with robust colors and sharply defined lines. What I saw wasn't an island so much as a platform with no defined base, a swirl of colors that could represent land or sea or air or maybe a bed of flame, but definitely something distinctly unsolid, dissolving and recreating itself anew.

Above that shifting base, however, was a city.

I'd read enough about the Platonic description of Atlantis to know I wasn't the first person ever to see this vista. The city was built as a series of concentric circles leading to a central tower, and it was surrounded by rich farmlands, vineyards, and fields, the perfect utopian center. "That's how it looks today? Or how it looked before all hell broke loose?"

"That would be before. Today the island is shrouded with what literature tells us is 'impenetrable seas and currents.' I can't pierce the mist surrounding it, but it exists. It merely has been broken and rebroken, no stone remaining untouched."

"You can't..." I tried to bend my mind around the

idea of something Armaeus couldn't do. I'd seen him rebuild streets in a blink, blast power around the world with a thought. What truly lay under all that mist, I wondered, that was strong enough to hold even the Magician at bay?

Armaeus took his hands away, and the screen faded, but he didn't move from his position, rendering me effectively trapped between his body and the table. I focused on the empty space where the image had been.

"So what's the point in me going there, if the place has been blasted to bits?"

"Because though all has been broken, nothing has been removed, to our knowledge." His words tumbled soft and warm across my neck. "Atlantis is forbidden to us."

And suddenly, I got it. "You guys can't go there, can you? You need a non-Council member to do it." I broke free of the cage of his arms, turning to face him. "And you *do* want to go there. You've been sitting around waiting for someone to send, and that someone is me."

He said nothing.

A new realization struck. "*Are* there truly weapons that can help me get those children back? Or are you simply manipulating me to get more trinkets for your collection?"

Armaeus regarded me with no emotion. "The weapons you seek should be within the central tower of Atlantis. In addition to assisting you, they will also prove instrumental in the larger war on magic. As I said, they were forged when the power that swept the world was far greater than it is today."

"Uh-huh." I crossed my arms and leaned against the table. "And how does that work, exactly?"

"Anything forged in Atlantis's fires will aid us. The merest cup could nourish a multitude, if held by the right practitioner. The slightest blade or spear..."

Armaeus gestured again. Below us on the table, a more traditional schematic appeared with illustrations. There was a dagger, a hatchet, and several star-shaped blades.

I glanced back at him. "Please tell me I'm not supposed to actually use those. I'm a little rusty on my hatchet throwing."

"The downfall of Atlantis was not that it grew beyond its military prowess, but that it bent and manipulated that prowess into magical form. Its wars were won not solely by might, but by the magic that powered its weapons. These pieces are all nondescript blades. In the hands of the Unconnected, they are simple tools. But in the hands of someone with psychic ability, they become far deadlier." He tapped the screen. "A shield can protect an entire army, a dagger can serve as the focal point for laser rays. Seas can be split with a staff."

"You're scaring me here with the biblical overtones."

"The greatest stories ever told often have their root in yet older stories, Miss Wilde. You more than most should know that."

"Okay, but...when was Atlantis officially destroyed? How long ago?"

"That is a subject of much debate. The artifacts of the civilization resemble those of ancient Greece and Rome, but its date of destruction is considered far earlier. Far, far earlier. Too early to make sense of the artifacts we have recovered, artifacts which made their way to friendlier shores before Atlantis's fall. Those pieces date to the golden age of antiquity, yet the records we have of Atlantis's fall date well before that time. As if it was destroyed before it could have existed."

I blinked at him, and he stood back to allow me space, but didn't move far enough for me to break our intimate connection, not completely. "You're saying it was shoved back in time somehow? That's why it can't be found? It was put back to a time when the island didn't technically exist?"

He smiled. I'd seen Armaeus smile lots of times, but this one seemed...fiercer. Stronger. More dangerous.

"It is one of the more intriguing theories, I suspect you'll agree?"

"You suspect correctly." A curious buzzing sounded in my head, and I squinted at him. "Something's different about you, isn't it? Something important."

Rather than answer me, Armaeus leaned close.

I stiffened. "What are you doing?"

"See with all your senses, Miss Wilde. Then tell me what is different."

He bent down to kiss me, and it was the most natural thing in the world for me to match the movement. As his lips brushed mine, I sensed the undeniable surge of power filling me up, almost lifting me off my toes. He placed his hands on my lower back, drawing me into his body, and I let him do it too, which was so shocking that my senses pricked, telling me that something was *wrong* with this, something was off...and yet so, so on.

"What's happening here?" I murmured against his lips. "Why am I not afraid of you?"

"You should never have feared me." As he spoke, whorls of sensation skittered along my nerve endings.

"Perhaps you're simply realizing that." Then he moved his mouth from my lips to trail a scorching line up to my ear, where his warm breath sent a surge of need through me, a mini whirlwind with nowhere to touch down. "You must prepare for your journey to Atlantis if you mean to go, Miss Wilde. The way is not an easy one. You will need to be strong."

"My...what?"

Armaeus's rumble of laughter sent shivers through me, and suddenly I couldn't think of anything but taking my clothes off, right there in the conference room. There was none of the usual panic that accompanied his touch, no resistance, nothing but a knee-buckling *want* that made my mouth water and my blood burn with need. I sighed against him, allowing myself to sink into the magic of his body, so sure, so perfect, so right that it made me wonder why I'd ever felt anything other than the incredible need to be with this man, to allow myself to —

The doors of the penthouse conference room opened with a bang, and Armaeus was suddenly five feet away from me.

Literally, five feet away, looking cool and unmussed as the Fool of the Arcana Council burst into the room with a laptop and a pile of printouts bristling in his grasp.

"I dove in as soon as I got your message," Simon said. He grinned at me as he strode forward. "How'd the hairpin work out for you in Germany?"

"Perfectly," I said. I could do cool. I could do unmussed. "How about five more of them?"

"I can do that." He beamed as he dumped his materials on the conference room and spread them out. Today he was wearing his usual knit cap, this one decorated with Day of the Dead skulls adorned with fat pink roses. Beneath, his wiry hair stuck out in all directions around his lean, pale face. He'd poured his slender body into a knit hoodie, ragged-hemmed jeans and Chucks, and he fairly bounced with energy. "Went low-tech to do the research on this one. It seemed...I don't know, less rude. Given they're kids and all."

I recovered and looked down at where he was pointing. The posters had been recreated with exacting detail, all of them except mine. Six children stared at me from the table with their camera-happy faces. Beneath each, Simon dropped blown-up photographs of the age-progressed images.

"A few anomalies right off the bat. As you noticed, that's not a computer-generated background behind these kids, and they haven't been Photoshopped onto other images. These are all complete photos. And they're *photos*, not computer graphics. The lighting shifts in each of them, and the quality is flawed in nonstandard areas, suggesting a snapshot. Their expressions match that theory as well."

"So where are they?" I squinted, trying to get anything from the painted concrete wall behind the faces. "Someone simply lined them up and took their pictures? That's a pretty basic wall. For all we know, they could be in a prison somewhere."

"Maybe, but if they are, they don't know it." Simon tapped keys on his laptop and hit return. The image on his screen reappeared on the table in front of us. It was the face of the youngest girl, Mary, reimagined as if she was Pinhead from *Hellraiser*. "The human face is a map of trackable muscle movements connected to emotional expression. Even faking a smile maps to a highly specific series of muscle movements and skin tone reactions that are significantly different from those affected by a natural smile." He moved his cursor, and

91

the pinpoints went away, leaving the smiling face of the older Mary Degnan, aged approximately seventeen. "This girl is smiling naturally. Her eyes are warm and engaging, her teeth are slightly mismatched, her face is turned slightly off center. She's not posed. If I had to guess, I would say she was caught leaning against a wall, talking to her friends, and was called to attention for a quick camera shot."

"She's real, in other words," I said.

"As real as can be." He lined up two more photos as well. One of a boy, the other a girl, both of them tilted slightly toward the other. I hadn't noticed that before. "The camera angle is such that the movement is cut off, but these two almost certainly had their arms over each other's shoulders, looking out toward the camera as a unit. Though they aren't looking at each other, their smiles mimic each other's, implying either a romantic relationship or a longtime friendship. A sibling relationship could also be indicated, and though the subjects aren't related, forced proximity for ten years could result in that kind of a bond."

I winced. "Okay, this is getting a little *Flowers in the Attic* for me."

"But notice again, there's no shame—not a hint of sadness. Nor the scars of long-term depression, which you'd find in sallowness of skin, discoloration here—or here." Simon pointed to the faces in quick succession. "These children all went through a devastating experience ten years ago, but the result of that experience appears to have been almost fully expunged from their features. It's fascinating, really."

I stared, wholly absorbed, the beginnings of excitement starting to warm the cold rock of loss in my stomach. "Actors?"

"Negative. The facial projections match. These are

the sixteen- and seventeen-year-old versions of your missing kids, down to dental imperfections. However, they might not realize they're missing."

I jerked my head up, staring at Armaeus. "Can he do that? Wherever he stuck them?"

"He, who?" Simon asked as Armaeus nodded.

"He could." He shot Simon a glance. "Viktor Dal, Simon. That's who abducted the children, and that's who, it would appear, now wants it known they were abducted."

"The Emperor," I added.

"The prodigal child returns." Simon whistled, rocking back on his heels. "In more ways than one. Viktor's been off the grid for about, what, two decades? Not practicing at all." He frowned at the images on the table. "At least not anywhere we could keep tabs on him. That's…interesting."

"What exactly are the Emperor's powers, Armaeus?" I cut in. "Or his abilities or whatever PC term you guys are using these days to explain your psychic skills? Because to convince traumatized children that they haven't experienced anything bad is kind of a scary trick, you ask me. Especially if you're the one traumatizing them."

Armaeus studied the posters with renewed interest. "The Emperor is one of the most skilled mental manipulators I've ever met, and I'd lived through my share of military and scientific revolutions by the time he was introduced to me. He was an adherent to Mesmer, but he'd taken his studies far beyond anything Mesmer had attempted. Brainwashing and implanting false beliefs are Viktor's stock-in-trade. Add to his considerable scientific skill the fact that he is a powerful Connected, and he is a formidable force indeed."

"Did he work for the Nazis?" I asked. There was no escaping the possibility, given the time and place where Viktor had surfaced. "Is that where he honed his skills?"

Armaeus's head came up at my tone, but his gaze remained impassive. "There are truths about the Council that are difficult to understand, Miss Wilde, without a perspective of history that spans millennia, not decades."

I shook my head, turning away. "You people should really listen to your own drivel some time."

Armaeus did not seem to take my censure personally, which was a shame, since I'd intended him to.

"In addition to Viktor's memory work, he became adept at managing perception of pain, pleasure, and physical challenge." Armaeus drifted his fingers over the old photo of me as Sariah. "He could make athletes stronger and faster without any pharmaceutical intervention. He could make militaries stronger. He could make the brightest minds smarter, all with the use of the power of suggestion. The human mind was his playground in 1937, and his work was invaluable to scientists and psychologists the world over."

I wasn't mollified — until a new realization clicked in place. "You put him on the Council to keep him in check, didn't you?"

Instead of answering me, Armaeus turned to Simon. "Have you located him?"

"*I* did, actually." Eshe's imperious whine echoed off the conference room walls as she sailed into the room in a puff of entitlement. "He's in Turkey. Surrounded by his fawning attendants, but not these children." She waved a dismissive hand at the missing persons photos. "These reek of normalcy. I can't imagine why he would waste his time with them."

There was too much derision in her words, even for the High Priestess. Like she took Viktor's actions personally. "What, were you and Viktor tight?" I asked.

"Hardly." Oh yeah, they were so tight. "But he is a part of the Council, and he has been sorely missed. He left when Roxie Meadows did, decades ago, and while she stayed close enough, he hasn't returned."

"We haven't needed him to return," Armaeus said, and his voice had an unmistakable edge to it.

"Now we do," Eshe countered with equal determination. "It's time that we provide a united front, Armaeus. You know that as well as any of us."

"But how can Viktor remain on the Council?" I asked. "You guys should be punishing him for *abducting children*, not wondering whose kickball team he's going to captain."

Eshe regarded me with familiar disdain. I found that more satisfying than insulting.

"We know he took these kids ten years ago." I jabbed my finger at the posters lining the table. "If he worked with the Nazis, he did a hell of a lot worse than that. According to Brody, he's suspected of trafficking drugs, humans, and military-grade weaponry. Don't you guys have *any* standards for the people you accept onto the Council?"

"You couldn't possibly understand the requirements of being on the Council."

"Uh huh." I scowled at her. "What are you doing here, anyway? I thought you were playing Ring around the Globe."

Her startled glance to me contained just enough pain that validation scored through me. "Hurts worse than you thought it would, doesn't it?"

"I have a new appreciation for your work and the work of the oracles, yes," she said, with more grace than I would have expected. "But it is a skill, like any skill. You improve with practice."

"Yeah, well, you have fun with that. I've astral-traveled enough for a lifetime." A sudden thought struck me. "Wait a minute. Please tell me that's not how I'm expected to find Atlantis."

"Atlantis?" Simon's eyes flared wide. "I'm going with!"

"Council members are forbidden." Eshe looked at me with curiosity, then slid her gaze to Armaeus. "It's also quite dangerous for mortals."

"She'll have a map," he said, but Eshe shook her head.

"The price is too high for a map such as that, Armaeus. You know it, and so does Death. There are rules, and you cannot break them. Not even to maintain the balance."

Simon's brows lifted so high I thought they might fly off his face. I kind of knew how he felt. "Whose rules, exactly?" I asked. "And when were they made? Because if you guys are somehow okay with bringing on people like Viktor Dal, your rules suck."

Eshe rolled her eyes. "As I said, you couldn't possibly understand."

"Yeah, well, I'm beginning to consider that a badge of honor." I shifted my gaze to Armaeus. "I'm out of here."

He nodded, but Simon frowned, clearly certain he was missing out again. "But where are you going? And when are you coming back?" He poked his finger at the posters. "Aren't you going after them?"

"First, I've got to sleep. Then I've gotta see a woman about a map," I said, not missing Eshe's patent concern as she snapped her gaze back to me. I smirked. "Have to admit, I'm dying to meet her."

"Yes," Eshe said tightly. "You will be."

CHAPTER EIGHT

The parking lot between Dixie's chapel and Darkworks Ink was empty when I reached it the next morning, and I breathed a sigh of relief that Brody's car wasn't parked in any of the chapel's visitors' slots. I didn't think I could handle another of his and Dixie's meet cutes anytime soon.

I paid off the cabbie and stepped into the shade of the overhang of Darkworks Ink, noting the "OPEN" sign.

The public room of the shop was about what you'd expect from a tattoo parlor. Walls lined with panels of flash tattoos and pictures of happy customers, posters of superheroes and fantasy villains. All of it was dark and kind of grungy, with the not-so-faint scent of patchouli hanging in the air.

A bell gave a sharp ping as the door closed behind me, and I busied myself looking tattoo-curious.

I'd seen one man here before. A thin, long-haired smoker with sunken facial features and hollow eyes. Jimmy Shadow, the man we'd thought owned this place. The man who I'd secretly suspected was Death, when I'd first seen him beneath the flickering neon lights of the shop, next to a poster of a grim, flag-bearing warrior on a white horse—all Death, all the way.

Apparently Death was a she, however, and

apparently she was busy. No one came forward from the back room, and I double-checked the neon sign — yup, the place was open. And there was the fact that I'd gotten in the front door without having to pick any locks.

Idly, I flipped open one of the large hanging panels of flash tattoos, sizing up my options. I could get one of literally a hundred bumblebees, hummingbirds, or butterflies, or a full garden of flowers. I could go all tribal and have jagged, swirling lines inked on me for life, or imprint the complete works of Shakespeare on my skin. Eventually, I gave up on there being any sign of life in the place and focused on convincing myself that Hello Kitty deserved to become a permanent part of my dermis. That or a Gandalf symbol. Toss-up.

"Those wouldn't be nearly enough."

I have a lot of practice getting surprised in stupid places, and I drew on that wealth of experience as I managed not to jump out of my skin. Instead, I glanced over to the woman speaking…

And nearly jumped out of my skin.

Death leaned up against the doorframe, her gaze raking over me like she was going to have me for lunch. Taller than me by about a half a foot, she was clad in black leather jeans and a tight-fitting muscle shirt that showed off every heavily muscled inch of her. Her hair was cut in a severe up-shaved style with a shock of platinum blonde falling over her eyes. One arm was completely covered in a colorful sleeve of tattoos, the other one almost starkly bare. Her ears were pierced all the way along the curve, but her face was free of metal. She wore no makeup, so all there was to focus on was a double-barreled dose of her piercing white-blue eyes.

I was getting used to the touch of an Arcana

Council stare, but this was different. This was…old.

"Cigarette?" She waved a battered pack at me, her faintly British accent a surprise. "I'm taking a break anyway. Come on back."

Without waiting for me to agree, she turned on her heel, leaving me with no alternative than to trail behind her. Death walked with the easy grace of an athlete or warrior, loose limbed and long-legged, easily navigating the narrow hallway despite the fact that it was stacked with boxes and photograph albums. One large room opened off the hallway with multiple chairs, then private rooms followed, a half dozen in all. I'd never seen any tattoo artist other than Jimmy coming in and out of this place. Clearly, though, they must get some traffic to justify all the workstations.

Or the landlord was willing to let someone nicknamed "Death" slide on the rent, which I could totally understand.

The hallway ended with an industrial-strength door, and Death turned against it, hip-checking the door as she gave me another grin. It wasn't a friendly grin, nor a sexual one, despite its hunger. But it was primal, and as she held the door for me, I felt my adrenaline jack. Passing that close to the woman—demigod, whatever she was—took way more chutz than I'd planned on pahing today.

If she noticed my nerves, Death didn't mention it, instead nodding to the room beyond.

"Big enough room to smoke in, great ventilation," she said, the odd accent to her voice strangely fitting for the large, utilitarian chamber. "Need it for the paint."

The place was the size of a small airplane hangar, and the paint she referred to was being applied to vehicles—muscle cars, specifically, each of them surrounded with a bristling forest of airbrushing equipment, the cars themselves in various stages of heavy metal heaven.

"You do this too?" I asked, if only to fill the empty space around us with words. Behind me, I heard the flip of a lighter and the suck of smoke, but I couldn't bring myself to face her directly.

"It's what's kept me away so long, you want to know the truth. Grab a chair." Death hooked a folding chair with an easy grip and settled it next to a second chair, close enough that we could have been the first two attendees at a twelve-step meeting. Punching down my nerves, I pulled a different chair forward and sat opposite her, keeping five or so feet between us.

It wasn't enough. I forced myself to not lean back as Death hunched forward toward me, her elbows on her knees, her hands dangling. The cigarette hung loosely from her fingers, and the smoke wafted up around her, too much smoke, really. Then again, I suspected she was probably dragging on something a little stronger than Marlboros.

"Car shows all over the goddamned country, you'd think I'd invented the art. 'Course, helps that I look like this." She gestured to herself unselfconsciously. She had a point. She currently was doing a mean impression of Charlize Theron in full-on Mad Max attire, only taller. A lot taller. And without the metal arm. "Business is good."

"And that matters?" The question could have been rude, but Death didn't seem to mind. She grinned, and the only imperfection I'd been able to catch was visible, a slightly uneven smile, the teeth not perfectly straight. Not enough to detract from the overall severe beauty of her face, but enough to make her seem real, attainable.

Almost human.

I felt the frisson of connection stir between us, followed by the hiss of panic. Fortunately, she chose that moment to start talking.

"Matters enough. I'm having a good time. The ink, it comes and goes in waves. There's always enough of the flash business to keep the front up, but the more intricate stuff has been getting a little out of hand recently." She took another draw on the cigarette. It didn't seem appropriate to suggest it might kill her. "Lot of Connecteds using ink these days. Think it'll enhance their abilities."

"And you help them with that?"

"Me? No. Council rules, remember? But that's why I have Jimmy, and that's how I keep tabs." She waved her hand through a cloud of purple smoke. "Easier for me not to be super attached to the Council, though, given the circles I run in."

I decided not to ask if there were nine of those circles. She didn't give me a chance. "You know what I am. You want me to tell you what you are?"

"What? No," I said automatically. Then I hesitated. "You can do that?"

"Could." She shrugged. "Not what you're here for. You want the map to Atlantis. Armaeus sent you." She grinned as my gaze whipped to hers. "Been around a long time, sweetheart. He can't read your mind because he hasn't really tried. I can. It's a good mind. You'll need to work harder at shutting it down, but you can keep me out too if you stay focused." She let her gaze trail down my face. "And you are my type, since you're wondering."

I felt the touch of her mind then, and blanked my thoughts. It was exactly what I did with Armaeus without thinking, but the effort was more challenging here. More intense.

"Good girl."

"Do you have a name?" I asked, happy to move the conversation back to her. "Or do you only go by 'Death'?"

"Not likely," she snorted, rolling the cigarette. The smoke had turned a soft azure. "Most call me Blue, though I've been given the moniker Blue Ice for more formal occasions. Originally I was called Crow, so I guess I'm moving up in the world."

"Banbh," I said, pronouncing the word "banuhvuh." Her quick grin told me I was correct. "That's your accent, then. It's Irish."

"Close." She grinned. "Now it's a lot of nothing, sullied by centuries away from home." She settled back on her chair, her long legs outstretched. For someone who'd been around since before recorded history, she looked surprisingly good. "But don't call me Crow. Too many old memories. Blue is fine, and keeps things simple."

She eyed me over her cigarette. "So, what has Armaeus told you about me?"

"Not much. He says you can help me get to Atlantis, or whatever is left of it. And he told me there'd be a price for it."

"There's always a price." She shrugged. "Why Atlantis?"

I hesitated. She'd just been in my mind, but maybe she hadn't looked around much. "Short version, weapons. He's gearing up for the return of Viktor Dal to the Council. I'm gearing up to beat the crap out of Dal."

"The dark mage." Blue nodded. "That's who took those children, the ones you have foremost in your mind. Six of them, ten years ago. Viktor was a busy boy."

Irritation riffled through me. "Look, I get that six lives probably don't mean a lot to you, given how long you've been doing...whatever it is you do. But they were kids, and they had families."

She lifted a sardonic brow. "Families like yours?"

I bristled. "It doesn't matter what kind. They were taken from their parents, their siblings, and put God knows where. I want them back. If going to Atlantis will help me confront Viktor and do that, I'm all in."

"And if it won't?"

"Then Armaeus wouldn't be sending me there."

"Fair enough." Blue's grimace was a grudging one. "And you're not wrong, though the Magician is ever one for having multiple reasons to do everything. The weapons you gather from the ruins of Atlantis will help you achieve your goal. When it comes time, Armaeus will have very specific instructions for what he seeks. I'd advise that you follow his guidelines, and not to tarry. Atlantis is filled with both truth and deception, most of which would do better to stay where it is, buried out of time."

"Okay." I frowned, considering her words. "Why else is he sending me there?"

She dropped forward again, elbows on her knees. "When Armaeus ascended to his seat on the Arcana Council, he was barely a boy, for all that he'd lived to be a man. What he saw in the years since is what ruined him."

"Ruined?" That didn't sound right.

She shrugged. "You can't look into the face of evil for so long and so hard without making some sacrifices."

I sensed the truth of her words, but I wanted details. "What sacrifices has he made, exactly?"

"Not my tale to tell, but he's taken precautions to protect himself. To protect the Council," she said. "His immortality alone is a boon for that. It provides the ultimate safety."

That was news. And a problem since Armaeus was now mortal. "It does?"

She smiled. "You'd wondered if Viktor had been raised to the Council deliberately. He was. The merest mortal is more capable of human depravity than any Council member is ever allowed. Yet as dark as Viktor is, he'll never agree to become mortal again, not for an instant. The aging process commences, and he is far too vain for that. He ascended when he was already a man in his fifties. To him, his youth has already withered away." She shook her head. "But for Armaeus, the need to remain immortal isn't born of vanity. There are things he is capable of as a mortal that he cannot allow himself to do, not anymore. The world is a smaller place. It could not sustain such magic."

"Right." I thought of Mim's horn and the feeling of utter bliss on Armaeus's face as he consumed the last of the wine from it. Had his eyes seemed darker afterward? He remained under the influence of the rush of Llyr's magic, but was there something more to him, now? "Well, let's hear it for immortality."

"Yep." Blue stubbed out her cigarette. "You wanted a map, you said. Only it's not quite a map. It's more a… I guess you'd call it more of a key. Each to its own location." She extended her sleeved arm and regarded it with a rueful smile. "Better than stamps in a passport, I'll give you that."

I stared, mesmerized by the artwork on her skin. Now that I could see it more closely, I realized it was almost moving in the shifting light and smoke. "Those are—those are all keys? To places like Atlantis?"

"You've seen the energy waves, right? That image is also stuck in your mind — and it should be. Armaeus was right to show you. We're all interconnected on this plane, but we're also interconnected with other planes. Where there are connections, there can be travel. Where there is travel, there can be transformation." She lifted one shoulder, dropped it. "And I happen to be in the business of transformation." She nodded back toward the tattoo rooms. "Let's get yours started."

Breathing a little shallowly, I stood and trailed her into the main rooms. It was only a tattoo, I reasoned to myself. People got tattoos all the time. It wasn't a big deal.

Instead of angling toward the open doors, however, Blue stopped at a door midway along the corridor, marked with the number 3. She lifted her hand, placing it on the smooth wood, and closed her eyes for a moment. The door clicked open and swung wide. The room was dark beyond.

"Um — I didn't bring any cash with me or anything to get a tattoo," I said, edging away until Blue pinned me with her glance. "I can come back later if that's better?"

"Nah." She smiled. It wasn't a good smile. "First walk is free." She winked. "It's the second one that'll cost you."

CHAPTER NINE

"Ordinarily, I'd place this on your upper arm, where it couldn't be seen if you didn't want it to be. But Atlantis is a special place. It deserves better."

As she spoke, Blue moved around the compact space. It looked like any other tattoo setup—a chair that would make a dentist drool, a table filled with tools, stacks of books and papers sitting around. But as soon as she flipped the overhead light on, the detritus evaporated—all of it illusion. Only the chair and the tools remained.

"Keeps people from getting nervous, to have all that crap here," Blue said, though I hadn't asked. She gestured to the chair. "Go ahead and lose the hoodie. It's not going to hurt, you know."

"Sure." I shucked my hoodie and got in the chair, my tank top meager protection against the chill in the air. "If it makes you feel better, I'm this way with easy chairs too. I'm not a fan."

"You'll be fine. The skin is thin at your wrist, so you'll feel it, but it won't be like a usual tattoo. With these, the pain comes later."

"Oh, good." I looked around the completely barren room as she lined up her equipment. The whir of the needle in its gun made my stomach clench. "I don't suppose you have a strap of leather or something I can bite down on?"

"Extend your hand."

Obligingly, I straightened the fingers of my right hand, the left now gripping its armrest. Death released a lever and swung the right armrest out, positioning my forearm in a wide angle as she scooted her stool to my side. I couldn't see my arm anymore over her hunched shoulder, and jumped as she swabbed the skin below my wrist with something wet and medicinal smelling. "Fingers out, Sara," she murmured. "Like this."

The cool touch of her palm against mine practically shocked me off my chair, the electrical pulse almost as intense as Armaeus's.

"A little warning next time," I gritted out as she pressed my fingers down.

"I can see I didn't spend nearly enough time in your mind," was her only reply. Then the whir of the needle started up again. "Touching here. This won't hurt, but you'll think it does."

"What kind of —" Then the tip of the needle hit my skin, and I blacked out.

Lights rushed back toward me as quickly as they'd fled, and I surged, fighting the fear, the panic, the despair, the —

"It's over, Sara. Relax."

Blue's voice sounded way too far away, and I blinked my eyes open, my gaze swiveling around the room. We were in the main tattoo parlor, and no longer alone. Jimmy stood with his own eyes shining and round, swiveling his attention between me and Blue. My right arm hurt like hell, and a gauze bandage had been loosely secured to the skin above my palm. "You said it wouldn't hurt."

"I lied. Chin up, though. If you ever decide to get a regular tattoo, you probably won't pass out. And when

you get your second key, you'll know what to expect."
She gestured to the bandage. "You can take that off. I
didn't want it to get damaged while we moved you."

"How long have I been out?"

Jimmy was at my side with a water bottle, and I
jumped again as another whirring noise started. This
time it was only the chair moving upright, and I eyed
the bandage warily as I slugged down the water. When
I pulled the bottle away, I was surprised. I'd drained
the thing. "Is it going to bleed?"

"No," Blue said, her certainty bordering on
laughter. "Keys tend to have a cauterizing effect. One
of their many benefits, once you have it on you."

"Yeah." I slid a nail under the gauze and peeled it
up, expecting to see my skin blackened and charred.
Instead there was a raised design that hadn't been
inked into my skin so much as burned there with ink
frosting, though not forcefully enough to be a brand. It
was a slender, sinuous curve that looped around on
itself, at once reminding me of an ocean wave without
the typical jagged peak. If pressed, I wouldn't be able
to say what it was supposed to mean. I glanced up at
her. "You couldn't have just given me Hello Kitty?"

"In time." Blue was leaning back against the wall of
books, and Jimmy had retaken his position at the door.
I decided to ask the question he was dying to know the
answer to.

"How long are you in town?"

"As long as I'm required. I'll be making my
appearance to the Council later this week." She nodded
to Jimmy. "He can see them too, if you're wondering.
Probably one of the more Connected people in Vegas,
and I know that's saying a lot." She grinned, her eyes
crinkling at the edges. "Armaeus's little blast last week
about fried his brains, though."

"You sensed that?" I swiveled my gaze to Jimmy, who looked sheepish at the attention. "How did it affect you?"

He shrugged. "My sight's screwy, if that's what you mean."

"And by screwy, he means fixed," Blue put in. "Twenty-twenty vision without his contacts, and believe me, he was a mess before. His second sight is also improving." She made a face. "Gonna make it hard to ink the typicals if he keeps it up."

Now it was Jimmy's turn to grimace. "Nothing worse than trying to talk someone out of a romantic tattoo when you know flat-out the feeling isn't mutual."

I held up my wrist to the light. "Um… Does this come with an instruction manual?"

"You need a tether point here—I'd pick Armaeus, since you trust him the most." She grinned again, as if at some private joke. "Usually. You've tranced out before, right? You'll do the same with this."

"Ah…okay. Then what?"

"Like I said, it's a key. You pick the point where you want to go in your mind, and when a barrier kicks up, that symbol will get you through. No secret words, no map, no spells. This is more direct, trust me."

"And coming back?"

"You'll need to focus on whoever your tether point is. The tighter your connection the better. Blood is good, sex is good, even rage if you don't have a physical bond."

"Blood like family?" I wasn't touching the sex idea with a ten-foot pole. "Because I'm fresh out of that."

"Or blood brothers. There's a reason for that old practice," she said. "Whatever you think will be a strong enough tie to bring you back. That's really the

110

key. Coming back isn't about being able to jump dimensions so much. It's about reasons, belief. You have to know you're wanted, and you have to be wanted enough that you're pulled through, no matter what."

I nodded, though my mind was churning. Had there ever been someone like that for me? Maybe Brody, a long time ago, before I'd run. Before I'd left him wondering if I were dead for ten years. Would he come looking for me now if I vanished again? Would anyone?

Blue's gaze was steady on me, and I managed a shaky smile. "Sounds like a little bit more than a typical astral travel journey."

"It's—similar. But you will be traveling physically as well as psychically. Your body will be present in Atlantis, and you can be killed."

"Oh. That's...ah, good to know."

She shrugged. "Life is change. You'll get used to it."

A bell rang at the front, and Jimmy jumped. "You can stay here as long as you want," Blue said as I levered out of the chair. "Not like there's going to be a rush on tattoos."

"I don't know, word gets out that Blue Ice is back in town, you might have a run on the place."

She laughed easily, but her gaze never left me as I reached for my hoodie. "When you ink someone, blood's spilled, you know. It can be a messy process. I've seen a lot of blood in my day."

I winced. "If you're telling me the walls back there are covered in arterial spray, sorry about that."

"No, that's not what I mean." She shrugged off the wall and sauntered toward me. I held my ground, but I couldn't deny the jacking of my heart rate, the sudden heat in my wrist. "I mean I see *into* someone's blood. I can tell things by the mix and measure of it. Who lives, who dies. Who is strong, who is weak. More energy is contained in a single drop of blood than in the multistate power grids, if you know how to channel it. How to set it on fire."

"Yeah?" I pulled on my hoodie, careful not to scrape the tender flesh of my inner wrist. It may have sealed up, but that didn't mean it didn't hurt. "Did my blood have anything to say?"

"It did." She stopped in front of me and reached out with a lazy hand, catching my chin with her finger and tilting it up until I met her gaze. "It said you would be coming back to me. And soon."

She held my gaze for a long moment, and I felt the essence of her words burn into me. Another bell rang, and Blue glanced toward the front of the shop, breaking the moment. I blinked myself back to the present.

"If that's your sales pitch, it's a damned good one."

She nodded, allowing me the out. "I try."

The heat of the day seemed somehow less oppressive when I walked out of Darkworks Ink. I squinted up at the dusky sky. I'd apparently been in Blue's chair most of the day. It was nearing evening, and I felt out of sorts, off my game. Across the parking lot, Dixie's was deserted. I couldn't face the idea of an air-conditioned cab, though, so I set off on foot. My skin felt strangely chilled, and I was beginning to seriously consider the error of my ways by the time I got to the Strip. I blinked, looking at the skyline, then blinked again.

The Emperor's keep no longer gleamed like a dull, empty husk. Instead, it punched out of the ground with almost a demanding presence, its surface electric, almost blue-black in the light from the setting sun. It wasn't the only changed Tower either. Soaring above Treasure Island, the White Tower seemed bolder and fiercer too, suddenly as occupied as the Foolscap, Scandal, and, of course, Prime Luxe.

Was the Emperor already here? I could feel the crackle of energy in the air, riffling across my senses. If Viktor was on the Strip…

My phone rang. I clicked it on. "Sara," I snapped, more harshly than I intended.

"Mademoiselle Wilde." The voice stopped me dead in my tracks.

I'd worked for Mercault on only a few occasions, but they were memorable ones. Memorable and lucrative. Mercault had come to Vegas a few weeks ago just shy of body-bag status, however, and I hadn't heard that he'd recovered.

"Good to hear your voice," I said. It wasn't a lie.

"Yours as well," he assured me in his lilting French cadence. "And I suspect I will not get much of an opportunity to speak with you in private once it's learned that I have embarked on the road to recovery. Can you meet me?"

"In the hospital?" I frowned. I hated hospitals. More importantly I had a transdimensional journey to embark on. But Mercault was a client, a client who paid me really well. A client prone to fits of vengeful petulance when he didn't get what he wanted when he wanted. As badly as I yearned for Viktor's head on an Atlantean pike, Mercault could be a font of useful information when he was so inclined. I needed to keep him inclined. "I mean, sure. I guess."

"*Mais non.* I have taken a suite of rooms at the Bellagio. You know it, yes?"

My gaze shifted to the enormous casino and its

bevy of dancing fountains, far up the Strip. Simon's domain soared above it, but of all the members of the Council, Simon would have no problem with me roaming around his crib's subbasement. "Well enough."

"*Magnifique.* I will expect you within the half hour."

I made it up the boulevard in good time, skirting the crowds and entering the gorgeous hotel at a relaxed pace. For all that I'd seen the Bellagio from the outside, I'd never actually been inside. It was every bit as opulent as I'd expected, however, and my enjoyment was not dampened one bit by the fact that two Frenchmen with guns fell into step beside me almost as soon as I'd entered the lobby.

"Mademoiselle Wilde?" one of them asked, though I suspected the fact that I was the only woman wearing a beat-up hoodie and jeans in the magnificent lobby was probably a dead giveaway to my identity. I nodded, and they kept their guns beneath their jackets like good little killers. I was elegantly marched over to an enormous bay of elevators, and I tried to look relaxed.

We boarded, and one of the muscle men slipped out a key to allow access to the penthouse floor. A penthouse floor in the Bellagio? Mercault never did anything halfway, I had to give him credit for that.

When I finally saw him face-to-face a few minutes later, my admiration only increased. He was looking surprisingly good for a dead man.

"Mademoiselle Wilde." Mercault repeated his bodyguard's greeting, but with much more flair. After suffering the European kiss, I stood back from him and eyed him critically.

"You seem...whole."

"Remarkably so. My family, less so." Mercault

strolled to the ample bar against the wall and poured two balloons of cognac. "I have much to thank you for."

I winced. He'd suffered much—more than most could endure. "I'm sorry for your loss," I murmured, but Mercault waved off my words.

"This is not the important thing." He handed a glass to me. "Grief comes later, in private, when I have rebuilt. Until then, it is a raw and open wound, meant only to help me focus." He swirled the cognac in his glass, staring at the patterns it made. "I have a debt to repay, to you and your patron, I know. A patron who I suspect is going to exact his repayment from me via slow and rather torturous conversation."

I shrugged. "Or you could give him permission to read your mind. Unless you have secrets to hide. He'll probably find those out anyway, given enough time. But the upside is, you give him access to your thoughts, you won't waste an afternoon, and he'll be in *your* debt again. It's not a bad position."

Mercault surveyed me from beneath heavy-lidded eyes. "I see what you are saying, but this mind reading... Will he warn me of it?"

"Probably not." I grinned. "So if you go in and offer it, it'll catch him off guard. He's too polite not to accept it as the gift it is."

"Yes...yes. I want an alliance with your people."

"Not my, uh, call," I answered awkwardly. My instinct had been to disavow the Arcana Council as my people, but...they sort of were, I supposed. At least until I got the children back.

Mercault didn't seem to notice my hesitation. He leaned forward, his eyes intent upon me. "In the meantime, then, I have a job for you."

CHAPTER TEN

My eyebrows fought each other in an epic struggle to reach the top of my forehead first. "You are barely upright, Mercault. You should be focusing on healing."

"Believe me, this will help me heal." He gestured to the table, where two high-backed overstuffed dining chairs sat. "You are right, though. I will tire too quickly if I don't rest."

He took a chair, and I pulled the other one out and away from the table before settling into it as well. Mercault had been a good client, but he was devious, coldhearted, and an absolute nutter. That level of crazy could be directed at me at any time.

"Two weeks ago, you attended the Rarity show," he said. "There was another of the black market elite there, Annika Soo. Her loyalties are of great interest to me."

"I thought you syndicate guys weren't loyal to anything but your next infusion of cash."

He smiled thinly. "Soo's holdings have not, to my knowledge, been infiltrated by the scum that is SANCTUS, while that organization has been a patent thorn in my side," he said. I nodded. I had personal experience with SANCTUS, none of it good. The quasi-religious, quasi-military organization was dedicated to the elimination of all things magical. All things, all people, and, apparently, all suppliers. "I am losing money and facilities, while she is stepping in to control the flow where my supply chain is being disrupted."

My brows took up residence near the ceiling. They were comfortable there. "You think she's on SANCTUS's payroll?" I considered what I knew about Annika Soo. Chinese, tough, and reclusive, she'd been a warrior in another syndicate before she'd risen to prominence by cutting off that organization's head. Literally. A bloodbath of *Kill Bill* proportions had ensued, and she'd been in power ever since. That had been five years ago, about the time I was learning that there was something called an "arcane black market." Oh, what a difference a few years could make.

I refocused on Mercault, who hadn't answered my question, so I helped him along by asking a second one. "Is she trafficking Connected children too?" It seemed that for every rock of nasty I turned over, there was another larger one to follow.

"That, I would suspect not. Mademoiselle Soo started out her life as a slave. She is not known to be fond of the practice." He shifted a glance to me. "You said you met her?"

"Eyed her across the room at the Rarity. We didn't chat."

He pursed his lips. "I expected her to approach you there."

"Well, we got a little sidetracked." I frowned. "Last I knew, she was recuperating in Vegas."

"No longer." He rolled the cognac in his glass again. "She undoubtedly received the same influx of power I did, only I don't know how she was affected. However, I do know that she's out of the city, back in Shanghai. I want you to find her, tell me where she is and who is with her."

"Sorry, Mercault." I set my glass on the table and

stood before he could break my heart with how much he was willing to pay. "My dance card is a little full these days."

"No." He shook his head, his expression fierce. "You will not need to leave this room, unless I miss my guess." He pointed at my chair. "You can tell me everything I need to know right here."

It took me only a few seconds to figure out what he meant. I swore under my breath.

"You want me to travel—like I did when I saw you last. To find her in, um, spirit." I blew out a breath. I'd never tried astral travel without the direction of one of the Council. I waited for Armaeus to hit me with one of his trademark "Miss Wilde" cranial insertions, but my brain remained quiet. Then I remembered. I'd completely shut him out, unless I phoned home. The influx of ability had affected me too, enough to turn the dial down on the most powerful Connected in the world.

So…maybe I could travel on my own.

"Two hundred thousand dollars, Mademoiselle Wilde," Mercault purred.

Then reality kicked me in the head. I liked Mercault, but that didn't make him any less of a criminal. And I was decidedly outnumbered here. Not a problem while I was upright, but locked into a trance? No way could I protect myself then.

I glanced to the door, noting that Mercault's bodyguards had taken up their positions in front of it. To block people from coming in? Or to block me from leaving?

I shifted my gaze to Mercault again. "Five hundred thousand. And no guarantees that what I find will be useful."

His gaze never wavered. "You saved my life. And

will save my business, if this is successful. Five hundred thousand is more than a balanced trade."

"Okay, then." I was nervous. Greedy, but nervous. "This could get ugly, though. This kind of travel is hard on a body. Hard as in I could spew all over you."

"I stood in the blood of my own deputy less than two weeks ago. I assure you that even if you explode in front of me, I will be unmoved."

"Not super comforting, but okay." I blew out a breath. "What am I looking for, specifically? You want me to see Soo's location and who she's with?"

I reached into my jacket and withdrew my deck, then shuffled the cards aimlessly as I stood, getting a feel for them. This was my second-favorite deck, traditional cards with stylized coloring but retaining all the symbols of the Rider-Waite deck that I'd used so frequently to find the missing.

"Her location, her compatriots. I suspect she is harboring agents of SANCTUS in her domain. I would know that as well."

"Yeah, well. Agents of SANCTUS aren't doing so well, I've heard."

"Your modesty is unnecessary." Mercault smiled. "I'm well aware of your role in damaging their operation. Do you not know the impact of your actions?"

At my confused glance, he gestured to one of his men, who stepped forward and powered the large computer screen to life. A green-on-black map of the world flashed briefly to life, then zoomed in to Europe. Large expanding dots with ties to other dots bloomed in several locations throughout Eastern and Western Europe. "Before the burst of psychic energy, this was the general reach of SANCTUS. Rome, Istanbul, Budapest...Shanghai."

119

"Shanghai. Didn't know that one."

Mercault nodded. "Soo's headquarters have long been located in the historical district of that city. Now, look what happens in the days leading up to the pulse. Here." The man beside him hit another key, and the Vatican City stronghold winked out, while Istanbul bulged and small outposts blossomed in Paris and Amsterdam. "And more importantly, here."

Istanbul disappeared. My eyes widened. "That's where they were hiding? The Hagia Sofia?"

"Not within the walls of the cathedral itself, but in a nearby palatial estate. They didn't die, mind you. They merely—dispersed. Rapidly. We can account for some of them traveling to Shanghai, hence my interest. The rest…" He shrugged. "Are in the wind. Not for long, I suspect."

"Some of them are Connected now, or think they are. Those with more developed abilities, like you, got ramped up. That's going to set them back."

He nodded. "We've been tracking all known operatives, but the augmentation of their abilities has made traditional tracking somewhat problematic. We think the major players didn't run to Paris or Amsterdam—too close, too obvious. We think they went to Shanghai."

I frowned. "But what could Soo be thinking? She's a Connected. She knows what SANCTUS's end game is. They want to destroy all magic. By definition, that means her too."

"Annika Soo has always been able to control an end game. It does not stop her from making money along the way." Mercault gestured to my cards. "You will use those?"

"I don't usually work this way. This may not work at all. You've got to know that going in."

"I will wire half the amount to your usual account for making the attempt. If you have information that I can use to help undermine Soo's next attempt to move in on my trade, I will wire the second half."

Mercault always did know the direct line to my heart. That didn't make my stomach any less queasy about the thought of attempting an astral travel jump without the Council's protection. Then again, they weren't here. And Mercault was a loyal client with money to burn. I nodded.

"Wire the money."

As Mercault nodded to the man opposite him, who busied himself at the computer keyboard, I angled my chair closer to the table. If I collapsed, I didn't want to fall that far. I shuffled the cards a few more rounds, then spread them in a wide, sweeping arc across the table, my mind slowing down, my heart slowing down, the breath coming more easily between my lips. It was always this way when I was able to truly sink into the cards, this feeling of rightness. A sudden pang of pain flared along my right wrist, but I ignored it. Blue's tat would take time to heal, but I wasn't jumping to Atlantis on this trip. I wasn't going anywhere at all, not really. The shortest stroll around the garden, nothing more.

I pulled three cards from the deck in quick succession and flipped them over. Nine of Pents, Hierophant, Five of Wands. And in that moment, my stomach tightened for reasons that had nothing to do with the body-scrambling hop we were about to do.

With a knowing that could not be denied, I'd identified where Annika Soo was. I knew who was with her, and I knew what I was about to walk into.

I turned back to Mercault. "Here's what I need you to say."

121

BORN TO BE WILDE

The trance started a lot rockier than usual, no surprise. Mercault was Connected, but he was nowhere near the High Priestess's level, and he was saying the words for the first time. With his aid, I dropped into my mind in fits and starts, eventually reaching the place where my limbs extended outward and my body became diffuse in my own perception, angling out of the luxurious room at the Bellagio and up, up, soaring past the tallest spire of the Magician's lair. If Armaeus saw me through one of the million and one windows in his fortress, he didn't wave.

My breath seemed constricted, too tight, and I wondered idly at the pain as I soared west to the edge of the US and beyond, arching over the wide Pacific. Everything else felt right, and my vision wasn't impaired—I saw the world flowing beneath me as if it was a combination of a hundred different images, the bird's-eye view of dozens of satellites constantly shifting in time with my own gaze. The islands dotting the ocean came up to me in sharp relief, and then there was the cataclysm of Japan, and the teeming masses of mainland China beyond.

I angled down sharply to Shanghai, fighting with my own breath. I sounded gaspy, and refocused on my purpose. Annika Soo's domain was currently located in the Waldorf Astoria on the Bund. Like syndicate bosses of old, she commanded an entire floor in the elegant hotel, along with the elaborate solarium she'd had built for quiet contemplation. Most people didn't know about the solarium, but that was where she would be. The Nine of Pents showed a woman alone in her garden, enjoying the fruits of her labor. The fact that Soo hadn't labored directly for anything she was likely enjoying was well beside the point.

I arrowed down into the smog surrounding

Shanghai, and then I really did have problems breathing. I could hear Mercault muttering something in French, but I paid him no mind. He'd done the job he needed to do by launching me into this trance. Until I got out, he'd be little more than a recorder.

"She's here, atrium. Alone." I saw Annika almost immediately. She knelt before a small altar, apparently in prayer. She wasn't going anywhere right away, so I faded back through the beautiful rooms of her suite at the hotel. Opulence greeted me at every turn. Rich wood inlays, marble, gold. Thick carpeting over inlaid floors, rich paintings on every inch of open wall. Other than the artwork, which had an Old World Asian feel, and the clientele, who were also predominantly Asian, I could as easily have been in New York, not Shanghai. Especially when I got to the main suite of guest rooms on Soo's private floor.

The head of SANCTUS, Cardinal Rene Ventre, lay in an enormous bed, his face slack, his body loose. He was sleeping, but he didn't look to be enjoying it. Tubes ran from his nose and mouth to a medical cart at his side, and surrounding the bed were more monitors and keyboards amid the fancy overstuffed chairs and thick carpet. It might as well have been the world's most comfortable hospital room. A small force of medical-looking people stood beside him, grim but focused. On the screen, the cardinal's vital readings appeared to be steady. His mind might have been fried, but Ventre's ventricles were doing just fine.

I murmured his location and status to Mercault, who started cursing in French. Since I didn't know the language, I kept going.

In the antechamber, more of SANCTUS's men were collected. They looked shell-shocked. Skittish, edgy. One of them paced the floor. Another stood with his arms behind his back, staring down at a schematic. I didn't know his face, but I described him to Mercault as best as I was able. He looked like a leader. Or whatever passed as a leader while Ventre lay in state in the next room.

Something shimmered in the energy field surrounding me, and I turned. It was as if I'd been tapped on the shoulder. Which shouldn't be —

Pain blasted through me so hard, I thought I was going to black out. I whirled, and Annika Soo stood before me, clad all in white, her dark hair ruthlessly pulled back from her head. In her hands was a white sword, its blade stained crimson. Which proved an exact match for the blood staining the carpet at my feet. Except my feet weren't visible — none of me was. Supposedly.

Based on the reaction of the men around us, it was clear that *they* couldn't see me at least. Only my blood gushing out of a long, wicked gash, streaming onto the carpet. Soo hadn't intended to kill me, then. Merely wing me for the benefit of her men. I wasn't in the mood to appreciate the finer points of this distinction.

I turned, reflexively gripping my left arm with my right hand to stop the crimson flow from my wound. My right wrist spasmed as it came into contact with my own blood, and heat swamped me, somehow taking the pain away and replacing it with sharp, clear focus.

Annika was circling me now, ignoring the concerned shouts of the men around her. Suddenly, then, it wasn't only Annika I faced. Six other white ninjas flowed out around Annika, all of them with their eyes on me.

Note to self: I am not invisible to ninjas.

Annika started spitting at me in a language that I

had no chance of understanding, and irritation flashed over her features as she switched to English. "What are you doing here? Who sent you?"

It wasn't a bad question, but I had a few of my own. "Why are you harboring SANCTUS? You know what they're doing to the community."

My arm seemed to be done bleeding for the moment, so I dropped my hands to the side. I had no weapon, and I hadn't exactly been practicing swordplay. Something else to add to the to-do list.

"You're allying with filth," I continued. "It's a poor decision, Annika."

"I ally with no one." She held up her sword, but unlike every kung fu movie ever made, she didn't approach me alone. Nor did her men and women surge forward in a choreographed attack of ones or twos.

Instead...they all converged on me at once.

Rude.

As panic shot through me, I felt the very heavy weight of a Glock pistol pressed into my hand. Mercault was screaming, and I brought the weapon around, not to shoot it, but to complete a roundhouse punch, coldcocking the man closest to me. The unexpected move sent him back into his fellow, and I squeezed off two quick shots then, spraying in their direction as the SANCTUS operatives shouted in alarm and ducked out of the way, heading for the doors. I whirled and shot again in a battering spray, getting a wall behind my back.

The should-be-dead ninjas, however, didn't fall down or sprout blood on their cloud-white gis. They disappeared, leaving nothing but their swords behind.

"That's cheating!" I scrambled forward, barely able to scrape up one of the blades in time before the other four were on me. Using the sword as a blocking tool and not remotely as a weapon, I screamed bloody murder and charged the ninjas with my gun pumping bullets, waving the sword more to distract and confuse than to actually display any weapons skill.

Poof-poof-poof. One after the other, they all disappeared, except Annika, who stood watching me with a smirk on her face. "You're wounded."

"Were those guys even real?" I snapped. "Did I just get pincushioned by illusions?"

She didn't drop her sword. I held Mercault's gun trained on her. She could probably throw the blade faster than I could shoot, but I wasn't about to test that theory.

"I have many tools at my disposal," she bit out. "The others are wrong about me. I am stronger than they think. I am stronger than *any* of you think."

"Hey, I've no interest in a pissing war with you, so back it down." I steadied my gun on her. "You trafficking children too? Pinching artifacts not enough?"

She straightened. "You're a fool. SANCTUS is broken, and I will help them mend. In so doing, I will consume them."

"They're on a mission from God, Annika. They're not going to give that up. Not even for you."

She arched a perfect brow. "That depends entirely on what god they come to believe in more fervently." Her gaze raked over me and lingered on my gun for a long moment. Too long. I didn't bother glancing down, but I had a feeling I was using Mercault's personal firearm, which, knowing Mercault, he'd modified in a highly distinctive way. A way that Annika Soo clearly recognized.

I wasn't wrong.

"I have no quarrel with you, but you also should have a better care in the alliances you strike." Her expression hardened. "Mercault!" she shouted, as if I was simply an extended Bluetooth. "I will not give up my advantage. But you *will* give up yours."

Then she rushed me, sword high, expression fierce.

I braced myself for her attack. This...was going to hurt.

CHAPTER ELEVEN

I still had Soo's sword sticking out of my left shoulder when I came back to consciousness in a rush, tipped back in the chair being braced by one of Mercault's musclemen. "That's new," I gasped.

Mercault stared at me for a long moment, ashen faced, before exploding into a flurry of French. Three of his people rushed me and pulled the sword from my shoulder, immediately applying pressure to the wound. It was my left shoulder, the same arm that had gotten gashed earlier in the trance. I closed my eyes as equal parts pain and nausea swamped me.

"We good, Mercault?" I finally managed.

"Your account has been wired the cash." He dabbed a cold cloth against my brow. "The men you described are the highest-ranking operatives of SANCTUS, barring two. We will begin the search for those individuals presently. They are either dead, or defected, or disillusioned. In any case, they are good people for us to locate. If they can be turned away from SANCTUS's cause, we might be able to regain our advantage."

"Yeah?" I struggled to a sitting position. My lightheadedness was already easing, and I pulled the poultice away, unsurprised to see that I had no marks on my skin. It still hurt like a bitch, though. And Soo's sword hadn't disappeared. Which meant that, technically, I could courier items home via astral travel. At least if they were stuck through me. "And what good will that do you, exactly? You really think you can stop SANCTUS's holy war?"

"Stop it? Not at all. I want to encourage it." He grinned. "All our efforts for decades with the technoceuticals were designed with one thing in mind: to enhance the power of Unconnecteds, allowing them to taste the fruit that only the blessed had. And the market was good. Very good. But there was also the fringe element, those Connecteds seeking to *enhance* their abilities, albeit temporarily. That market was narrower, but much more lucrative. They could afford to pay for the best, and only wanted the best."

"Right." I slumped back in my chair, rubbing my shoulder. "And children paid."

"Sometimes." He brushed off my outrage with the fervency of a sideshow huckster. "But now we have seen so much more. With my own eyes, I have seen you do things I have never heard of before."

"Astral travel isn't new, Mercault." But I already suspected he'd reached the same conclusions I had.

I was right.

"You didn't travel solely with your mind, though. When I saw you, you held a weapon from my household. This time, you *carried* a weapon. There and back again." He pointed at Soo's snow-white blade. "And came back impaled by a weapon as well. That is new. That is important. How possible is it that you could astral-travel to a location and pick up an artifact? That would change the game significantly, no?"

"I have a bad feeling that the artifact would need to be impaling me. That'd be less of a good time."

"Perhaps. But something to study."

His complete lack of concern for my physical well-being was charming. And familiar. "You know, you really should meet a friend of mine. You and Eshe would really hit it off."

"It is good work today." Mercault looked up as a phone buzzed in the pocket of one of his minions. I turned to see a look of frustration settle onto his face. "Very well. My cadre of doctors is here to poke and prod me, running endless tests. I submit because I wish to understand what happened to me. My newfound strength."

I grimaced. "I think that might be a temporary high, Mercault."

"Oh—I'm counting on it," he said, his eyes practically twinkling. "But if it's a high I can replicate, well." He spread his hands. "A man must innovate to continue making money, no?"

We both stood, and I shouldered on my hoodie again. It wasn't torn where Soo's blade had pierced through me, nor was it stained. My brain cramped at the reality of feeling so awful when there was no physical manifestation of my pain, and I scowled at Mercault. While I was here, I could use the man for something else, though, besides his money. He knew things I didn't. Things I needed to understand.

"What have you heard about Viktor Dal?"

Of course Mercault knew who I was talking about.

"Him." Mercault curled his lip. "Dilettante. He tried to come in on my business a decade ago, and I stopped that flat. He had no sense of the artistic nature of my work. Only wished to secure a blunt-force effect. That is no way to run a business, no way to run an operation." He leaned forward, clearly intrigued. "He has been quiet for years, though. He makes money, I am sure, but he stays to himself. Why? Is he reentering the game? If so, let him come."

130

"Stop your chest thumping. He's bigger than you and Soo and all the other families as well."

That shut him up. His expression turned mutinous. "What are you talking about?"

"I'm talking about *scale*, Mercault. Worry about Soo all you want, but there's a bigger picture you need to be paying attention to. A picture that includes SANCTUS and Viktor and even stronger magic — magic that Viktor Dal is already tapping into, unless I miss my guess." I pointed at his computer. "Find out everything you can about Viktor, and tell me I'm wrong. Tell me he doesn't have fingers in every supply chain in Eastern Europe. Tell me he's not about to topple your power when you're already reeling."

It was a long shot, and a bluff, but Mercault bit. His eyes glittered dangerously. "I will find this information. And when I do, you will help me ensure that Dal does not succeed in this coup."

"Deal. Now, you show me to a bathroom before I get sick all over your hotel room carpet."

By the time I got back outside, I continued to feel the aftereffects of astral travel. Worse, I was feeling the before-effects of Atlantis travel.

Even thinking that phrase made me doubt my sanity.

Focus. Armaeus wouldn't send me unless I had to go, I was sure of it. And he was worried about Viktor, without question. He might be the head of the Council, but the Emperor was coming, and that meant trouble. Then again, Armaeus wasn't doing anything to keep the guy from hitting the Council either.

What was the Magician's plan here? Was he trying to box me in, somehow?

A dark thought occurred to me, sliding through my stomach. Had *Armaeus* hung those missing persons posters to draw me into a conflict with Viktor Dal? Was he pitting the two of us against each other?

Just how badly did Armaeus *need* me to get to Atlantis?

As I stood staring into the street, thinking about that, a sleek limo pulled up in front of me to idle at the light. In Vegas, limos weren't any big deal, especially on the Strip, and more especially in front of the Bellagio. The window whirred down, despite the oppressive heat of the evening.

But it was only when I saw the creature standing on the other side of the limo, smack in the middle of the street, that my brain came back online. Slowly, though. Way too slowly.

Over the roof of the limo, a woman stared at me with ice-cold eyes, her blonde hair lifting in the wind, her enormous wings tucked tightly to her back. The Valkyrie's voice lifted over the rush of traffic.

"Are you so ready to die, Sara Wilde?"

Only then did I see the muzzle of the gun in the open window of the limo.

I lurched backward, landing butt-first in the Bellagio fountains as the stone statue on the opposite side of the pool exploded in a million pieces.

Beneath the water, I could almost see the trajectory of bullets and identify by the widening spray of ammo when the limo picked up speed, racing away. It was peaceful down here. You could barely hear the screaming.

Sadly, there was no way that could last. Not given the whole oxygen thing.

A moment later, the issue was resolved. Strong arms pulled me out of the water, and I shook my head hard as a familiar voice snapped at me.

"Sara? Sara! Are you hit?" Detective Brody Rooks

hauled me out of the water and onto the concrete.

"Where did you come from?" I sputtered.

"You've been acting batshit since yesterday." His face looked bleak, worn beyond his usual low-grade exhaustion. "You never truly reacted to the news about your mother, never once. I've dealt with a lot of trauma victims, Sara. You qualify."

I pushed the hair from my eyes, trying hard not to think about what kind of chemicals were floating in the Bellagio fountain. "Seriously, Brody? You've been *following* me?"

"Well, I knew you got a tattoo from that shop next to Dixie's. I also knew you were talking with Mercault. I had plainclothes on you at that point. When you came out and settled in at the fountain, they radioed me. Said you looked despondent." He scowled back at the street. "Your reflexes remain good, at least."

He reached for my left arm, and I winced, shifting away from him.

"You *are* hurt," he said. "I'm calling an ambulance."

"No, you're not." I got to my feet. "I'm fine. This was another message, a nudge from Viktor, if I don't miss my guess. He knows I'm looking for him."

Brody didn't seem convinced. "He *shot* at you."

"And missed. If someone had wanted me dead, they would have succeeded." I pointed up to the looming casinos on the Strip. Not the Council's digs, but the actual casinos — the Flamingo, Paris. The Bellagio behind me. "Lots of places for a sniper."

"Sara..." Brody's voice was tight. "Look, we need to talk."

I jerked my gaze to him, hearing the new tone in his voice. "What now, Brody? Is it Nikki? Is she okay?"

"She's fine. She's as worried as I am, with a hell of

a lot more reason." Without asking, he took my left arm and moved me down the sidewalk. I managed not to bleat in pain. "I know about the Council, Sara. I know about the work you're doing. I can fucking see their buildings up and down the Strip, and I can't believe they've been here this whole damned time."

I went for cool. Failed. "Oh?"

"Yeah, oh." Brody squeezed my arm, and I tried manfully not to pass out. "You want to do this in public or private?"

I opted for public, and we ended up at the bar of Paris, with both of us drinking scotch. Seemed a good way to start the conversation.

"Why specifically is Viktor shooting at you, do you know?" Brody asked, ruining the buzz of my first sip. "Is this because of the latest job this Armaeus Bertrand has sent you on?"

Staring at the richly colored liquid in my glass, I considered my options. They weren't great. I didn't know how long Brody would keep his amplified intuition, and I didn't know how much of his information was homegrown or fed to him by Dixie. That seemed a much safer avenue to walk down. I glanced up at him again. "Did you see the Council's digs on your own, or did your new girlfriend help you? Or, I'm sorry, your old-new girlfriend. Whichever."

He didn't back down. "Dixie doesn't figure into this conversation."

"Yeah, she kind of does." I sat back in my bar chair and swiveled toward him. "She showed you the Council's homes, explained them. After that, they were easy to see. Am I right?"

"It doesn't—"

"It does. Then she told you I did work for them,

134

and that's why I'm back in Vegas. How am I doing so far?" I didn't begrudge Dixie the revelation. Having a secret is a heck of a lot more fun when you could share it with a few select people. And inviting Brody into her little club was a temptation she knew he wouldn't be able to resist. The man liked intel. A lot. Almost as much as he liked perky blondes. "All I'm saying, Brody, is be careful of what she tells you. There's a lot of truth in there, and a lot of what I'm sure she thinks is truth. But what she thinks is reality and what actually is reality don't always match up. Look at her recollection of ol' Viktor."

"Then maybe you could help me out, because you're the one getting shot at here, Sara. Not her. You're working for this Council, finding magical artifacts for them. You're also working freelance for clients like Mercault. You tipped me off on that Nigel Friedman character, and he's hit Interpol's radar too, only come to find out—he's an artifact hunter too. You're in kind of a dangerous business."

"I'm kind of a dangerous girl."

"Well, you're bringing your brand of danger to Vegas, and people are going to get hurt. I can't have that. I can't have you hurt either."

"Either, as in here, or either, as in anywhere? Because you're not going to stop me from going after Viktor, if that's what you're thinking. You don't want that to happen here, I'll try to work that out, but he's coming to Vegas, and there's nothing I can do about that."

"Correction, he's already arrived." Brody took a sharp swallow of his drink, giving me the opportunity to stare at him. "Viktor Dal landed via private jet early this morning. We couldn't hold him, because, technically, nothing sticks to him. He cleared customs and left with his entourage for the city. We had eyes on him, and then we didn't. Lost him here, actually." Brody pointed up. "Big black monolith overtop Paris, lit up like a Christmas tree. That means he's, what, in residence?"

I looked up as well, as if I could see through the ceiling. "I have no idea."

"Yeah, well, it's the only thing I can figure. His baggage was bugged, and it disappeared as well. Guy's a ghost. A ghost with guns trained on you. Sooner or later, he's not going to miss."

"Anyone else with him?"

"Not that we can tell. No special cargo either. We've had border checks set up to intercept any unusual transport, and have nothing for our troubles. The kids aren't here, Sara. He's stashed them somewhere else."

I blew out a breath. "Somewhere else" indeed.

"That's not all," Brody rumbled. "I asked Dixie why Viktor was shooting at you."

"Dixie," I snorted, eyeing him. "You're serious."

"Remember, she knows Viktor. Her memory is flawed because she remembers him as a good guy, but she has a network on the Connected community that goes back for years. She has information on everyone who's anyone, and quite a few as 'uncategorized.'" He eyed me over his drink. "Including you."

"I'm honored," I said dryly. "And this explains why I'm getting shot at?"

"According to Dixie, Roxie Meadows did once let drop that Viktor Dal is, um, something called the Emperor of the Council. If that's the case, his position entails highly specific duties. Duties that haven't been carried out in hundreds of years, apparently."

"Well, he had time to take care of those before this

week. Viktor came on board in…" I hesitated. "You get the whole immortal thing, right?"

"I'm working on it."

"Right, so Viktor came on board in the nineteen thirties. If there was some ancient practice from hundreds of years ago he was supposed to resurrect, he's kind of late to the punch."

"Maybe," Brody said. "Maybe not. According to Dixie, there used to be an entire network of, well, 'mortal' supporters for the Council. She referred to it as the house system."

I set my drink down. "The house system. As in Cups, Wands, Pents, Swords? Those houses? Or houses like Slytherin, Gryffindor, and Hufflepuff?"

He grimaced. "I'm out of my depth here, Sara. All I know is, she thinks he might be recruiting you for one of these houses."

"By *shooting* at me?"

"It's apparently gotten your attention."

"It's also almost gotten me dead." I shook my head. "Does he plan to interview me through a body bag?"

"All I'm saying is, if you want those kids back…"

And suddenly, I got it. My eyes widened, and I turned toward Brody. "You *want* me to pay a visit to him, don't you? Straight up. I'm the *bait*." I grinned and lifted my glass to him in a mock cheer. "It's not a bad idea."

"Viktor wants to talk to you. Urgently and for reasons we haven't figured out. If it's merely a matter of him releasing the kids in exchange for a favor granted, he wouldn't have been playing these kind of games. He'd simply contract with you like anyone else, except for the fact that he committed a crime."

"That wouldn't make him unique among my clientele."

Brody grimaced. "And, if he wanted to kill you, he could probably already have done that."

"No probably to it." I shook my head. "Try definitely. I ran into Nigel Friedman in Germany, and his job was to tag me, not bag me. Viktor wanted me alive."

"That guy," Brody muttered, pulling out his notebook. "Give me his information—"

I waved Brody off. "Not the point. If Nigel had been instructed to bring me in at any cost, or to kill me, he could have done so pretty easily. I got away because I was supposed to be unharmed. He didn't understand why, but he wanted his paycheck, so he went along."

"Sounds like a charmer."

I grinned. "He has his moments. So whatever Viktor wants me for, he wants me intact. Which means he either wants to harm me himself, or he needs to use me. Either way, he's already dangled the possibility of finding those kids once. You'll know he'll do it again. We might find out where they are, what he's done to them."

Brody nodded. "I'm counting on it."

"When can we get started?"

He shrugged. "Now sounds good. I've already cleared backup if we need it." He shot me a glance that I was fairly sure was intended to be reassuring. "You'll be wired, of course."

"Oh, I'll be better than wired." I smiled, relaxing the barriers that had become more second nature to me than breathing, the ones that had moved from a furtive defense to a fortified wall. I dropped them away with a mental sigh, letting in the shadow at the door. The shadow that had always been there, watching and waiting, prepared to support, defend, or push me beyond any rational limits. The shadow that I craved more than I should, the shadow I hungered for, though he could never know it.

The shadow I didn't yet have total faith in.

I felt the touch like rain on a summer day, flowing back to me with an unquestionably sensual thrill. It was right, it was good, and it was about damned time.

"Hello, Miss Wilde."

CHAPTER TWELVE

"Mental telepathy." Brody's face betrayed his skepticism. His derisive tone didn't help. "Your client on the Council can read your mind."

"Sort of." I shrugged. I looked around the bar, vaguely surprised we were still having a conversation. "He's not the only one with that kind of gift, though. I would have expected Viktor to have put in an appearance already, him or one of his minions."

"His abilities are more specific than that. He controls by direct and personal contact with his subjects, but within that scope, his control is absolute."

For Brody's sake, I didn't share Armaeus's response. There was only so much that a cop from Memphis could take, no matter how jacked up his psychic abilities were.

"But, um, since he's *not* putting in the appearance," I said instead. "I'm going to walk around and think really positive thoughts. Sooner or later, the guy's got to show up."

"I'd rather have you wired. I can't help you otherwise."

"You sort of can't help me period, Brody. These casinos aren't part of the normal world—your team can't see them. So where would you and all your backup go if I got into trouble? Up to the rooftop of Paris? This is better."

He bristled. "I can see it, though. I can go with you."

That wasn't a bad idea, but Armaeus shot it down with a hard laugh. *"Viktor used Detective Rooks's number on those posters. He knows the detective is emotionally engaged. He will accept him. But in so doing, Detective Rooks will be put at risk of Viktor's abilities."*

"Right." I looked at Brody. "No. Armaeus will keep you posted. If something happens that needs to have a legit police action, you'll be tapped in. If not, you'll wait here."

Brody frowned. "He'll, ah...let me know? Mentally?"

I could tell the moment that Armaeus touched Brody's mind. The detective sat up straight, blood draining out of his face. Armaeus's touch couldn't help but be intimate, it was the way his magic worked, but I'd never considered what that would feel like to a heterosexual male. Apparently, it wasn't super comfortable. "Christ," Brody muttered.

I patted him on the hand. "I'll be right back."

It took me going outside the bar area and into the casino section for Viktor to get the memo, but he caught up with me soon enough. I recognized the stamp of his men as they rounded the corner beside an enormous Wheel of Fortune kiosk. Very Eastern European, very thick. Very no-nonsense. I didn't touch them, but I didn't have to. They were low-level Connecteds. Enough to see and believe, but not enough to cause Viktor any trouble. The perfect psychic minions.

They marched me toward the elevators, and I kept my peace, though my mind yearned to connect with Armaeus again. The Magician, for his part, remained silent. He could be totally stoic when he wanted to be.

141

I knew without the Magician saying so that Armaeus wasn't happy about my decision to visit Viktor directly, but he wasn't unhappy either. I wasn't on the Council, and that gave me the opportunity to do all the dirty work Armaeus couldn't do, or wouldn't do. Technically, Armaeus was mortal now, but that didn't seem to be relaxing his iron hold on noninterference. At least not direct interference. Indirect, he was all good with.

The doors slammed behind us, trapping me with the Euro goons. We shot up with ear-popping speed to well beyond penthouse level, and the doors whooshed open again.

Right about then, I realized my mistake.

Viktor hadn't been around anywhere near as long as Armaeus had, but he *was* a member of the Council, and he presumably wasn't an idiot. He knew the skill sets in play. He might not be as strong as Armaeus, but he'd had time to study the man and how he worked. The Magician had limitations. Of course Viktor would exploit those limitations.

The Magician's ability to read minds was always impaired by water. It was why I'd preferred to keep an ocean between us when I'd first begun working with the Council. Now, as the doors of the elevator opened onto a large penthouse domain, I blinked in surprise. The walls of the Emperor's domain had been transformed into waterfalls.

"Sariah Pelter, it is so good of you to join me, at last."

My attention snapped to the center of the room.

Viktor Dal was a tall man, but not as tall as I remembered. He stood maybe six feet, his body whipcord thin, his face lean and weathered. He'd ascended to the Council in his midfifties, and his hair

142

was mostly blond, with a few fierce tufts of white proclaiming his age. It was cropped close to his head and contributed to his hawklike appearance along with his aquiline nose and strong chin. His eyes were a curious shade of gray, so pale that you wanted to look away, but you couldn't. He wasn't an ugly man, but he wasn't attractive either. He was…compelling. I thought of Armaeus's description of him: a mesmerist. Someone able to persuade others with a glance and a few words to do what he wanted. Looking at him here, I could believe it.

I didn't see the point in wasting time. "I want those kids back, Viktor. Alive and as whole as they can be."

"I'm glad to hear it." His smile was gracious, almost affectionate, and I felt the weight of its warmth as a physical touch. I found myself shifting closer to the man, without any reason to do so, and steeled myself to remain where I was. "I was charmed by your attempts to recover them ten years ago and realized the threat you posed. Had you continued on your journey, you would have found them, and that would have been far too soon. Still," he sniffed, "how quickly you were able to forget all those poor children once a challenge was put in your way."

An unexpected wave of shame scored through me. Despite knowing this was Viktor's modus operandi, I was startled at how rapidly I shifted from angry to embarrassed. Because, of course, he was right. I *had* abandoned those kids. Brody hadn't, but I'd run and never looked back.

I'd abandoned them.

As if he could read my mind, Viktor continued his genteel condemnation. "Imagine my delight at finding Detective Rooks here as well. Now he I have to commend. He continued to look for the children, to

143

maintain ties with the parents. Ties that grew ever more strained over time, of course, but he persevered as long as he was able."

I hadn't known about the parents, Brody had never told me. Still, I could see him doing something like that. All those years. All those birthdays come and gone.

While I had done everything I could to forget.

I tried to regain control of the conversation. "You killed my mother."

"Oh please, Sariah. We both know she wasn't really your mother. Surely the detective ran to you with that news the first time he saw you again. He took that death harder than most, felt responsible. And he was. Had he kept Sheila Pelter out of the investigation, she never would have died. Not by any direct attack anyway. Eventually, the alcohol and prescription drugs she was taking would have done her in, but she wouldn't have been bludgeoned to death and dumped in a river."

His gaze flickered over me as I blanched.

"Oh my. He didn't tell you that either? That must be challenging. Knowing that all this information is out there and yet being unable to do anything about it…and knowing that the information you require is being willfully withheld from you. Makes it difficult for you to do your job, I should think."

I folded my arms, his censure finally reaching the tipping point where it couldn't hurt me anymore. He seemed to recognize that as well and flashed me another smile. "You must be wondering why I've brought you here. Not to torment you with the children you let slip through your fingers, I assure you. As enjoyable as that is for me."

"Are they dead?"

"Of course not. There would be nothing of value I could offer you if they were dead. And I want to be of value to you, Sar — oh, but it's Sara now, isn't it? I may call you Sara, can't I? It's such a well-suited name to you."

Once again, I found myself slipping into the cadence of his words. They created a sort of walled space around me, one filled with comfort and security, keeping everything that was dark and awful out...

I shook my head, forcing myself to stay focused. "I don't care what you call me. What's your price to release the children?"

"It's a tricky subject, that. You see, I can't release them myself. I can see them, ensure their safety, their growth. But I can't quite *get* at them. It was something I didn't realize, ten years ago, but I was too hasty in my preparations. I didn't account for the nuances of where I was placing them."

I stared at him. "What are you talking about?"

"Forgive me." He seemed to come back to himself. I had no idea if he was acting or not, but if he was, he was doing a good job of it. "They are quite safe. But also quite trapped."

He turned to the side, and the panels of the wall split apart to reveal a large-screen TV. The image that immediately came to light brought me up short. Six teens at what looked to be some sort of boarding school, interacting with other students, each other, all of them laughing and carefree. "They believe they survived a terrible accident while on a class trip together when they were children," he explained glibly. "They were all from the same general area, so their accents and mental touch points were quite similar, which made the frame easier to accept. Their parents were killed and the state placed them in this school. Distant relatives visited for a while but then flowed away. Now, they have only each other."

I snapped my gaze to him. "That's the load of crap you fed them?"

"We all tell ourselves stories, Sara." His smile remained gracious, but he regarded me with shrewd focus. "Think of the stories you willfully believed your whole life."

Another queasy burst of shame slid through me as Viktor kept talking.

"This story, however, served its purpose. It kept their minds whole and healthy until the anomalies of their new existence became accepted fact. It was a far more humane approach than letting them believe they were abducted from loving homes and thrust into an alternate universe guarded by demons."

Oh, for the love of... "Demons."

Viktor nodded. "Six of the most powerful entities that ever walked this earth. They were banished when Atlantis fell."

"What?" I blinked at him. "Atlantis?"

He waved his hand. "Yes, I'm aware that you've met Llyr. These creatures are nowhere near his level, but they are powerful in their own right. Should they return to this plane, they would infuse the world with magic once more, down to its very core." His smile flashed. "It will be glorious. You will see."

"Right. Because everyone associates demons with good times." I jabbed my finger at the screen images of the children. "Explain to me again why you can't get them out. You put them there. It shouldn't matter who you signed up to guard them."

Viktor sighed, looking a touch abashed, which I immediately distrusted.

"To understand that, you must understand what I

146

was attempting to accomplish ten years ago." He turned from the screen and looked out one of the windows lining the space, the thin wall of water spilling in front of it turning the skyline of Vegas into a wavy abstraction. "Magic in the world may currently be under attack from groups like SANCTUS, but that is not the greatest threat we face. The Council has ever been consumed with the idea of balance. But if there is no magic, then balance becomes a pointless endeavor."

I shifted uneasily. I'd made this argument to Armaeus myself. "I thought magic was a self-sustaining force."

"It is, or it can be. But the Council was not always so diligent about its commitment to the cause of noninterference. There have been times—many times—when it has acted forcefully to remove magic that it considers too extreme to be balanced."

I thought about Llyr. He hadn't been ejected once from the earth, according to Armaeus, but at least twice. "And that matters why?"

"Attrition. Extremes promote growth. Pushing all magic toward some homogenous center promotes atrophy. Eventually, magical properties weaken to the point that they can't transmute into different forms. When an ocean dries to a pond, it has a much harder time reaching the sky to return to ice crystals that then can become rain."

He gestured to the world outside. "And, too, population explosion has played a role. Magical abilities are not necessarily inherited, but they can be. When one psychically skilled forebear has a child, that inheritance is undiluted. When six or seven children are born, who then go on to have six or seven children, it becomes a hit-or-miss proposition."

"Nobody has that many children anymore.

Especially if they're psychic."

"Not anymore," he conceded. "But the damage has long since been done. Add to that the forced removal of magical creatures deemed too strong for this world to balance, and the gradual weaning away of Connecteds from natural sources of magic, and you create a state in which a war on magic is a lopsided war indeed."

"Don't tell me those children were part of your *defense* against a war on magic, Viktor. I'm not buying that."

"They were…an experiment, which I neither regret nor have any need to defend. There is a time and a place for balance, and a time and a place for active effort. I grew weary of waiting for the time for the latter to arrive. We must move forward if we are to create a new world order. And the time for movement is now."

"Sounds like someone got a little too turned on during his stint with the Nazis."

His lips twisted. "You speak about things you know nothing of. There will always be unbalanced people in the world who are willing to do the things that no one else can fathom. Most of the time, nearly all of the time, their insanity is also their infamy. Hitler was no different. But you also cannot discount the power of a truly focused mind. Look at what one insignificant sociopath was able to do, almost exclusively by the force of his sheer will. Look at what is happening around you with insurgencies throughout the world, militant leaders who command tens of thousands to their cause. The human mind is the most fascinating psychic weapon at our disposal, and all too often it takes a maniac to show us its true potential."

148

"Do you have any idea how much of a nutball you sound like right now?"

"And yet, you're still listening." He leaned toward me slightly, and I found I didn't want to lean back. There was something about Viktor's crazy that truly was compelling, as loathsome as I might find it. "Hitler's regime was riddled with wrong thinking, but in one particular well-documented area, he had something right. There *were* forces beyond the understanding of man that existed in this world, forces that he very much wanted to control. The accumulation of occult artifacts and items of magical power was not just some haphazard game to him, an adjunct to his accumulation of precious art. He had a purpose and a plan for those items."

I thought of all the artifacts buried underneath Neuschwanstein. How many more cubbyholes of the arcane remained around Europe? "And, what? You were part of that purpose?"

"No." Viktor's grimace was regretful. "I'd ascended to the Council by the time Hitler truly came to prominence. I could only watch as he moved directly toward his goals."

Listening to Viktor's words, I understood more clearly why Armaeus had agreed to accept him onto the Council. His abilities had been cresting and apparently, the Council needed an Emperor. But perhaps more importantly, the Allies needed Viktor on the sidelines, not in the thick of the war…and working for the wrong side. I kept my face carefully blank.

"Okay, Viktor, I'll bite. Why did you take those children ten years ago and stick them God knows where? Why did you harm innocent lives, destroy families?" I hardened my gaze. "And how many more children did you take?"

149

He smiled and waved again at the computer screen. It flickered and went black. No, not quite black. There were images there, negative reflections against the darkness of the screen. "What the hell is that?"

"Those are the reasons why I took the children—and there were six, and only six. I took them from the heartland of America, from small towns and cities. The requirements were exact. They had to be linked geographically, they had to be educated, or what passes as educated in this world. But not too educated, not yet. They had to be healthy and well nourished. They had to be pure of heart." He twisted his lips. "Even six- and seven-year-olds were challenging in this last regard, I can assure you."

"And in exchange you got..." The answer was obvious, but I couldn't wrap my head around it. "Those guys?" I gestured to the screen. "Six demons of destruction?"

"You have a child's view of psychic abilities." The words were a sharp rebuke, but Viktor never changed his tone. "There is no ultimate destruction where there is magic. There is only creation. What one man considers to be darkness and loss, another sees merely transformation."

"Uh-huh. And yet I'm sensing a distinct lack of goodness and light with those guys." I peered at the screen, sensing the wave of derision that rolled back toward me. Derision and age and fury. I stepped back. The creatures knew they were being watched.

"Because that is how the perspective of this world sees them, and, to be fair, the sentiments they most deeply espouse would curl the toes of any Sunday school teacher. They house every vice, you could say. Every sin."

I flicked my gaze to him. "Don't bullshit me,

150

Viktor. You said there are six demons, not seven. No one ever referred to the *six* deadly sins. I would've heard of that."

He smiled. "Not at all. But they do figure into that same conversation. In addition to describing what became known as the seven deadly sins, Solomon mentioned another six entities, but he gave no name to them." He gestured to the screen. "Those six hold the power of pure potential for the human spirit, untrammeled by the need for our petty morality or concern for goodwill."

"They're amoral."

"They were when they were blasted from the earth, yes. They have spent the intervening millennia studying our world, but there remained one missing piece for them, one thing that no remote study could replicate. Before they could return, they required the souls of six children."

"Their *souls*?" The word came out on a screech. "You mean to tell me you delivered these kids' *souls* for demons to pick apart?"

"For the opportunity to have magic reenter the world, reenergize the planet? For the opportunity to refill the well that we have drained with our wars and creeds and dogma?" He scoffed. "I would have gladly traded six hundred thousand. Six million souls. And if you had seen what I have seen, you would too."

"I want them back."

"I know." He smirked. "I want that too." He waved at the screen. "You'll notice, those demons remain on the other side of the veil. They did not kill the children, as I expected, but created the elaborate shell in which they live, drawing upon my abilities to keep the mortals' minds whole and sane. The demons also did not come through, as they promised they would.

151

Instead, they've bonded with the children."

"Bonded." My lip curled. "What the hell does that mean?"

"For our purposes, it means that they will not leave without them, nor will they remain behind without them." His gaze shifted to me. "You want the children back, then go get them. But in doing so, you will also bring six demons into the world. It's the only way."

CHAPTER THIRTEEN

The moment I entered the elevator, flanked once more by Viktor's thugs, the Magician was back, flooding my mind with a comfort I hadn't realized I needed.

Please tell me you could hear that.

"Viktor could not keep me out entirely. I could not hear, but I could see what your eyes saw, feel what you felt. I saw the children, and that there is a way." He hesitated. *"But the demons you saw must not return to this plane."*

No kidding. But Armaeus offered no other pithy advice, like how I was going to get the children out without their tagalong masters of darkness. I was beginning to understand the limits of his reach in all sorts of areas.

The elevator stopped well short of the ground floor, and I tensed as the doors swung open.

"Exit here," one of the guards said gruffly, gesturing me out. "Take another elevator down in five minutes. Leave the casino area immediately. Understood?"

"Oh. Sure."

Obligingly, I stepped out, debating the relative likelihood that I was about to be shot, but the men stayed where they were. The doors whooshed shut, and my knees almost instantly wobbled, the full magnitude of what I'd seen and heard taking over for a moment. I made my way to the bench in the elevator bay and leaned against the wall. "Armaeus," I whispered.

"I am here, Miss Wilde. I am always here."

But I knew he wasn't. He couldn't be, not for where I needed to go. He was a member of the Council, and I was his hired hand. I was paid well for that. "Those weapons in Atlantis. Can they fight, um, demons?"

"They were forged in the same era of those beings. They were intended for such a battle."

I nodded. "Then I'm going to go get them."

Before he could respond, I closed my mind again, shutting out the comfort of his touch. I would have to get used to being without it, even when I wanted it. I grimaced. *Especially* when I wanted it.

The chime of an elevator pinged, startling me. The doors swept open, and I stood, feeling a million years old. I shuffled into the elevator and, when it opened again, made my way off the casino floor. Brody was waiting for me in the bar of Paris. He wasn't alone.

"Dollface, you need to learn the value of taking backup with you."

"Hey," I said as Nikki grinned at me, resplendent in a Sgt. Pepper's Lonely Hearts Club Band conductor jacket and hot pants, a pair of John Lennon vintage sunglasses on her nose. "How'd you get here?"

"Detective Dishy here got tired of waiting for updates from the man in black." She winked at me. "Fortunately, I've been around you long enough that I'm no slouch at seeing what you're seeing." She looked at me over the rim of her sunglasses. "Those kids are alive."

Brody sat at the table with his laptop propped, his phone at his side. His gun remained holstered, but his jaw was tight. "Where are they?"

"Trapped. They don't know it, though. They think

154

they're living normal lives." I shifted my gaze to Brody. "But if I go get them, they won't be coming alone."

He scowled at me. "Meaning?"

"Meaning Homeland Security is not going to be happy. Six very bad…Connecteds will be coming out with them." I tried to remember the shapes in the screen, the shadows. "Very bad. The kind of bad we'd want to lock up immediately and run screaming in the other direction. You have any sort of facility for that?"

"Homeland Security isn't exactly set up to handle a Connected insurgency, Sara." He looked at Nikki, his gaze resting on her Sgt. Pepper outfit, then sliding away. "You have any sort of holding pens for your own kind?"

She frowned at him. "We don't work that way, love chop. We're much more a live-and-let-live kind of group."

Irritation was plain on Brody's face. "You don't police your own?"

"Well…no. We focus much more on keeping souls out of harm's way versus attacking those who would do them harm. We have to choose our battles. There's only so much of us to go around."

"Well, there's about to be less." He shifted his glance to me. "These men. What are the odds they'll ally with the dark practitioners?"

"Just north of a hundred percent." I hesitated, but I knew I needed to tell him the full story. "They're not men either, not precisely," I said, as gently as possible. "They're demons."

"Actually, my dear Sara Wilde, they're quite a bit more than that."

We all turned as Aleksander Kreios stood at tableside, resplendent in a midnight-black tuxedo, unbuttoned to show the full length of his ocean-blue silk shirt. Gold glinted at his neck and wrists, and I could see a new feature as well. The edge of a tattoo at his neckline, gleaming against his sun-gilded skin. An illusion? Or had he paid a visit to Blue as well today?

I tried not to think about that too hard as Kreios nodded to Brody, then turned to Nikki, picking up her hand in his. "It is always my most sincere pleasure to see you." He bent to kiss her knuckles.

Nikki fluttered but held her own as Kreios turned to the rest of us. "Armaeus suggested that it was time to provide some illumination on the challenge you face. Viktor Dal's demons are, in fact, one-time Atlantean sorcerers, banished at the same time as Llyr. Their role in Llyr's ascendance to power has been lost to recorded history, but they came from a race mentioned perhaps most prominently in the Bible. Giants of men who commanded an unusual power over the crops and the weather, and the mortals around them."

"Canaanites." I knew my biblical history, and I knew my *History Channel: Aliens* too. "You're talking fallen angels here."

Brody made a noise that sounded suspiciously like a groan. "Please tell me you're joking."

"They've also been known as djinn, demons, watchers—the list is endless. But the salient part is this. At the time of the Great Flood, the Canaanites were wiped out, along with a prodigious amount of humanity, if you believe historical accounts. The Council records paint the story a little differently, of course. Either way, the six djinn of Atlantis were banished."

"Banished where?"

"Unknown." Kreios shook his head. "That Viktor

found them at all is…remarkable, and bears further study. We suspect he doesn't know their precise location. He summoned them, and they responded to the pull of his magic but kept their dimension safely hidden. To reach them, he needs a mortal of sufficient strength and training — and with a connection to the children. He believes he has that with you. Where before you were an obstacle to his objective, now you are a path, Sara Wilde. His only path."

"Well, that's great, but we've got a problem. According to Viktor, bringing those kids out means bringing the demons in the world."

"Perhaps." Kreios smiled, and for the first time, I picked up on his peculiar energy. He was fairly buzzing, his eyes too bright, his manner edgy. "Alternatively, the children could come out possessed by the djinn. Alternatively, no one could come back, children or demon. The possibilities are endless."

"Those all sound like really bad possibilities, for the record." I thought about it. "How bad are these guys?"

"Did Viktor characterize them as bad?"

"Viktor worked with the Nazis, Kreios. His perspective isn't reliable."

When the Devil simply stared at me with that infernal smile, I shrugged.

"No, he didn't call them bad. He specifically said they were amoral, unbound by any of the preconceived notions of our time regarding things like crime, laws, or human relationships."

"Is that all?" Brody put in dryly.

"And we don't have any record of what these bad boys did back in, um, Atlantis? Before they were shipped out as No Return to Sender?" Nikki had recovered herself and was rolling her drink in her hand, her long manicured nails painted an eye-popping red to go with her conductor's outfit. "For all we know, they could have gotten a bad rap."

"Viktor chose his marks well," Kreios said. "The six djinn were considered the most powerful sorcerers of their time, but they were not men schooled by traditional means. They arrived in this world fully arrayed in the light of their power. According to our records, they could alter the hearts of men to a cause, command armies, change weather patterns, move with the speed of wind. They were also unusually tall and tremendously strong."

"Sound like my kind of guys," Nikki drawled.

Kreios winked. "The rumors of them eating the children of their enemies has never been substantiated."

Nikki blanched, so I pushed on. "What else? Why did he want them, specifically?"

"The very nature of their magic is what draws Viktor, I suspect." Kreios shrugged. "These are not trained sages or seers. Their abilities are purely natural. As djinn, they also are immortal and fertile. They could infuse the world with magic through natural means should they desire to do so."

Viktor had said something similar. I grimaced. "If they're so powerful, why didn't they come back through on their own?"

"Because they were sent to the other side of the veil forcibly, their power stripped." Kreios lifted his elegant brows. "It's speculated that their abilities here, should they return, would not be anywhere near their powers during Llyr's time. The flooding of the earth changed the climate and atmospheric plane dramatically. Lives that had extended for hundreds of years became dramatically shortened, and the ability for man to traverse the land at great speed was never spoken of again. The djinn may find the world a much changed place once they come through again." His gaze shifted to me. "*If* they come through again."

"And this is where Viktor decided to stash the children," Brody mused. "To, what, give the demons a primer on humanity?"

"The dimension in which the children believe they are existing does not have any innate characteristics of Earth, and yet—those characteristics were created. An elaborate illusion was constructed to keep the children's minds safe and whole. To accomplish that, the djinn would have had to have studied the world very closely."

"You're saying they built that world for them?" Brody asked.

I nodded. Viktor had already indicated as much.

"Not the world," Kreios corrected us both. "The illusion. They kept the children alive and their minds engaged with an elaborate act of collaboration that involved all their cooperation, and they've been at it for ten years. If Viktor had intended this, it was masterful, but I don't believe he did."

"You think he merely wanted a trade. Six for six," I said.

Kreios nodded. "It's the least complex of outcomes. He could not have envisioned the demons would not have wanted to come through immediately. Freedom was the only thing they craved, in his mind."

"And instead, they pulled babysitting duty. Why?"

"The motives of the djinn were never clear." Kreios shrugged. "They were—"

"Sweet Christmas. They wanted to play God." I sat upright in my chair, the reality of what we were dealing with hitting home to me. "Maybe they'd seen what had happened on Earth, maybe they hadn't, but if they were going to come back here, they knew there would be changes. Maybe changes they didn't want. Maybe manipulating these kids..." I shook my head, immediately rejecting my own theory. "No. They would have tired of the game long ago." Regardless, something about my idea resonated with me. Something deep and primal. And scary.

"Maybe it was more of a dry run?" Nikki suggested. She glanced up as we turned to her. "They start to consider the realities of coming back, but humanity has changed. People have changed. What would it take to dominate a modern mind the way they apparently did in the bad old days?"

"Maybe." Brody shook his head. "Ten years is a long time, though."

Nikki lifted her brows. "To a demon holed up in darkness for millennia?"

"Fair point."

"There is no certain date for their banishment," Kreios agreed. "Some position it at more than ten thousand years ago. Some further. The lifetime of a child is but a blink to them."

"Okay, but back to the main point." Brody tapped the table. "Why are the djinn willing to come through now, after all these years?"

"It's not only a question of whether or not they're willing, it's a question of whether or not they could," I said. "Viktor thought the child swap would do it, and he was wrong, apparently. Something more is needed. And he thinks I'm that something, and that I'll do it, given the children involved. And Brody..." I met his gaze. "He showed me more images. They're alive. They're safe."

I read his cop skepticism and turned to Kreios.

160

"Right? You think they're stable?"

"It is impossible to tell. Their minds may have fractured long ago, or may fracture when they return to this plane. The human brain is capable of great things, but it is also fragile. They may not accept what they see."

"But we have to try." I looked at Brody. "We can get shrinks, right, for when they come through? Therapists?"

"We can. It'll take a day or so to assemble a team." He hesitated. "And I'm not sure what we'll tell them when we do. Kind of questionable to say we might have some kids who were kidnapped by demons."

I looked at Kreios, who stared steadily back at me. Brody didn't know what the Devil's innate abilities were, or how far they reached. But I did. Kreios had a knowing of a person's innermost wants and needs, and he was a master at being able to meet those needs, should it suit his purposes. However, like everyone else on the Council, he didn't do anything for free.

"I think having therapists there is a good idea," Kreios said, but though Brody and Nikki nodded, it was my gaze he held for a moment longer. I looked away from him quickly enough, but the message between us was clear. The children would have his aid, to help them make the transition. And for that, I would owe him.

Owing the Devil was not the world's best position to be in, but it beat the alternative.

At that moment, Brody's phone buzzed. He pursed his lips while he read the screen. "As it turns out, I have a job that exists only in this dimension." He looked at Nikki. "Promise me you won't leave her alone?" And then to me. "And you promise you won't do anything until I have backup assembled?"

I shrugged even as Nikki saluted a firm "yes."

"I don't think I'm going to need backup for this job, Brody."

He stood, shaking his head. "I'm not talking about for you, I'm talking about for us. If we have an army of ancient demons screaming into Vegas, I'd like to be prepared."

CHAPTER FOURTEEN

Armaeus was waiting for me at the Council's conference room, but this time, I didn't come alone.

"Sweet baby Jesus on a tricycle," Nikki breathed. "Would you look at this place?"

Nikki had taken Brody's request to heart, and had refused to let me out of her sight, even after I explained that I wouldn't be tackling Viktor's demons for at least another day. I had bigger oceans to navigate, quite literally—I couldn't face a demon horde until I faced Atlantis. But I didn't have the heart to ask her to leave either. With so many people lining up in the "people I owed" category, I was beginning to lose track. It was refreshing to have someone who legitimately seemed to be on my side for no other reason than that she wanted to be there.

"Miss Wilde. Miss Dawes." Armaeus stood at the head of the table and had not turned around to face us. Instead, he watched the skyline of Vegas through the soaring penthouse windows. It was an impressive sight. Not merely the glitter and flash of the Strip, but the extraordinary residences of the Council: Scandal's lava lamp neon show, looming above the Flamingo; the glittering Foolscap above the Bellagio; and the Emperor's monolithic black tower, crackling with electricity as it soared above Paris. The homes of the Council members shone brightest from this vantage point at night, and Nikki stopped and stared as well, caught by the splendor.

"What is she doing here?" Eshe and I asked the question at the same time, and Nikki blinked beside me, taking a step back as the High Priestess swept into the room. She looked magnificent as she eyed Nikki with withering scorn, and I was happy I'd brought Nikki along.

"She shouldn't be present," Eshe said, turning to Armaeus. "She is nowhere near skilled enough to contribute."

"She walks, I walk," I said, shrugging. I'd been able to help Mercault on my own. How much worse could Atlantis be?

Armaeus remained standing but lifted a hand to stop the argument. "I have asked Eshe to join us to assist with your travel, and Simon for mapping purposes, based on what you find. I trust that's acceptable. Kreios will arrive later."

"Yeah, well, all the more reason to keep Nikki here."

Eshe groaned. "This is insufferable."

"You'll get used to it." I gave her a smile with more teeth than necessary.

Nikki had long since gone silent beside me, and I thought about the scene from her perspective. She'd seen each of the Council members before, of course, but I wasn't sure if she'd seen them all together in their joint magnificence.

It was an impressive sight. Armaeus was sporting one of his trademark one percenter suits. Eshe, on the other hand, struck a pose in her favorite fashion style, the gilt-edge toga, with gold bangles around her wrist and what appeared to be gilded flip-flops on her feet. She was made up heavily enough for Halloween. "You got a hot date tonight, Eshe?"

"C'mon, c'mon, I can't wait to begin." Dressed in a long-sleeved tee shirt, jeans, skullcap and tennis shoes, Simon strode into the room and set his laptop on the table with a hard thump, hauling out another tablet and tossing it down as well. "I've got the coolest new mapping software that I bastardized from the Darkweb. It says it can account for interdimensional and intertemporal discrepancy, but of course no one has been able to test it. We'll be the first."

"Joy," Nikki muttered.

He popped open his laptop and tapped furiously on the keys for ten seconds, then looked up at us again. "Oh! Nearly forgot." He jumped up and moved to my side, slipping out a thin chain from his pocket. "You should wear this." He winked. "For luck."

"Luck," I said flatly as he slid the chain over my neck. "That's a recording device, isn't it? In case you can't hear me while I'm there."

"Like I said, lucky." He scampered back to his workstation.

"It is best that we begin, Miss Wilde." Armaeus moved forward. "From everything that I can tell, Viktor's conversational channel with the djinn has remained open since you left his apartments. While he expects you to journey to them at any moment, he appears unaware of your sojourn to Atlantis, which means that the element of surprise is in our favor."

"It won't be for long unless we move quickly," Eshe snapped. "He's not an idiot. He'll suspect that Sara is going to arm herself in some way. What better way to do so than by going to the source?"

Something about her words struck a wrong chord with me, but then again, this was Eshe we were talking about. Irritating me was her stock-in-trade.

I stepped forward and pulled out a chair. When Nikki didn't move forward with me, I turned.

"I'm good here," she said, and her voice brooked no opposition. I frowned at her, and she leveled her gaze at me. I realized she was up on the balls of her feet, ready to take someone down. "You do what you do, but remember, when you're in there...I'm right here, waiting for you. And I've got your back." She squeezed my hand.

I squeezed back and immediately thought of Death's advice, to have as strong a connection as possible on this side, the better to bring me back home. I smiled somewhat crookedly, then turned back around, yanking the chair out as I did. "Let's get this over with."

"Such enthusiasm," cooed Eshe. "I've been experimenting more with astral travel. It's nowhere near as difficult as you make it out to be."

"Oh yeah? And yet I don't see you lining up to take this trip."

Her eyes flashed, and I'll admit it, I was smug. Council members might be creatures of amazing power, but they were also constrained by their position. They couldn't go where I went, couldn't do what I did.

I returned Eshe's gaze steadily, perversely pleased by her annoyance. "If we're done chattering here, then let's move."

"Eshe and I will both be performing the opening ritual," Armaeus said, his voice preternaturally calm. "Your familiarity with me will help bring you back, if anything should go wrong."

"And what might that 'anything' entail?" I watched with growing unease as he and Eshe moved to flank me. My seat was tucked tight against the conference table. I knew from experience that this would help when I eventually collapsed. Way closer to land on a table than a floor, even if the surface was hard. "What's waiting for me in Atlantis that I should be aware of?"

"Nothing that should pose an obstacle." This was Eshe again, and her voice too had taken on a different character, almost an edge. "But you will not go in unassisted."

She leaned forward and placed a small box on the table—the ornate blue-and-green case that held the Atlantean deck. I stiffened as she opened it. "No. I don't know those cards."

"The Atlantean deck makes sense here. More sense than the newer decks," Armaeus observed. I felt his gaze boring into my temple, but he didn't speak in my mind. Apparently he was content for everyone to hear his thoughts. "They can help provide direction. Atlantis's capital city is an enormous structure."

"But these cards are different." Mesmerized by the idea of touching the cards, I scooped them out of the box, feeling the weight of the deck in my hand. "They're too heavy for regular cards. You can't shuffle them."

"Try." Armaeus's words swirled through my mind like smoke, and I focused on the cards. Hefting them awkwardly, I sorted them in my hands, one over top of the other, all facedown. There were only about a dozen cards, and I hadn't looked at any of the faces except the eyeball card. Would I know what any of them meant?

Without thinking further, I spread the cards in a wide arc on the table, only vaguely aware that no one in the room was speaking. Everyone's gaze was fixed on the arc of cards, with the backs gleaming up at us, their strange interlocking design at once evoking Celtic, Norse, and Greek inspiration. The cards seemed to glow with an internal fire, and I stared down at them for another long moment. Then I picked three at random and pulled them out, all facedown.

Unlike many of the Tarot decks in current usage, the backs of these decks were not symmetrical at both the top and bottom. It was clear which side was upright, which was reversed. Fine by me. When it came to finding artifacts or even people, I always read the cards in the upright position. I didn't have time to split hairs over what a reversed card might mean. Not if I was being tracked or if someone's life was on the line. But here, assured of the cards' positioning, I turned them over in quick succession.

And blanched.

These cards were nothing like what I was used to seeing. The markings at the bottom, signifying the name, meant nothing to me. The symbols at the top, intended to be numbers, I assumed, were strange slashes. I didn't know this script, I didn't know these symbols. There was a full constellation in the first card — not only the Star but moons and planets as well, all crowded together. The second card wasn't merely the Tower, it was chaos. Multiple structures crumbled inside a thickly rimmed Wheel, while demonic creatures danced in one corner and angels raged in the other. The third card was the most disturbing of all, though it really shouldn't have been since I'd seen it before: A single eye staring out, unblinking, all knowing. Arcing over and below it were the rays of what could be the sun, or could be the onset of a killer migraine.

I had no idea what any of it meant.

Even as I stared, I felt moved to draw another card — beyond moved. Held in the all-seeing clutch of the sacred eye, my hand reached out and secured a final card, but though I could pull it forward from the deck, I couldn't turn it over. It was as if it slowly dissolved, as if everything was dissolving around me. I turned to see Armaeus and Eshe speaking to each other, their mouths moving, their eyes intent, me all but forgotten between them. Nikki stood behind them, but she was too far back — too far. I couldn't reach her, I couldn't speak, and beneath me, on the table, the cards began to shimmer, bursts of light breaking free from them and bathing me in a golden radiance.

It all felt perfect and good — until the rays arced across the tattoo Death had burned into my right wrist.

Agony swept through me. The table seemed to blow up, the cards flying and wind howling around me in a furious maelstrom. I stayed centered and sure for another moment more, then I blew up too, blinded by the bursting star.

I dropped swiftly — no, not dropping, *rocketing* down into a clear azure ocean, far down. Too far down. I shouldn't be able to breathe, but I was falling so fast and the water was so warm and I didn't need to fill my lungs, didn't need to breathe, didn't need to —

The skies opened up beneath me, and I hurtled to earth again, smashing onto a patch of dirt beside a crumbling paved road.

Oof.

Every bone on my body should have been pulverized with that crash, and I lay on the ground for a long moment, afraid to move. "Hello?" I managed, without shifting position.

There was no response. At length, I moved my fingers, then my toes. My arms responded, my knees as well. I wiggled on the ground like a bug, and my spine obligingly wiggled back. So far, so good.

I shakily got to my feet and looked around,

drawing in a questioning breath before realizing the import of that.

Apparently, Atlantis had oxygen. Good to know.

I heard a whirring in my ear, and I turned, then turned again. If that whirring was Armaeus, it wasn't going to do me any good. Which was unfortunate, based on what I was seeing.

I stood in the middle of a war zone.

It wasn't difficult figuring out the imagery before me. Buildings lay in ruin, shattered, their roofs caved in and their walls blown out. Not a single stone stood on top of another one from what I could see. The dirt strip I stood on looked like it had once supported grass, maybe trees — but those had been scorched to the ground. Nothing remained but dried-out wisps of something undefined sticking out of the ground. The sky was blue, but that was the only bit of cheer afforded this place.

Despite the carnage, it was clear it'd once been beautiful.

It appeared that I was in some sort of courtyard, in front of a large central building. There were stone walls — those had not been shattered, at least — which ran the circumference of the courtyard in silent testimony to what lay within. Another broken set of walls was only a few feet away, and I walked toward them. More empty space lay beyond. There wasn't dirt beneath my feet this time, only stone. I scuffed aside some of the sand, and dull, white marble peeked through. Apparently, I was inside the central building. Or at least closer to it.

I tried to report. "This place is totally destroyed." Nothing but whirs and clicks sounded in response, and I sighed. Atlantis had lousy cell reception. I was on my own.

At least I was alone in here.

I'd no sooner thought that than I recalled the cards I had drawn. The destruction card had been surrounded by the wheel, and on the outside of the wheel, angels and demons awaited. I squinted at the high walls surrounding me in a perfect arc, and shuddered. There was no sound, barely a rustle of wind. But I had no interest in finding out what lay beyond those walls.

Besides, what I needed was straight ahead.

As I walked forward, I thought of the other two cards I'd drawn. A constellation of stars, sun, moon, and supernovas, and the all-seeing eye.

I figured I'd know that last one when I saw it, but the constellation was confusing me. I'd already moved through space and time to get here, but I hadn't seen any of that imagery — nothing but mist and water. Since I'd arrived, however, nothing remotely resembled a constellation.

There was nothing here at all, in fact. No sound, no animals or birds, hardly any breeze. Then again, I'd moved through time. What was before me was now behind me, if Armaeus was to be believed. I was standing in a country lost not only to the world, but also to its timetable. Did that have something to do with what I was or wasn't seeing, and its order?

My head began to hurt.

Armaeus had told me the artifacts he sought would be at the very core of the central building, and that was where I was walking toward, or what was left of it. The place was enormous. With the wreckage, I couldn't get a true sense of the scale, but I felt like I was crossing a football field, with the central building at the far end. I picked my way through the rubble, trying to keep my footing. As I walked, I noticed something peculiar about the stone floor through the tumbled rock.

It was growing darker. Specifically, it was growing a darker blue. As I crept through the wreckage toward what I assumed had been the center of the building, I began to pick out a pattern on the floor—stars. I thought about the stars lining the ceiling in the Bavarian castle. How many centuries and lifetimes had been linked by a fascination with the heavens? How many dimensions as well?

I squeezed between two extremely large rocks and blinked, trying to process what I was looking at. Then I turned around. Instead of going up, as I'd subconsciously been expecting as I'd entered the ruins, I had been moving slightly downhill the whole time. I'd not seen the center of the building at all, but the very tip of a mound of rubble that had fallen together to make a large room. An enormous dome the size of a cathedral lay half-balanced on a shattered rock wall, creating a slitted opening. If I was correct in what I was seeing, the dome was sheltering the very center of the main building. Or, more succinctly, my destination.

I lifted a hand to wipe my hair out of my eyes, and something strange caught my attention. The palm of my right hand was deeply imprinted with marks—not burns, but deep ink stains that ended right above the symbol that Death had tattooed into my skin. I touched my fingers to the marks and felt no pain, then my mind flashed back to my actions right before I traveled.

I'd drawn a card. Drawn it, flipped it, and blanked out.

Squinting into the light, I tried to make sense of the images cresting over the palm of my hand. This image looked similar to one of the Major Arcana cards of the traditional Tarot system.

Justice.

A figure stood with a scale in front of her, the balance of the two objects held on the scale weighing out as carefully even. Unlike Justice, however, this figure was not blind. Also unlike Justice, this figure did not have a passive sense to her, cool and detached. She held the weighted scales in one hand, and with the other she brandished a sword — or brandished something. The image ran off the edge of my palm at that point, and it was impossible to tell what she was carrying. It felt very swordlike, though.

It also felt kind of useless.

Disgusted, I stood back and looked around. Common sense indicated I should stay away from the dome, but I'd been running the artifacts hunting game for a long time. I had a feeling it was the right place to be.

Nevertheless, it didn't hurt to understand exactly how big that dome was — and how sturdy — before I crawled under it. I took a running jump toward the wall...only to come up on it so much more quickly than I expected that I almost face-planted into the side of the dome. Scrambling to the side, I caught an outcropping a good three feet above where I thought I'd land and hung there, confused, my feet dangling for a moment as I tried to get my bearings.

I was easily fifteen feet up. And I'd gotten here in two quick jumps. What was going on? Scrabbling for purchase again, I spied the next ledge up and lurched toward it...

And missed it entirely.

Instead, I plowed into a different ledge, my head cracking against the stone, my hands flailing until I could pull myself up and onto the next ridge. Not a ridge at all, I realized. A shelf. And as I turned to peer down at the dome again, burnished gold and silver, brilliant in the harsh sunlight, I saw what I'd been both dreading and hoping for.

The all-seeing eye.

CHAPTER FIFTEEN

"Ohhhkay."

The entire surface of the dome had been etched with a large, Egyptian-looking eye, heavily lined as if with kohl, its center refracting the sunlight back to me. I teetered a little and took a step back, hugging the rock wall.

I was dizzy, I realized with a start. *Very* dizzy.

What had Armaeus said about the results of the Great Flood? It had changed the atmosphere of Earth in some way, rendering the demigods of old less fleet of foot, weaker, more susceptible to the vagaries of age?

By extension, if Atlantis had gotten blasted to never-never land, that would mean its atmosphere was different, wouldn't it? Not different enough that I couldn't breathe, but different enough that the quality of that breathing was dramatically impacted.

Of course, so was the quality of my speed and ability to leap tall buildings in a single bound. So there were potentially trade-offs.

Either way, I was much more concerned about breathing than I was about running and jumping. I couldn't afford to stay here too long.

I half slid, half jumped back to the ground level, approaching the crack between the rock and the dome. It didn't seem completely dark on the inside, which made no sense either. Taking a deep breath, I closed my eyes to prepare for the gloom within and ducked inside.

My eyes popped open, and the breath went out of me completely.

"Sweet Christmas," I managed, more in my mind than in words.

Light filtered down from an enormous oculus in the center of the dome, the iris of the all-seeing eye. It illuminated a floor that was absolutely stunning in its beauty, preserved unexpectedly due to the falling dome.

The full explosion of stars from the Atlantean deck was visible in the center of the room. Constellations chased each other across the visible floor and into the shadows beyond the light from the oculus. I wondered at that—when it was in its proper place, would it have provided enough light to illuminate the entire room? Probably.

There were no walls left to see if additional windows had been cut into the structure, but the interior of the dome was painted with perfectly preserved imagery that recalled Michelangelo and the Sistine Chapel. This had been a place of importance and lavish beauty, that much was clear.

Oddly, there were no bodies or remains anywhere in sight, as if the entire place had been evacuated before its crumbling. Had the Atlanteans been warned? Not all of them, clearly, if six had been sent into permanent time-out. But what of the others? Weren't there servants who would have been forced to stay behind? Priests? How had this place been completely swept of bodies?

A soft rustle of a breeze caught my attention, and I turned back toward the shadowed opening of the place. Was someone there? Surely not. This place had the feeling of a tomb.

Granted, I'd been in my share of not quite empty tombs. So once again, I jolted into action.

I turned back to the center of the room. The floor was translucent in some places, hinting at lower levels. The mere thought of what might be lurking down there had me quickening my pace once more. Artifacts would be fun. Screaming creatures in the dark, not so much.

When I got to the center of the room — all wide-open floor — I realized my mistake. The dome had fallen at an angle, not straight down. The true magic of this room lay beyond the edge of the shadows. Shadows I was moving through at last.

A grand throne rose up from a dais of steps, the top of it barely clearing the edge of the dome as it had sliced down onto the floor. Carved to appear like it was rising out of a roiling ocean tide of horses, dolphins, and fish, the chair looked large enough to fit three people, and I thought again about Kreios's comments about the stature of the average Atlantean. The Canaanites had been referred to as giants in the Bible. The story of David and the Goliath had centered on a Canaanite, and even given literary hyperbole, that had been one seriously big dude.

Was that what I'd be confronting when I went to find the children?

Nothing I could do about that, if so — but for the first time, I considered the likelihood that the weapons of these people might be proportionally sized for giants as well.

I peered more deeply into the darkness, stepping forward and to the right as I began to become accustomed to the gloom. I immediately hit pay dirt.

Beside the throne were two long cases, flung open and tumbled through. And in those cases were weapons.

A spear as long as two men, a sword that was almost as long as I was. Knives with blades the size of my thigh. Throwing stars the size of Frisbees.

I picked up one of the knives and heard it again, the sudden rushing of wind outside the dome. I whirled, but the doorway was far away from me — too far. I couldn't see anyone standing inside it, blocking my exit, and I turned back to the pile of weapons. In my right hand, the knife felt easy, unusually light for its size. I hefted it as I considered the remaining spoils.

Armaeus had been clear — I needed blades or weapons of any type, spear, axe, or sword — and I'd not only have a weapon to fight the demons, I'd have a tool to use to help pry the children out of their interdimensional dungeon. It made a certain sort of sense. The demons were Atlantean; so were these weapons. Bringing them together could only cause some sort of cataclysm, and that cataclysm might be all I needed.

I cast around and found a long, slender arrow as thick as my arm but buoyantly light, with a wickedly pointed tip. That would work. I picked up two for good measure, along with a sheathed knife, double-checking that the blade was still intact before I straightened. I scooped up a few throwing stars for good measure. Everything seemed good, so far, despite the fact that I couldn't hear Armaeus or Eshe.

Even the cards hadn't been a complete train wreck. The wheel surrounding the destroyed buildings could have been a blueprint of what was left of the center of the Atlantean capital. The all-seeing eyeball had proven to be a worthy X marks the spot. The constellation had been on the floor, and it'd led me once more to where I needed to be. Sure, some of the elements hadn't worked out, and the image imprinted on my hand hadn't proven useful, but Justice was sort of a tricky card. Sometimes it could mean that you would get your rewards for making the effort to do the right thing, or that you would get the good things that were coming to you.

Of course, it could also mean that you'd get the bad things that were coming to you. But details.

I turned around and let my gaze lift again to the oculus at the top of the dome. What must this place have looked like in its heyday? Before its ruination, before the destruction of every rock and statue. It was such a beautiful space, with the floor a rich panorama of stars, the throne made of pure gold atop a staircase of silver and bronze, and the carvings of fish and horses and sea dragons coiling around the base, bursting up out of the stonework as if they'd just emerged from the sea.

"Who lived in this place, meting out justice?" I jolted as I realized I'd spoken the words aloud, but once they were hanging in the air, I couldn't ignore them. I looked at my palm once more, then cast another glance at the rubble littering the throne room.

It took only a few more minutes to find it.

Kneeling reverently, my weapons forgotten, I spread the broken scales out in front of me. Two shallow golden bowls hung from a chain whose links had been cut or shattered, it was impossible to tell which. They were suspended askew from a long, graceful crossbeam that had formerly sat atop a center spire. The entire apparatus was about three feet high and two feet wide, but when I held it up, I found it curiously light, almost delicate.

A crash sounded outside the dome, and I sprang to

my feet, scrambling back to pick up my weapons. I realized I hadn't heard a buzz from Armaeus's domain in some time. Not since I'd entered the dome, certainly. Had that severed the contact? Was I truly cut off? From everything I could tell, there was only one entryway into and out of the fallen dome. Even if there was something out there waiting for me, I had to go that way.

I stepped forward, only to crash heavily down to one knee as my foot got tangled in the broken chain of the scales. I moved my boot, but the link wouldn't budge. It'd gotten locked onto my boot buckle. "Oh, give me a break," I muttered. Shifting the weapons to my left hand, I hauled up the center spire of the scales with my right. Shaking my boot experimentally produced no help. The plates dangled from their chains, but the whole thing looked a little like a mace. Maybe it would work as a weapon as well. It was light enough, almost comfortable to carry.

I simply didn't want it attached to me. Setting the scales down temporarily, I dropped the other weapons as well and slid the long knife out of its sheath. With one swift cut, I sliced through the chain…and into the stone floor.

Whoa." My eyes bulged as I hauled the knife back out of the marble, and I stood for a moment longer. If this was indicative of the Atlanteans' strength, no wonder they were viewed as gods. Suddenly the ol' "sword in the stone myth" took on new resonance. How many Atlanteans had survived the Great Flood? I suddenly wondered. How many still roamed the earth?

I gathered up the weapons and the scales once more, then moved back quickly across the large, constellation-strewn floor, toward the triangle of light that marked the opening. As I walked, I realized that the clinking chains of the scales weren't hindering me. The weapons too, once I got used to their ungainliness, were no hardship to haul across the floor. I seemed to be gaining strength, not losing it, and I drew in a deep, experimental breath.

Oxygen flooded my lungs. I felt light, almost buoyant, and despite the unknown of what was outside the dome, I was feeling unreasonably excited, practically filled with glee. I shook my head, muttering to anyone who should be listening on the other side. "Atlantis to Earth, do you read," I tried. "I have no idea what I'll be able to bring back of this, but I'm ready to come home."

Silence.

Great. I got all the way to the sunlit opening of the dome and peered out. No one was congregating in the small clearing that marked the break in the last round wall and the center dome. I swallowed and stepped outside.

More silence.

The wind whistled around the dome, making an odd keening noise, and I frowned up at it. Was that all that I had heard? Clear of the dome, I focused again, more desperately this time, trying to fix on Armaeus's face, his hands. His eyes. What was it Death had said? I needed to remain tethered to the person in my own plane who had the strongest hold on me?

There was no one who really fit that bill, of course. Nikki was a friend, but we'd met only recently. That left Armaeus, and even that connection was a little pitiful, now that I thought about it. I had nothing and no one who really wanted me, needed me. I was alone.

I was alone, and I was never going to get back.

Sudden despair leached through me, and I faltered,

slowing to a stop in the center of the courtyard, weighed down by chains and weapons and the inescapable truth of my life. I was no one's. I had no mother, no father. I had no lasting friends. I had come into this world a mystery, and it seemed I would go out that way too.

And I was so, so far from everything I knew.

A flickering buzz sounded in my ear again, but as I lifted my head, the sudden wellspring of emotion caught me so quickly that I staggered back. That emotion wasn't coming from me, though. It was coming from outside of me, a force ripping through the universe with a single word:

Mine.

Suddenly, Armaeus stood in front of me, as clear as if he were standing there. Relief washed through me. I focused and could hear words, demands—something I couldn't understand, couldn't quite catch...

And then a solid silver spear zipped right by my face, and Armaeus disappeared.

"Crap!" I scrambled backward, dropping the scales, and the chain tangled into my boot buckle a second time. I dropped the arrow as well but held on to the long knife, whirling around. The spear lay on the ground beyond me, almost to the makeshift door of the dome, useless. It was as tall as I was, though, and no sooner had I bent toward it when another blade soared by me, black as pitch. This was a knife, thick as my head, and it clanged against the far wall before dropping to the ground. Its obsidian length gleamed in the hot sun, and I stared at it, mesmerized.

"Um, this would be a good time for me to come back, Armaeus."

But it wasn't Armaeus who responded to me. An unearthly scream rose from one side of the wall circling the dome, and as it rose in crescendo, its owners rose with it—literally, hovering in the sky. At first I thought they were the Valkyries again, come to serve me with another death notice, but these weren't the fierce Nordic women I had met before. These were something altogether different.

I let my own blade arm drop, my jaw dropping with it.

Angels.

A horde of angels hovered on the far end of the wall, glowing bright white with enormous white-gold wings soaring above them.

A roar of fury met their cries, and I whirled, no longer trying to protect myself, no longer trying to understand. A new host of creatures surged over the far wall—not with wings but with arms and legs and…well, tails. Practically glowing with darkness, they growled and snarled, their humanlike figures as twisted as the angelic host was pristine. Then, as if both groups remembered I remained down in the makeshift pit, they turned their combined fury on me.

And not merely their howls. As if as one, they flowed down the walls—angels flying, demons racing—both of them hurtling toward me as if I were the last jelly bean at the bottom of the bowl.

"Crap, crap, crap!" It was too far to make it back to the dome. Even as I moved, the chain clambered after me, so I bent down and scooped up the rest of the scales holding the artifact by its base. The golden disks swung precariously, and I was reminded once more of its mace-like features. I whirled around, and I brandished the scales with a war cry of my own. "Get away from me, you freaks!"

The screaming chaos in my brain surged forward, and I swung once, twice, shocked on some level that I wasn't cleaving through muscle and sinew, claw and bone. The tone and tenor of the howling demons changed, but I couldn't stop—wouldn't stop.

Everything that had been boiling inside me surged to the fore. The revelation about my mother, Viktor's manipulations, even the petty betrayals of Nigel and Brody, people who owed me nothing and yet whose actions pricked at me unreasonably hard. And then there was Death with her cryptograms, and Armaeus and Eshe, and—I was weary to my bones. Tired and sick and so furious I could barely keep the scream wailing inside me from ripping me apart.

I slashed again and again, meeting no resistance, and almost stumbled as I realized what was happening.

The two groups had stopped. Completely stopped as if mesmerized by me and my mace-like scales. I shook the thing again, and they fell back, whispers rushing through them like a sickness. I didn't know why. More to the point, I didn't care.

"Get back from me—back!" I screeched, jabbing the scales forward as though it were a lit torch thrust against the darkness. It had the desired effect, or it started to anyway. The creatures fell back, but only until they formed a tight circle around me, a sentient wall of angel and demon or whatever the hell they were, as sturdy and impassable as stone.

And then...the front wall of them knelt down.

Whoa.

I stood up straight as I struggled manfully to keep my eyeballs from popping out of my head. This wasn't your ordinary kneeling either. Both angel and demon alike bent forward at the waist and put their foreheads on the ground, dirtying their pristine wings and getting dust on their claws, respectively. They held that position for a full thirty seconds while I spun in a tight circle, trying to find a way out.

For the record, thirty seconds is a long time to be venerated.

But there was nothing doing. Beyond the first wall of combatants, a second one stood, all of them looking at me as if they'd seen a ghost. I thought about the card burned into my hand. I did sort of resemble that figure, wielding my scales like a weapon. Were they picking up on the image's energy? If so, I would totally take it.

The interior circle stood again, and two of them stepped forward, like captains of opposing football teams. I tensed, holding out my scales, ready to bludgeon anyone who got too close.

"Stop right there," I warned, and they stood, whether because they understood what I was saying or from the tone of my voice.

"Miss Wilde."

Relief spiked again, but I couldn't spare the words. In front of me, the two creatures brandished the same kinds of weapons I'd seen inside the dome. Delicate arrows, a long curving blade, throwing stars, a narrow sword. They held these up like an offering, and I frowned. I'd lost my other weapons somewhere, other than the broken scales.

Finally, I found my voice. "Any weird contractual obligation I should be aware of before I take these things?"

The Magician was silent for a beat, then his voice whispered in my ear again. *"Take what, specifically?"* he asked, sounding worried.

He wasn't the only one, though. A rustle of concern seemed to be slipping through both the angelic and demonic hordes, the sound of confusion, almost dismay. The last time that had happened, I'd gotten

185

spears thrown at me.

"Screw it. Never mind." I thought about Justice and her scales, each side evenly matched, her eyes blindfolded so she wouldn't make an inappropriate choice. Even though the Justice etched onto my hand didn't buy in to the blindfolding part, I didn't want to offend either party by choosing the other first. I bent and set the scales down by my side, then reached out both hands.

It seemed to be the right decision. The two creatures stepped forward and placed their weapons onto my hands and forearms, while bracing my arms and hands with their own. The demon's long-clawed fingers dwarfed mine, while the angel's hands were smaller, smoother. I stared at both figures close up, and realized...they looked remarkably humanoid. Even the demon's image shifted and roiled, like a projection that had slipped its tracks. Beneath its imagery of a snarling-mouthed creature, it looked almost mannish as well. A very big man, but a man.

They seemed to be waiting for me to say something, but I didn't know Atlantean.

"Thank you," I said. English wouldn't have been the universal language in their time, but I threw in a short head bow as well, and their response was swift and sure. They spouted a line of nonsense to me as if I should know it, and I managed a smile.

I shifted my attention back to Armaeus, sensing the tide about to turn. "A little assistance here would be good," I muttered.

"You have but to say the word."

Frowning, I rolled my eyes. "Help me!" I called, maybe a bit too loudly, holding the weapons closer to my body.

Apparently, that was the wrong thing to say. As

186

one, the horde took flight around me, their screams a furious bellow — and attacked.

CHAPTER SIXTEEN

I burst upward with a scream, throwing my arms out wide to protect myself. Shouts of alarm brought me back into focus as metal clattered against glass. I felt ripped apart, shredded, like some sort of spiny-armed creature, and everything *hurt*.

"Yo, Sara!" The clattering stopped, and Nikki's strong arms were around me, hauling me back as my arms flailed and legs churned, my eyes not seeing the conference room around me but hands and claws and wings converging on me, my limbs being stretched and pulled in all directions. "Whoa! No more Red Bull for you, sister. Take it down a notch — I said take it down!"

Her words were light, but Nikki's hands locked on my shoulders as she talked, and I realized a moment later that I was no longer flailing but held fast in place, one of her large booted feet bracing my left leg wide, which felt like the only thing keeping me upright.

"Can't breathe," I managed, and she snorted somewhere above me.

"Well, if you can't breathe, you can't kill me, so I consider that a win." She held me for another long three counts. "You good?"

I blinked my eyes open, but my head still hung forward. I saw a series of polished shoes that cost more than I made in a month. The Council ringed me, not those…people. Things. Whatever they were. "Yeah," I gasped at length.

"Take it easy, dollface. The adrenaline will wear off in a few."

Armaeus's voice crackled through the room. "Look up at me, Miss Wilde. Only at me."

I turned my head toward him, and his gaze trapped mine as Nikki eased her hold on me. Eased it—but she didn't let go. Still, her words proved prophetic. Every fight-or-flight urge seemed to dissolve to nothing as I came fully back to present, and I sank into her grasp like I never wanted to leave it, my mini collapse all the more pleasurable because I had somewhere soft to fall.

"Simon."

The Magician's words vaguely penetrated my skull as Simon's Chucks came into my peripheral view. He edged in close beside me, but I didn't see him, not really. I couldn't see anything but the Magician's gold-and-black eyes. "You fed us all the imagery we need, but I want to take the device off you, submit it to further testing," Simon said. "You good with that?"

"Mmph," I managed as I felt his light touch at my neck. He removed the chain with a delicate tug. Then there were more tugs at my arms, my legs. Gentle at first, but one made me flinch away. All the while, Armaeus's gaze held mine, his wordless energy surrounding me.

"Can we move this along, please?" Nikki's voice sounded unnaturally strained in the silent room, but it wasn't Armaeus who responded. It was Eshe.

"It would be best for her to black out," she said dispassionately.

"I'm not going to black out." I shook my head, shrugging off Armaeus's stare and Nikki's light hold. No one moved as I took a step forward, my hands coming up for balance. I was surprised at the state of my arms. They were chapped and raw, like I'd had to run through a fire pit. "What the hell?"

Another realization came to me as my senses slowly bounced back online. My clothes were in tatters, with long rents in my leggings, and angry blisters beneath. I stank of charred leather too. And when I glanced up to the room around me, I didn't look for the Council members' faces, I looked at Nikki's.

It was frozen in horror.

"Not good?" Before she could respond, the pain swamped me like a tidal wave. Every bone and organ in my body seemed to explode outward, radiating agony, then to pull all that misery back tight, compressing it into a ball. Fire, slashing, blade and bone all crashed together in my mind, and I realized why I'd felt so...spiny when I'd first come out of the trance.

There had been things sticking out of me.

Knives. Arrows. Stars. And one long spear.

I blacked out.

CHAPTER SEVENTEEN

What seemed a millennia later, Armaeus's warm voice brushed over me, solid and comforting. "You're doing well, Miss Wilde. Don't rush it."

I was lost in an enormous pile of soft pillows and blankets, as I somehow knew I would be. Memories leaked through my comfort barrier, and I stiffened, my breath catching at the pain. "Do not remember," he soothed. "Not yet. Drift."

That was an idea I could get behind, particularly as I felt the bed dip, the weight of Armaeus's body running the length of mine and beyond. His heat radiated over me in a soothing arc, and I groaned, willing myself back to sleep but knowing it wouldn't come. With him so close, my breathing regulated, though, and his soft touch against my cheek felt good and right.

It also felt like I still had skin on my face. Which seemed an important consideration.

"What happened to me?" I managed. My voice was raspy, but my teeth were intact, along with my tongue. I couldn't quite bring myself to open my eyes, but that meant I had eyelids. Things were improving all the time. "Did I...did I catch on fire?"

"Your reentry from Atlantis was much faster than your exit, and the transfer through the dimensional veil did not go as smoothly. Simon and Eshe are trying to figure out why."

"It seemed a little rocky."

"Yes." He leaned forward and drifted a kiss along my temple. I didn't resist it. I didn't want to resist it. Where the Magician's lips touched my body, everything felt whole again. My headache eased, my eyes rested more easily behind their lids, my cheeks felt smooth, their skin unbroken. "You carried back weapons as we directed."

"Um…they were stuck into me."

"Unfortunately, yes. Until we pulled them free. But the mission was a success." He moved his mouth down to my chin, and the mini vortex of healing expanded again, a cool wash of relief against the roof of my mouth, my throat easing its constriction. I shifted my hands beneath the blankets, and my fingers flexed easily. My arms as well.

Then my legs.

I opened one eye. I saw the Magician in duplicate, my third eye fluttering to life with him so close. He fairly glowed with power, surrounding me in a cocoon of magic.

"You've been at this awhile, haven't you?" I murmured.

"You were far more injured than we first realized," he said without apology. "And injured in ways not consistent with astral travel as Eshe has directed it over the centuries."

"Well, you know. Atlantis." I sighed and let my eyes slip closed again as he levered his body over mine, dropping a light kiss on each of my brows.

"That certainly accounts for some of it," he agreed. "But your clothes and skin were torn. You looked like you'd been in a fight."

Um, yeah. "I thought Simon recorded all that."

"He recorded everything you saw and reported on until you reached the dome. At that point, we lost all contact with you. When you emerged from the dome, we could hear you, but your words were mainly a distress signal after that, and nothing transferred to the scouting device." He paused. "What did you see? What happened to you?"

I considered responding, I really did. But I was…so tired. Besides, this was Armaeus, and he'd been over the ground of my brain before. The idea of him plumbing my deepest, darkest secrets didn't appeal, but I couldn't bring myself to speak of what I'd seen. Far easier to let him see it for himself.

He must have sensed the moment my mental barriers gave way, laying open my mind for him. When his lips brushed mine, the electric jolt ripped through me, threatening to fry my already abused nerves.

Armaeus spoke words I couldn't follow as I watched the tumble of images stream through my mind once more, a visitor to my own brain. The beauty within the dome, the light following from the center oculus. The whistling winds that had so unnerved me. The weapons and the golden scales. With another breathed word, he slowed the passage of images as I picked up the scales, turning them over in my hands. He saw what I had seen, the imprinted image of Justice on my palm, so similar and yet different from the original Tarot deck. He played my shifting hands over and over again, me weighing the weight of the scales, hefting the weapons. Me turning back toward the door, becoming entangled in the chain trailing from the scales. Me hauling the golden artifact with me, some sort of treasure-hunting Quasimodo, hunched beneath my stolen spoils.

When I breached the outer courtyard once more, the images sped up again. I watched in growing fear as the armies of light and dark amassed around me, hurling spears and weapons as I ducked and ran.

"You could have warned me about those guys," I murmured against his lips.

He was silent above me, his mouth barely touching mine.

"You there?" I prompted.

"Shhh."

The images sped more quickly then, as if Armaeus realized that his time for brain exploration was rapidly nearing an end. He stopped abruptly, though, when I was surrounded by a circle of angels and demons — and they knelt.

"Yeah," I muttered. "That threw me too."

The rest rushed by in a blur. He didn't comment as the angels and demons stood once more, didn't murmur any surprise as their weapons were placed in my hands. He didn't comment, and I contented myself with watching a rerun of my life in fast-forward. The gift of weapons, Armaeus asking me to say the words, me saying them, and then the attack. The angels and demons converged on me until an explosion of white-hot light propelled me from the scene, and then there was only darkness.

He reran that piece a second time, then a third.

"You asked for help," he murmured at last.

I shifted away from him to look at his face. His eyes were the color of black gold again, as if an infusion of dye had somehow slipped into his irises without permission. But those strange eyes held me fast. "I told you to say the word. I needed a vocalization. You said 'help.'" He tilted his head. "Then they attacked you."

"That's pretty much how I remember it, yeah." I

moved my arm out from beneath the cocoon of blankets and studied it. A new web of fine white lines danced down the length of it, the scarring from the attack. "They seemed on my side, then suddenly, they weren't." I shrugged. "Of course, I was able to leave Atlantis, so maybe they did it on purpose. Maybe the full threat of their attack was what was needed for me to break free. God knows it didn't feel like it was going to happen on its own."

"They weren't speaking English to you, but a language that has not been spoken on Earth for millennia."

"And yet you know every language ever born, so spill. What were they saying?"

He hesitated. "Did you show them the card you had etched into your hand?"

I turned the offending hand and let my gaze drift over its now-clean surface. "Sort of a souped-up Justice card, but not the whole thing." I frowned. "Where's the deck?"

"Focus would be appreciated. Did you show them your hand?"

"Fine," I snapped. "I honestly can't remember. I think so, at least the two at the end who gave me the weapons. But I was running at them with a set of broken scales, so if those cards are from Atlantis, then they could have recognized me from that. Minus the flowing robes and outstretched hand holding a whatever."

"She holds a sword." Armaeus was studying me in his favorite pose, that of the earnest professor bent on discovering the mysteries of the universe from his prize bug. "You were brandishing weapons as well as the scales."

"Yeah, well, everything felt a lot lighter there." I

pushed myself up on one elbow as I remembered. "I was a lot lighter. I could climb more easily, run faster, jump higher. There was...flying too." My eyes widened. "Those angels and demons—I hadn't thought about that. They weren't actually flying, they were jumping."

"That holds with the ancient records, those that remain." Armaeus seemed lost in thought. "But to recognize you..."

"I make a fierce Justice, I guess." I considered that. "Is there a Justice currently on the Council?"

"There is not. Similar to Death, it is a card that is an abstraction and yet can be embodied by a mortal, but only Death has made the leap down to the Council."

I frowned at him. "What do you mean, 'down'? You guys are the junior league?"

"Your attempts at defining the Council are, as always, entertaining. And wrong." Armaeus seemed to come back to himself, and he leveled the full impact of his gaze against me. "You're feeling better?"

"I'm good," I said. I looked around the room. It had no windows, and I suddenly felt claustrophobic. "Where's everyone else, anyway?"

"Kreios offered to take Nikki home," Armaeus said, pointedly ignoring my lifted brows. "Eshe and Simon are studying the weapons you came back with, including the blade stuck in your shoulder."

"Ouch." I reached up and rubbed my shoulder, though it no longer registered pain. "I seem to be making a habit of that."

"A full night has passed since you returned, and most of the morning as well. It is nearing noon."

"Noon! That can't be possible." That made me sit upright. Armaeus obligingly rolled away from me, and I realized he'd been fully clothed this whole time.

196

"Viktor is waiting on me to go fetch the children, Armaeus. If I've disappeared for a whole day…"

"He knows what you've been doing. I've kept Detective Rooks apprised of your progress, though not your side effects. The detective seems unreasonably distracted by any injury to you."

"Noted," I said wryly. It was good to know someone cared. "What do you mean, Viktor knows?"

Armaeus's words were noncommittal. "He seems aware of your travel and is demanding to be advised of where you went, and why. We have advised him that you traveled in seclusion."

I frowned. "He can't think I went to wherever the stolen children are. I have no idea where that is."

"I do not know what he thinks. He's demanding a meeting."

I grimaced. "You guys should go into corporate. No one loves meetings as much as you do."

"You'll be happy to know he wants you to attend as well." Armaeus regarded me. "He's expressing remorse over the kidnapping."

"Right. He's got about as much remorse in him as a lizard does. " I flexed my fingers. "I tell you what. You guys meet, I'll go get more intel. I have a feeling I'm going to need all the help I can get."

Armaeus hesitated. "You've shuttered your mind from me again."

I shrugged. "I gave you what you needed, right?" Without waiting for an answer, I rolled out of bed, dragging a sheet with me as I padded over to get my clothes. I scowled down at the pile. "These are new."

"I think you'll agree that wearing your ripped and burned clothing would cause comment, even in Las Vegas."

"Fair enough." I picked up the trousers and light,

long-sleeved shirt. Everything felt like it was made out of spun silk. "What is this, mithril?" I waved them at him. "I would have been fine with the same brands I had."

He shrugged. "Indulge me."

I got it then and put the clothes on without comment, totally playing it cool. I'd be losing these clothes the moment I hit the Strip, but what he didn't know wouldn't hurt me. The likelihood that he'd infused tracking devices all the way down to my underwear was way too much of a chance I was not willing to take.

By the time I returned to the bedroom, Armaeus was gone. My phone and wallet remained, and I sighed. I was going to miss the wallet, but I couldn't risk it. Maybe I'd give it to Dixie for safekeeping until I found a way to strip it free of bugs. Or maybe I'd go buy another five-dollar wallet. Decisions.

But that wasn't all Armaeus had left behind. I lifted the set of large throwing stars, which seemed unreasonably light, even though we weren't on Atlantis anymore. They were wrapped in a heavy cloth. A small padded shoulder pack rested beside them, sized exactly to carry the lethal blades. I smiled. He knew what I planned to do. And he wasn't going to stop me.

Not five minutes later, I walked out into the sunshine, ready for my date with Death.

CHAPTER EIGHTEEN

I could smell the burned skin when I walked into Darkworks Ink, and I winced in half-remembered pain. My Atlantis key gleamed from my wrist, none the worse for wear. I'd expected it to be destroyed in the triumphant return, and I wasn't sure how I felt about the idea that it remained. Its presence meant that, technically, I could go back. Back to the strange mix of angels and demons who'd reacted so strangely to me, back to the mysteries that Atlantis held close.

Jimmy Shadow was hanging out at the front counter, and he grinned at me from his stool as I hefted the pack onto the surface, opening the flap to display the blades inside. "Nice stars."

"Gift from a friend," I said. "Hold 'em for me?"

"Yep." He nodded. "Blue said you'd be by. She's working a big project, though. Said you could wait for her in room three or hang out up here."

"I'll hang here." Room three was where I'd received my first key, the faux tattoo parlor that masked a setup that would make a horror movie director salivate. I could avoid checking that out again for as long as possible.

I took a seat on one of the stools in front of the counter, positioned at a large book of flash tattoos. The pages were open to seafaring nymphs and anchors, waves and whales. Sharks and dolphins lined the right-hand page. "You get a lot of requests for dolphins?"

"You wouldn't believe how much." Jimmy's smile showed his weathered teeth. Coffee and cigarettes had worn down his body the same way the Colorado River had carved the Grand Canyon. "Blue doesn't handle those so much anymore, but it's a gateway for a lot of people, so we do our share."

"Gateway — meaning they come back for additional ink?"

"Some of them. For others, it's a literal gateway, the piece they need to access their deeper selves. We're always up for helping that process out, especially if it gets a low-level Connected to a point of accepting their abilities and moving forward."

I nodded. "When did you know you were a Connected?"

He shrugged. "First time I could do this." The pages in front of me riffled and then blew to the side, taking me deeper into the book, where I saw dozens of wave images and every type of sailing craft. "Stupid trick, really, but it was cool and different, and it kind of freaked me out. I was maybe seven at the time."

Seven years old. The same age the children had been when Viktor had taken them. How aware had their parents been of their gifts, I wondered? How many of them realized their children had psychic abilities? "Your parents handle it okay?"

"If by okay you mean I was stuck in support groups and therapy, yeah. They did okay." He smiled. "I learned pretty quick to hide it. Wasn't until I got my first tat that I felt like I could start owning who I was. So I get it, man. I get the need to make that kind of a statement." He pointed to the book. "Even if it's a statement of a bunch of daisies and bluebirds. It's all in what helps the client."

"You ever get a request for something you won't do?"

He shook his head. "Ultimately, it's the client's call, but there are designs Blue flat-out won't do, and I can't say I blame her." At my raised eyebrows, he waved a hand. "RIP designs — death memorials, that kind of thing. Not Death itself — she'll make that image all day long, every day. But when people want to ink the images of their lost loved ones, she balks."

I considered that. "There's a lot of those images out there."

"They're everywhere. Doesn't make it right, though." He looked weary, then, thinking about it. "People get all up in arms about the biblical injunctions against tattoos, but scripture is pretty clear on this point. Whether or not the Bible is against any sort of tattoo, full stop, for sure any mark to honor or recall the soul of a dead man is not cool." He shook his head. "The worst is when pastors come in for ink to remember a loved one. That's not a conversation you ever want to have."

This conversation was having its desired effect, though. I felt myself relaxing, loosening up, the work of Armaeus to repair the damage caused by the Astral Travel Train Wreck settling into my bones with Jimmy's soft cadence. He nodded as if he knew what I was doing, but amiably kept talking.

The door bells jingled, and Nikki strode in, dressed in combat boots, camouflage cargo pants, and tight black tank top, her hair back in a ponytail. She spotted me and cut her forward movement short. "Armaeus thought you'd be here." She eyed my clothes. "And he thought you'd ditch the outfit he gave you too. Gotta give the guy props for trying, though."

"I guess." I bounced my heel on the foot rung of the stool, eyeing her as she settled in, her back against one of the few bits of wall that weren't covered with flash art. "You my babysitter?"

"Nope, I'm your friend. Hey, Jimmy, you got any coffee in this joint?" Nikki prattled on while I blinked hard, shifting my head down and away to hide my face. It wasn't that I didn't think of Nikki as my friend, but to hear it out loud gave the words a weight and grace I wasn't expecting. And it was possible that I was ever so slightly fragile at the moment. So there was that.

Nikki was still doctoring her mug of caffeine when Blue poked her head into the front room. "Jimmy, could use you on the finish work." She eyed me and swung her gaze to Nikki, her brows lifting. "You both doing a jump?"

"No," I said before Nikki could finish choking on her coffee.

"You came back, like, five seconds ago," Nikki managed, turning her attention to Blue. "Is that too soon for her to do whatever it is you mean by jumping? Because she was fried to a crisp and poked full of holes last time, and while Armaeus knows we're here while he's entertaining Viktor the Cruel, he's not physically on-site to put her into a cocoon when she comes back. And that seems like it'd be a problem."

Blue studied me intently. "You were damaged in transition? That shouldn't have happened."

"Well, good, that makes me feel better about what's coming next, then," I said, standing. "We should probably get moving."

She stood aside and gestured me back, her gaze dropping to my wrist as I passed her. "You shouldn't have been hurt that badly," she said again, sounding more curious than concerned. "The transition to Atlantis was smooth?"

"It happened on the way back." Nikki provided the color commentary as we moved to room three. "She was fine, doing her thing, then she got a tank dropped on her head and Armaeus couldn't yank her out of there fast enough."

"Stop." We turned at the change in Blue's voice, her eyes wide and hard on me. "You were attacked? By whom? There's nothing left in Atlantis but ruin."

"Well, there were two sets of creatures there — they looked to my eyes like angels and demons, but I admit I was a little hazy on the details. The atmosphere was strange, I was moving fast. But that's what they looked like."

"And they attacked you." She was looking at me as if expecting me to reveal a secret. "That's all they did."

"Well...no." I blew out a breath as Nikki watched me. She'd seen what I had seen in Atlantis, no recorders required. "I wanted to talk to you about that. They... It was almost as if they recognized me. I was carrying the scales of the Justice card, and I get that I might have seemed familiar because of the card in the Atlantean deck. But at first, their recognition seemed to be a good thing. Then — not so much."

"Right." Blue wasn't looking at me anymore but busying herself with her workstation. I sighed as I saw the familiar tools. If I kept this up, I was going to have a sleeve of my own by Christmas. "The creatures you're describing are tied to the card you are speaking of, yes," Blue finally said. "They do her bidding. But she's not Justice in the Atlantean deck. None of those cards tally exactly with the Major Arcana. They were more powerful, but also more flawed. It proved their downfall."

"Seems like a lot of folks met their downfall in Atlantis." Nikki poked her finger into the illusions lining the walls. "Does anyone actually fall for this?"

"It's not meant to hold up to close scrutiny, merely to appease the lookie-loos. If it bothers you…" Death waved her hand, and the room returned to its austere lines—the chair, the tools, and four walls.

"Ew, no," Nikki said, and the image of bookcases and posters resettled in place. "I'm good with illusions."

Blue smiled as she turned back to me, but her gaze was searching. "The card you drew is called Vigilance, not Justice. The creatures who serve it are known as Watchers. They obey unquestioningly, and their wrath is unstinting to any that stand in their path. Anything in particular trigger them to make the move on you? You incite them in any way?"

"Not that I thought," I said. I got into the seat as Blue pulled her chair closer. "I was talking to Armaeus, not them. I couldn't speak their language."

"Mm. And what did you say to Armaeus?"

I sat back in the chair as the now-familiar sound of the whirring needle stirred to life. "I asked him to help me," I said.

"Ah." Blue bent down to scrutinize my right arm, then glanced up at me. "This will be a lesser mark, but a more costly one. I warned you."

I forced my arm to stay still. "I know. I'm ready."

"No," she said faintly. So faintly I barely heard her. "But you will pay the price nevertheless."

She bent toward me, and the moment the needle touched my flesh—this time on the inside curve of my arm—pain exploded around me in a burst of agony. I vaguely realized that Nikki had bounded forward, at first to protest but then to hold me down as Blue murmured words I had no intention of deciphering if they brought with them this much pain.

The slash she half inked, half burned into me was small but intricate, an out-of-control Möbius strip that wove in a tight circuit over my skin, looping back on itself at the last second when it seemed obvious that it would stretch out into a wider trail. I didn't black out this time, though I wished I had, and it surprised me how quickly she was done. She backed away from me and motioned to Nikki, whose hands didn't leave my hip and shoulder right away. They only slightly loosened, their hold remaining firm. Like a handler setting loose a fawn in the wild, providing comfort until the very last moment.

"I'm fine," I rasped at length, and Blue turned away before I could see her face, attending to her tools once more.

Jimmy was at my other side with his omnipresent water bottle. "It'll help," he said in his soft voice, and given Nikki's mute nod, I took it. The water tasted cool and chemical free, and I was about to ask for pain relievers to go with it, when I realized there was no more pain.

"Why did this one hurt more?" I asked, staring down at the angry symbol on my inner elbow. "Is the skin thinner there?"

"Many reasons," Blue said. She swiveled back around to me. "You didn't know what to expect the first time, and were prepared for the worst. This time, you'd had an experience already and expected it to be the same. When it wasn't, your mind reacted with an outsized sensitivity."

"Right." Handing the water bottle back to Jimmy, I inched myself higher in my seat. "Why else?"

"Because of where you're going. There are several

layers of dimensions that surround us, each more complex than the last."

"Like the nine circles of hell?"

She smiled. "You might say that. Atlantis, for all its flaws, remains fairly close. It's an island sunk out of time and mind, but there is nothing there..." Her lips twisted. "Well, there's not supposed to be anything there. For the Watchers to have found you is an anomaly I haven't had time to fully consider." She lifted a hand to forestall my protest. "And no, I won't tell Armaeus until you are ready. You both will be busy enough."

That didn't sound good, but I needed to focus on the task at hand. "What about this place I'm heading? Viktor showed me, it looked pretty much earthlike."

"That's an illusion, as you'll see when you reach it. The demons that Viktor mentioned are known as the Syx, with a y. Contrary to popular belief, they are not allied with the Devil, certainly not the Devil as we know him on the Arcana Council. They're older creatures, from a time when the earth was formed, but they ruled as generals and were swept out when the Arcana Council destroyed Atlantis." Her expression was wintry. "Viktor is ever fond of reminding the Council of the sins of its fathers. The wholesale eradication of magic was a result unforeseen when the Council was formed to take on Llyr. At the time, the sacrifice was considered worth it. And magic did recover, eventually. The Syx have watched this evolution with an untamed hunger, as they watch all things."

"And Viktor thought the children would be *safe* with them."

"Not at all." Blue leaned forward, her elbows on her knees. Her ice-blue eyes were bleak in her pale face, her platinum-blonde hair spiked high. Today, a set of intricate cuffs trailed down her right ear to the tip of her lobe, before ending in chains that looped back up to the top cuff again to begin the cycle once more. She wore no other jewelry, no makeup, and her thin lips caught my attention next as she spoke again. "Viktor thought the Syx would kill those children. He offered them as payment."

"Payment for what, though?" Nikki's voice was sharp. "That was, what, ten years ago? He's been nowhere on the map since then. As far as we know, he hasn't been trafficking in human cargo either, or knocking over any third world countries. What could he have gotten in return that would have been worth getting caught?"

Blue shrugged. "Perhaps it is not what he was paying forward, but paying back. We simply do not know. When Viktor left the Council and entered seclusion, we were as barred to him as anyone else. It was his right to do so, and our rules have lasted too long to discount. We did not know of these children, much as we did not know of you."

That sounded ominous. "What do you mean?"

"Ten years ago, you saw Llyr in the midst of a confrontation with Viktor's magic, and yet — hundreds of miles away, the Council was unaware of any ripple in the veil. We only learned of it when Armaeus decided to use you for his work and realized you were nothing like he expected. He hates that."

"I've noticed." I considered what she said. "You think Viktor is a lot stronger than any of us realize, and that these Syx have something to do with it?"

"I offer it only as a possibility. The web of magic is fraying in some corners and reforming in others, a constantly changing weave. I do not have all the answers."

In that moment, I didn't believe Blue on that score, but I realized I didn't need to. I had work to do. "So these Syx. Will they know I've shown up in their, um, dimension? Because I totally slept through the demon-slayer portion of my training."

"You too are a key," Blue said, pointing to my wrist. The red flare surrounding the ink was already fading, and all that remained was the intricate Möbius strip, a Celtic knot of misdirection. "Your only task is to go in, get the children, and get out."

It was Nikki who pointed out the obvious flaw in this plan. "Except there's only one of her, and there are six of children. They're all grown up too. And if what we've been seeing on this side is all an illusion, they could be a hell of a lot worse off than we think. How is she going to pull them all back?"

"The same way she brought back artifacts from Atlantis," Blue said, standing. "What she touches can move in space and time with her, if that is her intention. So" — she turned to me, her eyes a mocking challenge — "be careful what you touch."

"Um, as I recall, those weapons were impaled in me, not touching me."

"Because that is their nature. Mortal hands are not intended to pierce, but to hold."

That seemed reasonable enough. I looked at Nikki. "Now?"

She drew her cap down more firmly on her head. "Not like I've got anything else going on today. Let's hit it."

CHAPTER NINETEEN

We stopped at the front desk to reclaim my throwing stars, then left Darkworks. We didn't need to go far—I was already abuzz with energy. Nikki had seen me go across and had helped bring me back. She could do that again.

Nevertheless, Blue had left me unsettled. She hadn't said anything specific, but her cryptic warnings and meaningful looks made me think she knew a lot more than she was letting on. And her reaction to the weird reception I'd had in Atlantis from the Watchers struck me as off too. I didn't know enough about Death to truly understand her moods, though. It would take time to understand that. And time wasn't on my side right now.

"We're going to need backup, Nikki," I muttered. "I don't know what I'm going to walk into, but I can't be shadowed by someone from the Council. If they know, Viktor might know. I have no idea how deep their hive mind goes."

"Agreed." She pointed at the chapel.

Not surprisingly, Dixie's white convertible was parked in front of it. A little more surprisingly, Brody's brown sedan was beside it. The two looked odd next to each other, but no odder than the couple itself, at least to my mind.

"Dixie and Brody?" she suggested. "They're both

amped and Connected at this point. And you know as well as I do that Brody will be chafed to the bone if you don't bring him in."

I blew out a breath. It made sense, and they both were here. Of course, they seemed to be everywhere together these days, Dixie using their newly rekindled romance as reason enough to embroil Brody into every Connected quarrel within ten miles of the Strip. But I needed backup, and one didn't look a gift detective in the mouth. Let alone someone with the Connected abilities of Dixie Quinn. Even before the augmentation had hit her, she was channeling some serious psychic ability — stronger than Nikki, potentially.

"I don't have a ton of patience for explanation," I warned Nikki, and she snorted.

"Trust me, I don't think Brody will either. Let's hope they're not canoodling. I'm full up on canoodling today."

"Power, sister."

Fortunately, we were spared that visual. Coming around the corner to the wide-open door of Dixie's office, the first thing I noticed wasn't the two of them, but a map of the Strip laid out on a foam-core board stuck full of pins, many of which were linked together with colorful thread. Brody and Dixie stood on opposite sides of the thing, scowling down at it like it'd just said a bad word.

Nikki voiced the question paramount in my mind. "What the hell is that?" she blurted. "And why low-tech?"

"Nikki!" Dixie brought her head up, her smile wide enough to take us both in. Once again, I felt my innate resistance to Dixie chip away another bit. It wasn't her fault that she was beautiful, sweet, good-hearted, and dating the man I'd pined over when I was a teenager. It wasn't ideal, but it wasn't her fault. "And Sara. You're looking so well!"

I blinked at the unexpected compliment. "Um — thanks. What's that?" I pointed at the map, my curiosity easily masking my confusion.

"Danae is in a tizz, ditto her coven," Dixie said. "We're trying to untangle why." She gestured to the map. "Literally."

My brows went up. Danae was the witch from the Chicago coven who had proven so necessary to maintaining the integrity of the Vegas psychic power grid during the attack from SANCTUS. To do so, she had remapped and reinforced the magic of the ley lines beneath Vegas. "She's still in Vegas?"

"She'd planned on leaving yesterday, but no sooner had she packed her last bag than the bottom fell out of the city, literally." Dixie drew her long fingernail across the map. "The ley lines are jumping around like underground lightning strikes. It's been happening since yesterday afternoon. No one knows why, least of all Danae. And she's not happy about it. These pins are workplaces of Connecteds who have reported strange reactions. Adrenaline spikes, psy abilities surging or completely guttering out, visions and dreams they can't understand. We've got reports coming in by the dozen."

"Since yesterday afternoon?" I looked at Brody, who stared at me knowingly. "Viktor?"

"Has to be." He rocked back on his heels, his hands in his pants pocket as I unshouldered my pack. "We haven't been able to locate him for several hours. But to our knowledge, he hasn't used any form of public transportation out of the city — no flight manifest, no chartered vehicles. So he's here, somewhere, behind closed doors. No way of knowing if he's the one jacking the energy." Then his gaze dropped. "What the hell are you pulling out of that bag? Is that a table saw blade?"

"Close enough." I leaned the throwing stars against the wall and peered down at the map. "A lot's happened since yesterday afternoon." Nevertheless, I didn't feel particularly jacked. I didn't think I had any connection to the ley lines going on the fritz. "Does Danae have any explanation?"

"None," Dixie said, "and it's put a bee in her bonnet, as you might imagine. She was looking forward to getting home to her walled garden of pure Connecteds." She wrinkled her nose. "Our more liberal views were already not setting well with her. Add in this burst of unexplained magical power, and she's beside herself."

"No injuries yet?"

"Not a one." She shook her head. "It's like the world is holding its breath, you know?"

Nikki and I exchanged a glance. Brody caught it. "What?" he asked. "What have you learned?"

I couldn't find the words. Fortunately, with Nikki around, I didn't have long to wait. "Sara's ready to get the children." She held up her hand. "It's not going to be pretty, it is going to freak you out, and we do need to get started."

"I don't have my team in place yet." He glared at me. "We need doctors. Shrinks. You know that." Brody ran his hand through his hair. "I haven't started calling the parents."

"Parents!" I snapped the word more sharply than I intended.

But of course he should call the parents. That only made sense. Didn't make it feel right, though. I picked up the largest of the stars, taking comfort in its solidity.

"We don't know how they're going to come back, Brody," I said. "Or *if*. I've never done this before, not like this." I decided this wouldn't be a good time to discuss how messed up I'd been the last time I'd made the attempt. From the look on Nikki's face, that was a good call.

"All the more reason to have professionals here." He pulled out his phone. "I'm calling to put the EMTs on standby, at the very least. They come in unable to breathe, injured, we want to be ready. You guys — " He waved the phone at us, turning away. "Get ready."

Dixie led the charge. Shutting down a wedding chapel was less of a production than I would have expected, and within a few minutes, every entry was locked down tight with no clear indication of when it would open again.

The main wedding chapel seemed too large for our needs, but the secondary chapel, done up in a Mediterranean Mermaids theme at present, seemed small enough to manage but large enough to serve as a reception hall for six teens. Nicki and Brody moved the large stucco statue of Venus to the side, along with the goddess posse of wild horses pounding from the surf. That done, we moved to the front of the room. There was no altar here, but the stairs were thickly carpeted. The easier for collapsing on, I thought. I was a fan.

"We should have a squad here as well," Brody muttered. "If those kids are injured…"

"Mmm-hmm." Nikki cocked an eye at him. "You want to tell them that you'll maybe have six teenagers transported to an off-Strip wedding chapel via mental projection, and you want someone on hand in case anything goes wrong?"

He looked ready to argue, but she waved him off.

"You really think you put in an emergency call this

close to downtown, they won't have a whole fleet of EMTs and police here within two minutes? You'll get the support you need. And without the straitjacket if we're not right about what's about to go down."

"Fine." He slid his phone back into his pocket. "What now."

Nikki took up her position beside me on the stairs, looking from me to the carpet. "Might as well go ahead and sit down, dollface."

"Yeah." I nodded. "Beats falling."

Brody's scowl deepened. "And what exactly do you plan on doing with that saw blade, Sara?"

"It's going to help me get in—and get out, if I do things right." I laid the star in front of me on the carpeted step. In the glow of the chapel lights, I could see the etching on the metal tips of the blades. "Pretty, don't you think?"

"Speaking of blades, chop chop," Nikki barreled on. "You draw cards already?"

"Not yet."

Brody made a small strangled noise as I reached into my hoodie pocket, fishing for my Rider-Waite deck. I didn't look at him. The last time he saw me draw cards to find children was the day before everything changed in Memphis...and there was so much water under that bridge, I'm surprised we didn't drown in it.

The cards met my questing fingers easily, and I drew them out, three of them, as familiar as a favorite shirt. Turning to the side, I arranged them on the ledge before me, not minding as Dixie, Nikki, and Brody all edged in. It was one thing to have the untutored but curious crowd your space, but these people knew the cards, and they knew what I did with them. Having them see the spread linked me more strongly to this

214

space. From what Blue told me, that kind of link would be important here in a few minutes.

I eyed the cards dispassionately, memorizing their features. The first was the Moon—the card of illusion and deception, or alternatively the card of the ocean, dreams, night creatures. I didn't know what it meant, specifically, but that was its beauty: I wouldn't know until I was in place on the other side of my jump.

The second card was the Seven of Swords again. He was showing up a lot of late, and that never made me happy. The card depicted a young man traipsing across a pathway, clutching seven swords. Since I wasn't likely to be visiting an armory on this trip, I had to take the card for its more esoteric meaning: the need for an abrupt change in strategy, or the elements of deception and illusion. Sort of like the Moon card, but with a craftier undertone. The combination of the two didn't make me feel warm and fuzzy. The Moon card deliberately tried to cloud interpretation on the best of days. But I was about to set foot into unknown territory and needed all the clarity I could get. These two cards together meant I wasn't going to get it.

And the third card was yet more disturbing, though it shouldn't be. The Six of Pentacles showed a generous man giving alms to the poor, with six disks raining from the sky. There were six children that I was returning home, and the card was generally a pleasant one. But with the first two cards looming over me with their dual hits of confusion and deceit, I wasn't happy.

"You know what that all means?" Brody asked gruffly. It was the same question he'd asked so many times when I was a teenager, and he asked it in so much the same tone of voice that I had a hard time separating the past from the present. I focused on the spread as I answered, the words coming easily to my lips but sounding as if I was speaking them from a far distance, a decade and a lifetime away.

"I will when I see it," I said, and the reiteration of the old exchange made my heart a little lighter. I tucked my hand into my jacket one more time, wanting something—anything—to give me a little more guidance. I peeked at the card, then rolled my eyes, pushing it back in my jacket. I gathered up the three cards and met Nikki's gaze. "Tower," I said with a shrug. "I shouldn't have asked."

"We'll brace ourselves." Nikki watched me critically as I sat down at the top of the carpeted platform.

I blew out a breath, feeling the urge to travel welling up in me. Or at least that was what I told myself as my gag reflex triggered. Traveling was hell on a body.

To take my mind off my sudden nausea, I turned my arm and focused on the newest symbol Death had inked there, my gaze tracking the sinuous curve of the narrow strip. Then I reached out and laid my hand on the throwing star.

"You know the words?"

Nikki shrugged. "There wasn't much to it. All Eshe did was hold out her hand and say—"

I blacked out.

Once again, there was no sense of time passing as I came back to consciousness with a rush, my feet moving me forward without my mind fully aware of my progress until I realized I was about to walk square into a brick wall. I stopped short, then turned around carefully.

I was in the same location as I'd seen on Viktor's

screen, down to the cloud-strewn sky. I didn't know if that was a good thing or bad thing, though. Was I trapped in the same illusion that the children were? Would I even be able to find them? Across the grassy lot from me was a wrought iron fence fronting a brick building, very New England college-esque. Trees sported rich green leaves, and the lawns were perfectly manicured. Dozens of what looked like perfectly normal students milled and chatted around the building. It was the idyllic setting for an idyllic life.

A murmur at my ear startled me, but I recognized the voice, desperately grateful that I could hear Nikki in this place. We weren't so far distant as Atlantis had been. That had to be good.

"I'm solid, I'm fine," I said back, speaking aloud.

"Yeah, well, you're still clutching the star here. Do you have it there?"

"I…no." I stared down at my empty hands, but it was the image beyond my hands that held my attention. "There's a problem."

The few words seemed to have a ripple effect in front of me, and the image faltered, making me catch my breath. I tried again.

"Speaking…" I stopped. Started. "Changes things. Alters it. Something's definitely wrong."

With each successive word, the image in front of me cracked. I thought about the Moon and its penchant for illusion. I knew that this image in front of me was a mirage. But it still was alarming to see it shift and warp as I spoke. I waved in front of my face. "Clear it away, clear it away! I want to see."

The image suddenly disintegrated in front of me. I whirled around, trying to get my bearings, but I was in a large, white-walled room, containing six covered gurneys. I froze, my stomach clenched into a tight ball as the horror in front of me registered.

The gurneys were small—far too small, and the huddled lumps beneath the blankets were too small as well, the size of children, *not* of adults, not of young men and women on the verge of all they could yet become.

"No, no, no," I moaned, stepping back reflexively. But there was nothing and no one else in this space, not a murmur in the oppressively blank room. I walked forward resolutely then, forcing myself to scan the area. It was white, completely white with stark fluorescent light beaming from both the walls and the ceiling. It gave the room a surgical feel. The gurneys were covered in soft blankets, three blue, three pink. There was no indication of what lay beneath the covers, but I knew…of course I knew. The children had been so small when they'd been taken, a few of them only six years old.

Had I learned so much about them, come all this way, for this? It seemed impossible. Why had Viktor wanted me then? Why had he lured me if there was nothing here but *death*?

With a shaking hand, I reached out to the first blanket, pulling it down. And my heart broke in two. I didn't have to touch her throat. She was dead— perfectly preserved as if she'd just drawn her last breath. She'd probably been dead the moment she'd crossed into this dimension, held in its thrall forever.

Mary Degnan. I remembered her face as surely as if she was the little sister I never had, her laughing eyes and sweetheart smile winning me over from the start. I'd known her only in pictures, but she was perfect and precious—and now terribly, horribly still.

"God," I managed, though there was nothing of God in this place, nor of heaven or the angels. "They're here," I said aloud. "They're... I'm bringing them back."

If Nikki replied, I couldn't hear it. I seemed to be moving in slow motion, my own heart rate dropping to a sluggish crawl. I dragged the six gurneys together in a rough arc so that I could touch each of them at once. Then I paused. What if the gurneys came back, but not the children? I couldn't face this place again. Steeling myself against the horror of it all, I moved with brutal efficiency. I flipped the blankets down enough to uncover the faces of the children. They didn't breathe, but they didn't look dead either, and pulling up their arms was easy — their bodies were more like dolls than human cadavers, rigor mortis having long since come and gone. I couldn't — wouldn't think about that. I only wanted to be gone.

Failed. I'd failed them again. The mantra chanted in my head. I saw myself as seventeen all over again, the first time Brody had shown me the picture of sweet Hayley Adams. The hope I'd felt. The determination. I'd thought I could find anyone back then. I thought I could stop any crime. *All this time, all this hope, for nothing.* Nothing but loss and death.

If anyone can save them, it'll probably be you.

I tasted salt and lifted my hands to wipe the tears from my face as I positioned myself in the center of the gurneys. Reaching out again, I knelt until my arms were perpendicular to the floor, and resting on six too-small hands.

Tears started anew. "I'm ready, Nikki," I whispered. "Bring me — "

The hands clutched my arms.

I jolted back, rigid, but I was held fast as the small bodies beside me changed impossibly fast, lengthening, growing. Until instead of small children's

219

palms dwarfed by my arms, I was being clutched by hands the size of dinner plates, hands attached to long muscled arms and powerful shoulders. Creatures of immense size and shape lunged for me, and I couldn't think, I couldn't breathe, could only gasp out the final word with a terrified shriek of horror. "Back!" I screamed, trying desperately to pull away.

Talons pierced my skin as I howled with pain. The grip of the Syx held me fast, and I felt the veil rush toward me, bright light and magic exploding around us all.

"The debt at last is paid," the closest one said to me.

CHAPTER TWENTY

I awakened with the scream on my lips, scrambling off the stairs. The star fell from my grip and bounced down beside me. I wasn't burned, and my clothes weren't ripped to shreds, but as I swung around wildly, I saw damage had definitely been done.

"Brody — Dixie!" I gasped, only there was something wrong with my voice. It came out as a bare rasp, the attempt at speech like dragging fiery-hot coals through my throat. I stumbled forward to where Brody half lay on top of Dixie, as if he'd tried to shelter her against a fiery blast. Even as I reached them, they were moving, though, and I heard him moan my name.

I shook him hard, and he came up swinging, narrowly missing clipping me in the chin.

"Sara!" he shouted, bringing a bleat of distress from the half-dazed Dixie, who also looked to be clawing her way toward consciousness. "Sara, you're all right! What the hell *was* that?"

He was shouting too loud — too loud, and I slapped my hands over my ears to stop the roaring in my brain. I wheeled around, and something felt wrong, so wrong. I couldn't understand it. The door of the secondary chapel had been thrust open, the statuary of Venus and her horses shoved aside, but otherwise the room was as empty as, well, a church.

And then I realized what was missing. I turned

back to Brody.

"Nikki?" I croaked, surprised that smoke didn't drift out of my mouth.

"You're hurt," he said automatically. He was up on his feet in an instant, ignoring me as I shook my head.

"What happened?" I managed again. "What came through?"

"I..." He frowned, looking around. "I don't know. Nikki said you were bringing the children back. That they were dead but you had their bodies. She had a grip on you and then started yelling at us to run, to go. Dixie screamed and half fainted or something beside me, and I turned to catch her, dropping down to the ground as..." He shook his head. "It was an explosion of some sort. Strong enough to blast the door off its hinges." He stared back at me. "And it seemed to come from you."

"Where's Nikki?" My voice sounded garbled, and my knees wobbled as I stood there. Dixie gave a cry, and Brody turned back to her as I braced myself on the nearest church pew. I stared at my hand. The skin was darkening, as if from the inside. The outer dermis was still intact and perfect, but the inner...

"Miss Wilde!" Armaeus's voice shattered into my mind as a fell wind, cutting through the dark fog that was creeping through me. *"What has happened? You're hurt."*

"Armaeus." I tried to move forward, but I faltered, and suddenly Brody was at my side, barely able to keep me from falling.

"Holy Shit, Sara, what's wrong with you? You're on fire."

"Limo—out front," I gasped. "There'll be a limo."

Dixie was on the other side of me, her gasp audible as she draped one of my arms over her shoulder.

"She's right, Brody. Nikki's gone, and I'm not sure how to heal this. She needs to see the Magician."

"The what?" I heard Brody's growl as if from a far distance. In my mind I saw the rapid succession of cards, falling like dominos. The Moon with its shadow of illusions, followed by the Seven of Swords. I'd been deceived by Viktor, tricked and deceived. The children weren't alive; they were dead. They'd been dead for a decade. A decade of hopes dying with them, a decade of prayers gone unanswered. A decade of eyes looking to the horizon, hoping, begging for their safe return. All gone in a wisp of smoke and fire.

Inexorably, the fall of cards continued in my mind. The Six of Pentacles and the Tower. It was so obvious now it was laughable, but I hadn't seen it... I hadn't seen it. The Six of Pentacles was all about giving and receiving. Sometimes what was given was a gift, pure largesse, and sometimes what was given was a repayment for services rendered. It was the classic Minor Arcana card for a debt being repaid. A debt in this case with a double meaning. A debt of six, or Syx.

Viktor had promised to get the djinn out of their enforced purgatory, and I'd been his tool to do it.

My legs felt suddenly too heavy, but as we cleared the front doors of the chapel, I shrugged off Dixie and Brody, forcing myself to stand. The limo was there, idling at the curb, but I didn't head for it either. I headed across the parking lot, toward Darkworks Ink. I was fifteen paces away when I noticed that the lights were no longer flickering in the windows, and the OPEN sign was shut off.

I blinked, too shocked to believe it. There would be no solace in that place. Not this day.

I almost hit the pavement before strong arms stopped my fall.

The ride to the Prime Luxe was a blur of smoke. I didn't understand my body's reaction to returning through the veil this time. There'd been no attack of Watchers, no fight, no spike of adrenaline. I'd blasted back much more easily, slipping and sliding along the Möbius strip that Blue had etched into me before falling back through to this dimension.

But I hadn't brought weapons this time. I'd brought creatures of fire and death.

That couldn't...be possible.

I sensed myself being transferred from the car, but nothing else made sense to me. Nothing else could.

"You would do well to rest, Miss Wilde." Armaeus's words were soothing — too soothing. The kind of tone used in hospices, not hospitals.

I flickered my eyes open. The clicking noise they made was also unnerving. "Where's Viktor?" I rasped.

"He is back in his domain, presumably. He knew immediately what you had done, when you had done it." There was no censure in his tone, nothing more really than a quiet curiosity.

"He...lied."

"He did." A light hand touched my face, impossibly cool. I turned into it, trying not to whimper. Why was I so hot? I felt like I had been boiled from the inside.

"The djinn were forged in fire, Miss Wilde. The Atlantean blade you held in this plane kept you from incinerating, but only just. The moment you let go of it, the fire of their passage began to cook you from the inside."

I coughed, and smoke seemed to burn through my mouth. "You have a way with words."

"And you are very strong. I did not foresee the djinn using you in this manner. They are creatures of

224

an ancient magic, but like all demons, they need hosts to exist on this earth. You provided them their host..." He shook his head. "It should not have been possible." He tilted his head, regarding me. "And now they must find others."

I grimaced, and slitted my eyes open to focus on him. "In English this time?"

"You set six powerful djinn free into the world, all on your own. To stay here, they must possess six separate souls."

I winced. "Maybe we should try another language."

He gestured dismissively. "Demonic possession has been a mortal plague since the dawn of time, a staple of every known religion. There are those who may summon the dark ones forth from their home for brief discourse — mages like Nostradamus, for example — but never for very long. Since their banishment, to remain in this world, a djinn must either have a host or sacrifice their great strength and abilities to become mortal. As you can imagine, most have no interest in becoming mortal."

Something about his words nagged at me. "What happens if they don't have a host?"

"Unless their domain is destroyed, they are returned to it, usually within twenty-four hours. But they can get very creative about staying in the mortal plane. The stories of demonic possession have at their core an essential truth."

"Then how could I have brought all of them back?"

"I suspect that Viktor's expectation was that they would return within the bodies of the young men and women he captured. If they had done so, we were prepared. The ley lines have been fortified to contain the possessed."

"That was you!" I stared at him. "You didn't tell Danae."

"For a witch, she has a tiresome need for details. But had the children come back carrying the djinn, it would have been enough. We were not prepared for *you* bringing them all back, however."

I tried to lift a hand, but it was held beneath heavy covers. "They're dead," I croaked. "The children. All of them, from when they were—"

"No, Miss Wilde. Those were illusions. The six missing children remain trapped in their elaborate cage until the demons are returned. Viktor had to wait for them to reach maturity before they could sustain the demonic possession, but instead he now has the demons without the children—and he doesn't have control over the demons." Armaeus looked particularly intrigued. "This was unplanned."

"But where did they go when we came through?" A new thought occurred to me. "They're not in me anymore, right? I'd know that."

"You'd know it. They seek out others."

My eyes rounded as I stared at him. "Oh my God. Nikki—they took Nikki."

Armaeus nodded. "Dixie and Brody were passed over, perhaps because of their fledgling bond, perhaps in the confusion of the release. But Nikki—we have no sign of her. She's missing."

I half rose from the bed, fell back. "I have to find her."

"Detective Rooks has already issued the alert throughout the LVMPD, and Dixie is tapping her vast network within the city. They will find her. You, on the other hand, must heal."

"I can't!" Real alarm shattered through me. "I did this, Armaeus, I did this to Nikki. I can't let her—" I closed my eyes, jolting with pain as a tear slid down my cheek, scalding hot. "This will happen to her, won't it?" I whispered. "I did this."

"Miss Wilde." Armaeus was at my side again, leaning down. "You can do nothing for Nikki until you recover."

"Then heal me, dammit," I breathed.

"You are too weak," he rumbled. "Your body is barely a husk. The weight of six demons effectively incinerated you from the inside. The Atlantean blade served to protect you somewhat, but you will need time to return to normal."

"Oh my God, Nikki."

"She will, at most, serve as host to one demon. Not six. It will not affect her the same way." Armaeus shrugged. "And the demons can assume any form they choose for the first twenty-four hours of their time on earth. They may elect to possess no one at all for that time period."

"We can't take that risk! Please, Armaeus, I beg of you. Heal me. I will do whatever you want, be whoever you want. I can't let Nikki die because of me." My eyes flared. "And those children. If they're alive, I have to go back, to get them. Without the djinn there guarding them, the way will be clearer, right?"

"We have no way of knowing that."

"Death will know," I spat. "She probably knew all along."

He didn't respond, which was all the answer I needed.

"What *is it* with you people?" I snarled. "Are you just that damned bored? You'll let mortals go and do *everything* you can't do because you've forgotten what it's like to be human?" Unaccountably, the tears welled up inside me again. I didn't want to feel them, didn't

227

want to feel anything. My insides were cooked, despite the healing mist Armaeus had woven around me. Every breath in was a blessing, but it became superheated in my guts, and by the time it released, it was like exhaling acid. "I didn't think I could hurt this badly."

And what was that about, anyway? I'd known Armaeus for a long time, long enough to know the man pounced on me every time I so much as had a hangnail, all in the interest of me being at my best. Had I become too broken for him to save? Was he no longer interested in trying?

I hated that I cared, but I did. I couldn't help it.

Everything was falling apart. I hadn't saved the children. I'd lost Brody. I'd lost Nikki. I'd lost people I'd barely found, or re-found, and I might never get them back. And now, Armaeus himself was distant from me, his hands on my wrists clinical, not carnal. Not even caring.

What had happened?

The obvious answer bubbled up without me realizing how close it was to the surface, breaking through before I could stop it. "Am I dying?"

"No." The word was sharp, almost a slap. Armaeus leaned toward me, his gaze searching my face.

I hadn't looked in a mirror since I'd come back, but the coolness radiating off him was a balm to my abraded skin. I must look like five miles of bad road.

"No," he murmured again, more softly this time, his tone decisive, almost resigned. "Do not close your eyes, Miss Wilde. Maintain every connection with me you can."

"You usually just kiss and make it—ah…" Ignoring his directive, I winced as the blood rushed to my face, the embarrassment I felt at the ridiculous statement rewarded immediately by a surge of pain. "My God, I feel like crap."

"God has very little to do with your condition, but your extreme condition is why I cannot kiss you, embrace you...or pound you into the back of the bed. Miss Wilde."

I clicked my eyes open again. Yep. He had my attention. "Um..."

"And believe me, I want to." Armaeus was close enough that I wasn't merely inhaling the pungent healing mist he had surrounding me, but the cinnamon fire of him, the scent of deep spices and sensual heat...a heat completely different from the crumbling embers inside me.

He moved his face, his lips not touching mine, but his cool breath played over my skin, and my body couldn't help but react. A thrill chased along my nerve endings.

"I have wanted to stretch you out beneath me and fill you to the brink since the first moment I saw you. I've wanted to make you cry out in passion and exhaustion, to hear my name on your lips as you begged me to take you to places you've never glimpsed before. I have wanted it. Yearned for it."

"Ahh..." I couldn't help it, I squirmed beneath his non-touch, wanting more than anything for him to rip the blanket away and do everything he was telling me. "Really?"

"Open your mind to me, only a little. You will see."

Never had my mental barriers dropped so quickly. The hollow husk of my brain, blackened and crispy at the edges, was suddenly filled to the brim with images so intense and real it was impossible for me to tell what was happening and what was mere illusion.

Okay, scratch that. I remained under the covers,

229

and Armaeus was not. But in my mind's eye I saw him naked and glorious, bending me back onto his enormous bed and climbing up on top of me, every inch of him rock hard and trained solely on me. In my ears, I heard the rush of a language I'd never known, a language that triggered my nervous system to hyperawareness, from the balls of my feet to the crown of my head, each of my chakra points lighting up like signal flares. And though Armaeus wasn't touching me, not really, my senses believed wholeheartedly that his lips were on my neck, my collarbone, my breasts. His hands skimming down my body and between my legs, touching, exploring, learning me like a master sailor knows every inch of his instruments, his ship, and lavishing me with the same single-minded care that a man who made his life at sea poured out over the one thing that would either be his salvation or his ruin. I arched in the bed beneath the covers, desperate to feel the taste of his mouth, but Armaeus kept me just out of reach.

At least in real life.

My mind, however, was filled with what had never happened next between us, what should have happened next between us so many months ago when we'd been drawn together like twin flames and then burst apart so shockingly, and my mind had collapsed under a surge of panic because it couldn't—it wouldn't—

None of that panic filled me now. There was only Armaeus, his arms powerful and sure, his hands at my breasts, my waist, my thighs, sliding around the curve of my backside to lift me up to his questing mouth. All I wanted was this, more of this. All I wanted was him inside me. I breathed out a long, ragged sigh, a distant part of me realizing that even that didn't hurt anymore. There was no fear. "How…?"

"It's a dream within a dream. Your mind knows the difference."

His answer made perfect sense, yet something within me rejected it. That something was shunted off to the side as his mouth came down on the most intimate part of my body, and illusion or not, I fairly jackknifed in the bed as he licked and kissed and held me braced in his powerful grasp, riding my building reaction. Muted pleas fell from my lips, but there remained no fear, no pain, nothing but the glory and wonder and a rapidly building tide of need, of want, and of the incredible rightness of this moment.

"Please!" I begged, though I had no sense of what I wanted beyond this power, beyond this fulfillment.

Armaeus did.

The mental image of him lifted above me, sliding up my body in a long sinuous movement. When his shaft nudged against the vee between my legs, I gasped, lights exploding in my head, but there was still no fear. He raised his head and saw me — truly saw me — and smiled. A glorious, triumphant, almost primal smile.

And then he leaned down and kissed me on the forehead.

In real life.

The forehead.

I sank down into the covers as he levered himself away from me, not even a button undone from the crisp perfection of his suit.

"That," he said, with pure male satisfaction, "worked better than I would have imagined."

I gaped at him, but he continued. "Your body is regenerating at an extraordinary rate now. The healing process should be complete in approximately twenty minutes." He studied me, apparently not impressed by the confusion and latent desire I was trying to stuff down. What had just *happened*?

My mind latched on to his next words.

"When you are ready to find Miss Dawes, I can assist you with that." His lips twitched. "Since you are reclining anyway, you will not have far to fall."

I gaped at him. "You're kidding me, right?"

"I assure you, having gone through what you have, travel in this plane will not affect you nearly as much."

I suspected he was probably right. Worse, my mind was already losing the insane perfection of the images he had poured into me, already returning to earth. An earth where I had a job to do, and people to find.

An earth I'd just seriously screwed up.

I let out a long sigh and braced myself for the crazy again.

"Say the words, Armaeus."

CHAPTER TWENTY-ONE

I tranced so quickly, I thought I'd have permanent whiplash.

"Nikki!" I managed as lights once more exploded in front of my eyes, but this time not at all in a good way.

Armaeus had slipped both my hands from beneath the cover of the bed and taken them in his, and his calming voice overrode the terror that consumed me.

Noise — noise. Everywhere is noise. Nikki was in the center of a maelstrom, her eyes wide, her mouth open, screaming like a little girl. Her thoughts were so jumbled, there was no possible way I could figure them out, but I got the impression of wind rushing through me, around me, chilling me to the bone.

"What do you see, Miss Wilde? What is she seeing?"

Hands reached for her, tearing at her clothes, ripping at her skin. I blinked, wild-eyed, desperately trying to get my own bearings, my eyes watering in the wind as I kept batting away more hands, always touching always seeking, clutching picking trembling being — all throughout and around her.

Trying to get inside her, trying to breathe the way she did and think the way she did. And laugh and cry and see and sigh and be the way she was and trying above all else to STAY.

Armaeus snapped a word, and I burst back out of the trance in a rush, unable to stop myself from burying myself in his arms.

"It's all right, it's all right," he murmured, the words sounding awkward and foreign as he held me close. Waves of healing energy spun between us, filling me up, making me whole.

"There were djinn—demons. Whatever they are." I gasped, gagging on air. "They were trying to pull her apart."

And one of them, the largest one, had filled my vision even as he'd filled Nikki's, dark and menacing and full of power.

Warrick. His name was Warrick.

"Where?" Armaeus's words were clipped. "You did not provide a location when you saw her. What did you see around her, where was she?"

"I didn't..." I shook my head. "There were too many lights. It was some kind of rave, loud and insane, people writhing, dancing, and Nikki in the middle of it, pulled in all directions." I closed my eyes, trying to remember. "Black—everything was black, like midnight. The walls, the floors. The lights had all this color, but the walls were black."

Armaeus nodded. "Viktor's domain, the tower. He's opened it for mortals, and they've flooded in."

I pulled back to stare at him. "You can do that?"

"There are many things the Council can do. You don't truly think Kreios keeps Scandal going day and night for his own personal meditation?"

"I guess... I never thought about that. I've never been inside Scandal."

"The mortals who have aren't aware that it's Scandal either, if that's any consolation. And those filling Viktor's halls do not know that they have shifted

234

planes. Nikki is in the middle of the rave, you said?"

"She was, but I didn't get the feeling she was staying. More she was being pulled through it, to some other destination." My stomach twisted. "Life gave her a pretty raw deal, Armaeus. She doesn't deserve this."

"You can find her." He watched me. "But I cannot go with you. Viktor has committed no crime."

I pulled my hands away from him. "Did you miss the part where he brought *demons* into the world?" As soon as I said the words, however, I realized my mistake. "But I did that, didn't I? So he's off the hook."

"In a manner of speaking," Armaeus said. "Viktor's role in the release of the djinn is not to be discounted, but yes, you, as a mortal, were the agent of their summoning. He might have pointed you in the right direction…"

"But I did the running." I closed my eyes. "You don't seem really worried about all this."

He patted my hand, and I wondered how boring the Council's lives must have been before they met me. What do you give the immortal who has everything? Something new to puzzle out. Armaeus's next words confirmed it.

"Your abilities are growing with every challenge. You will come into your own soon."

What, I hadn't already?

His phone bleated, and he removed his hand from mine, reaching down for the device. He turned the screen toward me.

"Detective Rooks is waiting for you outside the Luxor," he said. "I took the liberty of summoning him."

"Viktor will let us in?" I frowned. "I wouldn't, if I were him."

"I've also taken the liberty of cloaking both your

and the detective's psychic imprints." He held up two small devices. "If you'll do me the favor of actually wearing these."

This time, I had no problem with that.

Several hours had apparently passed while I'd been getting my insides restored. Night had fallen on the Strip. As Brody and I set off on the short walk to Paris, the brilliant casino homes of the Arcana Council loomed large over us.

"When Dixie first showed me these, I couldn't believe it," Brody muttered. "Now it's as if they've always been a part of the landscape." He gazed up and around, his eyes as wide as any tourist's. "She said that I might not see them again, eventually. Not sure how I feel about that, but it's not as if I have much choice, right?"

I slanted him a look. That almost sounded like a request, but a request to do what? "I don't know how long you will either."

"But you will, right? You and Dixie and Nikki. This is how you always see Vegas."

I blew out a breath. "Yeah."

We walked on in silence then, our gaze on the looming Black Tower, so focused that we barely noticed the change in the night sky. It happened so fast, we almost didn't see it coming.

Shadows suddenly darkened the brilliantly lit Strip, like blankets thrown over a building fire. There was a rushing swoop of wings, a startled shout. Brody's hiss at me to get back.

And then we looked up…way up…as shadows soared up the sheer black walls of the Emperor's tower. The whole thing had taken precisely three seconds. Two people were gone from the street, but in the crush of people, it seemed that no one had noticed.

236

Except us.

"Christ, please tell me that you're seeing that too," Brody whispered.

"They're getting...bodies." I nodded. "Looks like the djinn want to stick around." I trained my eyes on Paris and on the black monolith rising above it. "Nikki is in there, Brody. And they want her too."

"Yeah. No."

We moved quickly, approaching Paris like two love-struck partiers, hand in hand. I'd been to Viktor's domain already. I knew where to go. The gleaming black elevator bay beckoned, and Brody and I moved toward it resolutely.

I punched the button, and the elevator doors slid open. We stepped inside, still holding on to each other, though it was no longer needed.

"She's going to be okay," Brody said, squeezing my hand. "It'd take more than a horde of demons to hold their own with Nikki."

He was right, but that didn't make me feel any better.

The doors opened on a huge rooftop party floor that started inside, then spilled out to an unfenced patio, surely a safety violation in any dimension that didn't feature giant flying creatures. Archways soared up and over the area, whether to serve as a framework for a retractable roof or for aesthetic appeal, I didn't know. One thing was certain, though, there was no roof blocking the action tonight.

"Here we go," Brody muttered.

As Armaeus had promised, no one bothered us as we moved through the writhing bodies. The dance floor was pulsing with music and energy, and I winced, wondering what kind of introduction the djinn were getting to the mortal realm. No wonder they were rounding up possible hosts.

We moved out into the wide floor, and immediately I recognized where we were. This was the platform they'd dragged Nikki across. I pointed Brody in the right direction, and he nodded, then stiffened, his eyes riveting on a point in the distance.

I followed his gaze. Two men stood at the very edge of the crowd, one of them completely losing his marbles. The other dwarfed the first by over a foot. There was no doubt I was staring at a djinn, though he didn't possess wings. He had the rich blonde elegance of the Devil, and I wondered at the similarity. After tolerating the shorter man's panic for several moments, he reached out and backhanded him.

The smaller man dropped like a sack of flour, and the djinn picked him up, throwing him over his shoulder. He stalked away from us toward another section of the patio as if he wasn't carrying a near-two-hundred-pound man on his back.

We hesitated to follow him, in unspoken agreement that a lord of the demon realm would probably hear a couple of regular humans lumbering after him, despite the rave music in the background. Keeping our distance, we followed the djinn and his hapless cargo as he stalked through the darkness, bypassing the glittering lights and sounds for a separate sitting area flanked by giant cabana-style tented seats.

He cleared those as we caught up to him, and we heard the raucous sounds of yet another party in progress.

And one unforgettable cry.

"Hey, sugar lips! Hoo boy, you found another one. Look at those shoulders! He's totally a keeper."

Nikki.

Brody heard it too. "What in the—"

"Shh!" I cut him off. "She doesn't sound right."

"Well, she doesn't sound wrong either," Brody grumbled, but we edged closer to the party area. There was enough of a breeze at this height to keep the cabana tents fluttering, and I gaped at what I saw. This couldn't be possible.

Beside me, Brody cursed tightly as he saw the same thing I did. "Why isn't anything ever easy?"

Apparently oblivious to the fact that she was surrounded by magical beings that made her seem positively petite, Nikki sat cozily ensconced at a baize-green table, deep in a game of poker. From the looks of things, she was holding her own, but barely. Her compatriots were all djinn, from what I could see. Three giant males, easily seven feet tall, and unlike the demon we'd seen first, they weren't all blonde Adonises.

They were, however, all in exceptionally good shape, at least to my untutored eye. Lean, battle-worn, and with the feral eyes of cats that had gone too long without their kibble, they watched the card game with an air of ferocious intensity. Nikki, for her part, was keeping up a nonstop stream of chatter.

"There you go sugar buns, and boom, I'm up again on you. This would be the time for all of you to get worried."

The cards were shuffled and dealt around, apparently a standard game of five-card draw. Nikki tossed in a few chips, then the creature across from her grinned and added enough to raise the kitty to almost half her reserves. I felt my stomach cramp. "What are they betting on?"

"I don't think we want to find out," Brody said. Nikki's face was tight and flushed, the glass at her side barely touched. "You're right, though. She doesn't look so hot."

"How are we going to get her out of there?"

Nikki played her cards, and the djinn surrounding her grinned, one of them drawing his hand lazily along her arm. That was the one she'd called Warrick. Had to be. She flinched but kept on smiling, and as she glanced up to meet his eyes, drawling something nonsensical, I shifted slightly in the darkness.

Nikki's smile blossomed across her hard face. "Well, baby, I think my luck has turned. Anyone for another round?"

"You are almost out of markers," Warrick said. "When you fall out of the game, one of us claims you." He leered at her. "I've decided it will be me."

Nikki's skin went a little paler, but she tilted up her chin. "The one thing you can never afford to do in poker is count your money at the table, sweet pea. Deal the cards."

That elicited a round of jovial excitement around the table, and I flinched as Brody touched my arm. "Get a load of the action by the palms."

Two djinn stood next to two kneeling humans, and argued with a third djinn. I could barely make out their words over the pounding beat, but I got a lot of "No's" and "Impossibles" mixed in with several colorful expletives.

"What's that about?" Brody asked.

"Hosts," I gestured. "The rule is if you're a demon, you can't stay here in your natural form, not for long. You have to find a body."

"And once you do, you're stuck with it?"

"That's…an interesting question. It appears so, at least for a while." I frowned. "But they've got twenty-four hours, Armaeus said."

"And he knows that how?"

"Shh. Watch." The djinn reached out to yank one of the humans to his feet, a well-built gym rat with wild eyes, his mouth agape in terror.

"What are you going to do with me?" the man asked. "What do you want?"

In response to his bluster, the djinn laughed—a soul-sucking, mirthless howl that made the dark-skinned man blanch with fear.

This wasn't right. "I have to do something—" I began, but Brody reached out and held me close.

"Chill," he hissed. "We don't know how many of them there are."

"I do. There are six." Energy sizzled along my nerve endings, and I whipped my gaze back to the tight cluster of men and djinn. Suddenly there was one fewer of the demons, and the man was on his knees, howling into the night, his screams keeping eerie time with the music wailing out over the deck.

"What the hell?" Brody growled.

"They made the transfer," I said. "And if the guy can keep his sanity, it looks like the take was good."

With that, the man convulsed on the ground, once—twice—then reared back, regaining his feet with a scream of rage and power.

"What have you done to me!" he screamed, but his human voice was wild, almost exultant, and another voice crested the wave along with it, two voices singing the same song. The second voice quickly moved to the fore, drowning out the first. "It is done!" the man shouted, flinging his arms wide. "It is done."

There was a commotion at the table, and we looked back over to Nikki, who in the intervening few minutes had seen her stake of chips dwindle significantly. "I don't mind playing all night," she drawled. "There's no need to go all-in."

"The transfer has worked, and the strong survive," grinned Warrick. The other two sat back, one already out of chips but drinking amiably, the other with an appreciably smaller stack than Warrick. No matter which way you sliced it, the game was coming down to the head djinn and Nikki, and Nikki did not look like she'd be ending the day a winner.

"And you're sure you don't want to pick someone a little more your own size?" Nikki asked with a saucy grin, batting her heavily mascaraed eyes. "Think about it. With you in human form, you and I could go a few rounds, right? Something to consider."

"Oh, we will, human," Warrick leered back. "There is no closer connection than possession." Nikki's smile wobbled, and I felt my stomach twist with fear. For all her bravado, even Nikki had her limits. She reached for her glass, draining half of it with a single gulp. Instantly, a foil-wrapped waitress was at the table to refill her drink, and I somehow didn't think the cool slide of clear liquid was water.

"We have to get her out of there," I said. "If that asshole sitting next to her is planning to possess her, we're going to have a problem. I don't know how to undo that."

"Hang tight." Brody scanned the floor. "Nikki's not finished yet."

Across the wide space, Nikki laughed with delight, and we both glanced up to see her raking in a large pile of chips, her stash suddenly restored. "I told you that arrogance would get you in the end, sweet cakes," she cackled. "If you're going to win in Vegas, you're gonna have to learn some patience."

Warrick leaned back in his chair. With this haul, they were officially the only two players in the game. "Who is to say that I will honor this game of yours?"

242

he asked, a thread of menace underlining his playful words.

Nikki was unbowed, though from where I stood, I could see the sheen of sweat on her brow. "You wouldn't play this long to chicken out in the end, if you're even half the—ah, demon I think you are," she said, winking at the creature.

If anything, the demon's smile grew deeper, more intense. Nikki was used to scaring people off with her bravado, not having them respond with greater interest. But again, not even she could handle this guy swimming through her bloodstream. Right?

"Brody," I said warningly.

"Not yet," he said, and sure enough, the demon signaled for another deal of the cards. "Until they line her up for possession, we're better off waiting and watching." He stiffened and pointed. "Time's up. Does he know we're here?"

I turned to see Viktor Dal enter the wide space. Tall and whip thin, he walked with an imperious stride that forced his long, coal-black robes to billow out behind him. His face was classically beautiful—blade-sharp cheekbones, flawless porcelain skin, high winged eyebrows over sharp aristocratic eyes. Those eyes swept the gathering of djinn with relish, then he turned in my direction.

"Come out, come out, Sara." His voice boomed over the gathering, answering Brody's question. "You should take pride in your accomplishments. I owe you a debt of thanks."

Eluding Brody's grab, I moved into the open space. "You owe me? Fine. I want the children. And Nikki."

"Ah yes. The children." He clasped his hands. "Had I known what you would become, I would *never* have sacrificed the children to the world beyond the veil. I paid mightily for that transgression, you should know. Every year they were lost to this world I will be subjected to a score more of torment, in the full space of time. It was part of the debt assigned."

"My heart breaks for you."

He shrugged. "It was a price I thought I had to pay. There is not enough magic in this world. The djinn will replace that magic."

I looked at the man at the far end of the room, who was now doubled over, weeping. "By possessing a human? That seems an imperfect solution at best."

He nodded. "I agree. When I first conceived this plan, I knew precisely how it must go. The children were chosen for their innate raw ability and a certain...malleability as well. Their power needed to be groomed, developed. Their minds needed to be open. Their futures here would not have allowed that."

I scowled at him. I knew a little bit about the children's parents. They'd come from all walks of life, some quite poor, but not all of them. And they'd *had* parents. Siblings. Families that loved them. "What did you do to them?"

"I gave them stability without heartbreak, learning without censure. They are fully open to their capabilities, and they are bonded to their demon hosts." He gazed thoughtfully at the djinn, who stood at respectful attention...all except Warrick, whose gaze remained trained on Nikki. Nikki, who was doing her best not to notice the creature eyeing her with enough intensity that I was surprised she didn't dissolve into a puff of smoke.

The man who'd been possessed stood up again. But he shook, and tears streamed down his face, indicating that his body resisted the violation. He was fighting, I realized. He was trying to remain human—trying too hard. With a wave of Viktor's hand, the man crumbled to the ground. Beside him, staring down, was the djinn who'd attempted to possess him.

"Didn't take," the djinn said disgustedly.

Nikki surged forward, blowing past Warrick as she strode toward the fallen man. "You touch another hair on anyone's head," she barked, kneeling down and throwing a protective arm over him, "and I will personally beat the undead shit out of all of you. Stand back."

"It seems we are at an impasse, Sara," Viktor continued in his thin, cruel voice. "My djinn are here, and the children were not needed as their hosts after all. All that is left is to find Connecteds of sufficient abilities and strength to serve in that role. Fortunately, the demonstration you so capably performed for SANCTUS served to amplify the abilities of the Connected in the city. There should be many capable subjects. So it would seem I simply needed you to bring my dream to life, in the fullness of time." He nodded to me. "My thanks."

I glared at him. "But what about the children?"

He shook his head. "With the Syx gone, their time is short. They will die before... Well." He tilted his head. "Soon, I think. I gave myself over to their deaths ten years ago. My debt remains the same whether they return to this plane or not."

He sighed a word, and the djinn froze—even Warrick. While Viktor seemed to grow in stature.

"But it has been worth it, so worth it. Look, and behold," he said, turning away. "A world made new with magic."

CHAPTER TWENTY-TWO

Still captured in their thrall, all six of the Syx reached straight upward with both hands, and the electrical grid in Vegas bucked like a bronco. Light crackled up through the Syx's bodies and burst into the sky. My third eye flicked open, and I saw the energy waves flare out from the Black Tower like a shower of Silly String, visible all the way to Spain. The explosion rocked the entire raving floor, and an enormous cheer went up in a roar of drunk, happy revelers.

Brody, Nikki, and I watched as the fireworks blasted over Vegas. The djinn remained frozen, but there was no doubt that they were fueling Viktor's little demonstration. Electricity arced over and around them, pulsing with a living fury. Beneath us I could feel the hiss and sputter of ley lines. Somewhere in Vegas, Danae and her coven of Deathwalkers were losing their minds, I was sure of it.

A moment later, Viktor and the six djinn disappeared from the rooftop rave.

Just…poof.

How powerful was this asshat, anyway?

"'Bout time you people showed up." Nikki had rolled to her feet and handed off the crying man to two willing females in the crowd. Now she strode over to us, grinning ear to ear, though I couldn't quite respond. My throat was choked with apologies. "You sure do know how to show a girl a good time, dollface. How are you doing?"

"Nikki." My voice cracked as Nikki held open her arms. Tears sparked mutinously behind my lids, and I squashed them by moving into her hug, holding her close as she laughed and patted my back.

"It's okay, sweetie, it's okay. They didn't hurt me. They only scared me. A hella lot, but I'm okay." She stood back as I recovered myself, and I searched her face. Her eyes were steady, her smile genuine. "I'm frankly not entirely sure how I feel about what just happened, truth be told. I should be...disturbed, and I'm not. That's not right, I know it isn't." She blew out a long, disquieted breath. "I could go for a drink, though. And definitely a new set of Spanx."

"Do we need to warn the community?" Brody asked. "If Viktor was serious, the Connecteds need to watch out. Especially the big ones."

"I think we have the full twenty-four hours, actually." I considered Armaeus's words. "You saw their first attempt. They won't want to repeat that until they have to. The children will remain safe for that time period too, I suspect. No matter how smug he sounded, if this infestation doesn't take, Viktor's going to need them to make another run at the djinn."

We couldn't talk for a while as we made our way back through the crowd. I considered the problem from every angle. We had maybe twelve hours to affect a rescue, I thought. That was too long to leave the children in limbo, and not nearly long enough to warn all the Connecteds in Vegas about a possible assault. Even with Dixie Quinn's impressive communications network, we couldn't get to everyone. And with the ley lines amped up to a million and two, no one was safe unless they were on the Council. That meant Danae and her coven were at as much risk as anyone.

Something else was nagging at me too, despite it not directly applying to the problem at hand...yet I had the feeling it *did* matter. Armaeus had healed me without touching me, which sort of seemed like cheating. But beyond that, I once again hadn't felt any fear with his approach. Only lust, frankly, and a whole lot of it. There was something important about this. Something I needed to figure out, and quickly.

The answer seemed to be there, out of reach, but I knew better than to ask Armaeus about it. He'd only redirect me. Death also was a no-go. Her answers came with a price, and after getting cooked from the inside out once today, I needed to keep up my strength.

But I did have options.

We broke free from the Paris crowd and onto the sidewalk, the typical throng of tourists on the Strip somehow seeming less oppressive than the crush of people inside Paris. From the looks of the scene above us, the party was still going strong. Whether the revelers would ever have any idea they were actually dancing their brains out in an alternate dimension as Armaeus had indicated, I couldn't imagine. Then again, with technoceutical street drugs available on every corner, there was probably more of that going on than I'd like to believe.

We moved up the street to Circus Circus, and Brody pulled out his badge, flashing it idly as he appeared to be staring at his phone.

Three of the tables nearest to us cleared of patrons.

"Love chop, that is the best trick I've seen all day," laughed Nikki. "Remind me to ask you out for New Year's Eve." We sat at the table and hailed a waitress, who also served us with remarkable speed. Being a cop apparently had its privileges, especially in Vegas. But once the drinks were on the table, we got down to business.

"What have we got, Nikki?"

She met my gaze, knowing what I was asking. She wasn't your ordinary kidnap victim; she was a seer. She could see things that people could not see, or what they saw but didn't acknowledge. And though she'd been the prisoner of the djinn, she hadn't spent her time merely rattling her chain. She'd been learning all she could about her captors.

"Believe it or not, they didn't shield themselves from me, and I don't think they had any knowledge I was poking around," she said. "It took a while to separate them out, though, other than Warrick. He was the big guy."

Brody snorted. "They all looked pretty big to me. All male too. Yet Viktor took three girls and three boys. Why?"

"Gender is kind of an afterthought for the djinn, if you catch my drift." Nikki gripped her water glass a little too hard. "They become whatever is expedient for the moment. The male forms they took were meant to frighten and stand out—males to them have the primary trait of physical power; females are the masters of emotion and cunning. I was appealing because I have both." She paused. "The lunkhead they picked up off the street looked to be a good option, but dude wasn't a poser. He had a lot of internal strength to go along with those fine muscles. He was fighting them back." She shook the ice in her glass. "Good to know you don't have to lie down and die during a possession. That there's always hope."

"Far better that we never give them the chance." Brody scowled. "They'll be targeting Connecteds, Viktor said. We need to warn them."

"Dixie will be your best bet for that." Nikki nodded. "I'll start there, unless you want to?"

He shook his head. "Text me when you've contacted her. I need to get down to the station." He looked at me. "Twelve hours — sooner the better, I'm thinking. That'll take us right up to dawn, and we can't wait that long. I'm going to need to assemble real medical this time. You were in pretty bad shape when you came back through."

He wasn't wrong.

"I'm hoping I don't have to consume six souls to get them back across the veil, though. There has to be another way." I scowled, knowing this really was Blue's province. I didn't like how much debt I was stacking in her favor. "I need to figure that out."

"Well, keep me posted as well. And whatever you do, *don't* move unless we're with you." His gaze was heavy on me, then slid to Nikki. "I'm not losing either one of you, not to Viktor. Not again."

"Man, I love it when you get protective," Nikki said. She caught up Brody in a bear hug, loosening him enough to give him a fast kiss on the lips. Then she drained her glass and stood, winking at me. "You're missing out, doll. But your loss. I'm going to be at Dixie's, battening down the hatches." She turned back to Brody. "Be a dear and call Dixie, would you, let her know what's up? I gotta get changed. There's too much demon stink on me for comfort."

He frowned at her. "You worried they can track you?"

"Not a risk I wanna take, to be honest. I've had enough of that crowd to last a lifetime." She grinned. "Except for the big guy. He was kind of cute."

"Warrick?" I stared at her. "You can't be serious."

"Hey, I wouldn't have to wear flats with him.

250

That's one sure way to a girl's heart." She waved and turned away, her long-legged strides eating up the concrete.

I turned to Brody. "She's not serious."

He shrugged. "She's not wrong. The guy looked like he wanted to consume her, body and soul. As long as, you know, that didn't mean 'consume' consume, I could see the appeal. Nikki is way too much for most any guy, I'm thinking. It'd be interesting for her to have someone who could hold his own with her."

"You're both nuts."

"Remember what I told you," he said. "No going off half-cocked until we have everything in place." He sobered. "It's not that you can't do it on your own, Sara. I've seen you do it. But we don't know what shape you'll be in when you get back. Or what shape the kids will be in."

"I know," I said. And I did. I appreciated Brody trying to rein me in because it needed to be done, but I was the one who'd come back with a fried liver. I wasn't going to bring children back here without proper medical backup, not anymore, when I knew what could happen. Sometimes, ignorance really was bliss.

But we were a long way away from that. "How long?" I asked.

He looked at his watch. "Couple of hours, no more. Middle of the night is pretty much broad daylight here, as far as getting people assembled." He grimaced. "Welcome to Fabulous Las Vegas."

I watched Brody pick his way out of the bar, heading for the crowded sidewalk, and I hauled myself up as well. I had to be ready for the next confrontation, which meant I had to understand a few things. Death could help me, certainly. But I needed something more than she could give me.

I needed the unvarnished truth.

The walk from Circus Circus to the Flamingo was short, even given the crowds, and I stepped into the old standby of the Vegas Strip with the same shot of nostalgia I always did…which was odd, since I wasn't an old-timer in Vegas. I hadn't lived here when the Flamingo was in its heyday, and I'd barely visited the old casino when I'd been in town more recently. Nevertheless, the retro chic hotel was not my ultimate destination, and I glanced around, finding the image-on-image visual trick easily enough. I made my way over to the correct bank of elevators and punched a button.

When the doors slid open, I had to smile despite my tension. Leave it to the Devil to make even his elevator a sensual experience. I stepped inside the space, admiring the heavy drape of white satin and thick white carpet. Apparently the Devil's cleaners had no fear of the outside dust of Vegas filtering into his inner sanctum.

The elevator moved up at a leisurely pace, so leisurely that I really had no sense of time passing. When the doors did finally open, it wasn't a pulsing wall of sound and lights that greeted me, but a sumptuous tropical paradise, draped in a million twinkling lights.

"Sweet Christmas," I murmured. "Where have you been all my life?"

I stepped into a room that was more Garden of Eden than hotel interior. After a short marble apron, the room exploded into a lush jungle of lush plants and large bubbling pools. At the far end, enormous glass doors stood open to what looked like an outdoor patio and I thought I caught a glimpse of another outdoor pool as well. As I stood, gawking, I felt the touch of Kreios on my mind. He never intruded the way Armaeus did. Instead, he made his presence known as gently as a whisper. It was that whisper that was beckoning me now.

"Sara Wilde," he murmured, and I turned to the center of the room, finally spying the canopied tent that waved in the breeze from ornate overhead fans. Tiki torches surrounded it, as did honest-to-God live ferns and palm trees. "It is always a pleasure to see you. How can I help?"

I steeled myself and walked forward into the garden room, bracing myself for whatever state Kreios would be in. But the Greek demigod surprised me. He sat at a teak table in loose khakis, a long linen shirt open at the neck, and beach sandals. A large pitcher of something fruity looking occupied the table, plus two glasses. Fairy lights flickered all around him, swaying from the trees. "Much more civilized to talk this way, wouldn't you say?"

His jade-green eyes followed me as I picked my way down the sandy path, my mind refusing to stop wondering how he kept his place clean. It was a transdimensional domain of a demigod, and I was caught up with housekeeping.

Kreios gestured me to sit, and I took the only other chair at the table, a huge wing-backed wicker seat that I could curl up in and sleep in for days. It was piled high with pillows, and he smiled as I tossed a few of them to the thick rug lining the teakwood ledge. "You'd prefer to sit on the ground?"

"Thanks, not today."

"Ah, but if not today, then when?" He watched me with hungry eyes as I pulled the chair closer. "I've been so looking forward to this."

I raised a brow. "You're not seriously trying to flirt with me."

"There is no need for that." Without warning, he leaned forward and placed his hands on either side of my face, his eyelids dropping to a sensual stare as he drew in a deep breath. "You know that I can tell your innermost needs and desires. I know what you want, Sara Wilde. I can give it to you. But there is no need for us not to enjoy ourselves while you work up the courage to ask me, no?"

I found myself staring at Kreios's soft mouth as he spoke, his words weaving a spell around me so strongly, I found myself wanting to surrender. How would it feel to give over to that spell, I wondered. Nikki had done so, and though she never spoke of it, she'd been glowing like a beacon for days following the afternoon she'd spent in Kreios's care. I knew better than to think he actually had any affection for me, but—

"You are wrong," he murmured. "I have nothing but the highest affection for you." He leaned forward and kissed me, so hard and fast that it took my breath away. The kiss was fierce, almost angry, and he reared back with such a look of intensity shining from his eyes that I forgot who I was for a moment, who I was and why I was there.

"Ah! We understand ourselves better, then," he said, smiling as I jerked away from him, scrambling back in my chair. "Armaeus treats you like spun glass, but the time will come for your testing, Sara, and he will find that you are made of sterner stuff than he could imagine." He turned to the carafe of juice while I gaped at him. "What are you drinking? Not scotch on such a fine night."

He poured a glass of juice and pushed it toward

me, and I lifted it gratefully. My tongue had suddenly cleaved to the top of my mouth, and I felt awkward, almost shy in Kreios's presence.

What is wrong with me?

The Devil prompted me. "You want to ask about…"

I let the cool mix of alcohol and fruit juice slide down my throat, the perfect blend of harsh and sweet. And went with the question that weighed the most heavily on me since I'd seen the morning in Brody's house when everything went upside down for me. Again.

"Do you know who my mother is? My father?"

If I'd surprised him with my priorities, Kreios didn't betray it. "I do not," he said, shaking his head. "If I did, you would already know. Armaeus does not know either, though he has his suspicions."

"And what are those? And if you tell me that I have to ask him directly, I'm going to punch you in the throat."

"I should welcome the attempt," Kreios said, his lips curving into a smile. "He believes that you are the child of a mystic of great power, possibly two. It is the only way he can explain your resistance to him, and your capacity to accept new power within you. Your potential is nowhere near tapped, and most mortals simply do not possess that much psychic ability. Not anymore."

I frowned. "So, what, Merlin is my dad and Enigma's my mom? That's what he thinks?" I shook my head. "That's ridiculous. I was left with a woman who was drunk more days than not. Not exactly the mark of loving parents."

He shrugged. "Who is to say the reasons of a father when it came to protecting his beloved child?"

I looked at him, my face carefully blank. "It's you, isn't it?"

CHAPTER TWENTY-THREE

Kreios burst out with such a bark of honest laughter that his entire face was transformed with delight. It took my breath away.

"No, my dear Sara Wilde, I can assure you it is not. Much to my intense satisfaction, I'll have you know. But it is a question that continues to nettle Armaeus. Which is not a bad thing. He's better when he's nettled on occasion." He shook his head, grinning at me with such collegial goodwill, I couldn't help but be drawn to him. "I would tell you if I knew, but I do not. What else do you seek?"

I considered my next question carefully. "What will happen when I bring the children Viktor stole back through the veil? Will those kids end up possessed?" It wouldn't change what I would do, of course, but it might change what I asked of the Council. The children deserved to live their full lives, not have their existence cut out at Viktor's whim or damaged irretrievably by possession. I'd be damned if I brought them back only to deliver them on a platter to him.

Kreios watched me with amusement. "Why did you hesitate to ask this question? I do not have any affinity with the djinn." He smiled. "The world is a big enough place for magic of many hues, light to dark. Viktor makes the same mistake you do. He'll see the error of his ways soon enough."

I frowned at him. "What do you mean?"

"The djinn are beholden to him, but they are not his slaves. They are also not wholly dark, as I am not wholly dark. There are subtleties and nuances to their magic that he has not fully grasped. But that is part of his value."

"Value!" I shook my head. "No. He should be destroyed, Kreios."

My vehemence didn't faze him. "You cannot destroy darkness, Sara Wilde. You can only overcome it. But Viktor does have his uses. Every Council must have those who leap first, consider second. Else nothing would get done at all."

"And what he's doing is something useful?"

"I can assure you, the Council has not been this engaged in the actions of man since the Second World War. That is partly due to SANCTUS, yes. But it is also partly due to Viktor. And it is long overdue."

"That's not terribly comforting."

His smile deepened. "It's not meant to be. But to answer your initial question about the children and the djinn, consider this. You saw the man the djinn attempted to possess, yes? A fine physical specimen. I looked in on him after his ordeal, since in effect, the Council helped put him in harm's way."

I lifted my brows. "He'll be okay?"

"He will." Kreios nodded. "But more to the point, he was easily six foot three, well built, sturdy, and in his late twenties. Contrast that with the six children Viktor has taken."

I frowned. "What's wrong with them?"

"Nothing at all—but they have not spent the better part of their young lives in a gym, or training on a combat field. They have been given the illusion of an idyllic childhood and education, and that is all well and good. But not, perhaps, of interest to the djinn, if you catch my meaning. Since they'll be utilizing their own mental faculties."

"They want the Avengers."

"Indeed. Not six teenagers who will be trying to reacclimatize to a world that has gone on without them. Viktor should have known that from the start."

"Yeah." I blew out a breath. "I'm not really sure how that's going to go, assuming we bring them back safely."

"It will go as it must," Kreios said, his words unexpectedly gentle. "Bringing them back will be the difficult part. From that point, their way will be made as smooth as possible."

I met his gaze, and in it, I saw something solid and sure. The Council. They would take a personal interest in these children, in helping them return to a world they were ripped from. Their families, their friends. Their parents...

I frowned, looking away sharply. To his credit, Kreios didn't speak, but let me stare at the burbling pool not ten feet away from the table until I could finally move past the knot of emotion that had lodged in my throat.

Finally, I turned back to him. "I want to ask something else, but first... What do you get in return for all this information? Blue seems to be keeping a ledger of every question I've ever posed, yet you've given me everything I've asked for. That seems...unbalanced, if you'll pardon the pun."

"Not at all," Kreios said, his smile positively decadent. "What is the point of information if it is not shared? What is the point of giving if there is no one to take?" He leaned forward again, and I felt it, the stirring of awareness between us, two predators circling, wondering when to strike. "I give freely because I *take* freely, Sara Wilde. But I never take what is not given with equal freedom. And I prefer an educated conversation, don't you? That's far more challenging than when one party remains in the dark, in ignorant subjugation to the other."

He edged forward a touch more, truly seeming to enjoy himself. "So ask your question, the one you hold closest to your heart, the one I see shimmering on your lips. You'll find I have the ready answer."

"Why am I no longer afraid with Armaeus?" I blurted the question before I stopped to think of how stupid or silly it sounded. Instead, I plunged on. "I mean — I've known him for over a year, and never once until recently have I not been scared out of my wits whenever he moves in close. As much as I want it — want him to, well..."

"Say it," Kreios breathed, and embarrassment flooded me, quick and hot.

"Fine. I want him to *be* with me. To touch me. I do — but I can't. My brain shuts down, my heart seizes up. It's like I have posttraumatic sex disorder, only we've never actually had *sex*."

Kreios sat back, his face smug with satisfaction. "And that fear has recently changed."

"Very recently." I nodded. "Now, he comes near me, and it's like...a door has been opened. A door I'm finally ready to walk through. But I don't know why."

"It's a simple answer." He shrugged. "He's mortal."

I frowned at him. I'd expected this, but that didn't mean I understood it. "So? He's no less powerful, no less Armaeus than he's ever been."

"True, but he has changed fundamentally. That change will have to be reversed and soon — there are dangers to remaining mortal that go beyond simple aging, particularly for someone with Armaeus's past. But for now, he is mortal, and therefore, he cannot harm the essential part of you that he threatened before."

My head was spinning. "You're not being clear. Why, specifically, is he…"

"I think, once again, you are asking the wrong question, Sara Wilde." Kreios's gaze was intent on me, his smile lazy. "Instead of asking why, you should be asking what. As in, what will you do with this window of opportunity, now that you have it? Since you are finally allowed the possibility of connection with the one man you've never been able to have but have secretly yearned for despite your mind's fears. What will you do?"

I blinked at him. "Wait. Are you telling me to jump him?"

"Me? I would never suggest that." He waved off the idea. "But if you did, I suspect you would both find it highly…educational. And you know how much I prefer education over ignorance." He shifted his hand toward me, halting my words. "Before you ask, Armaeus knows your barriers have dropped. It's given him an access heretofore unprecedented, and he is equally unsure of how to proceed, which is a fascinating development in and of itself. His indecision is a feature of his mortality that he hasn't quite acknowledged yet, but its timing is unfortunate. You might simply need to act first."

"Act…first." I scowled. "So you *are* telling me to jump him."

"My role is simply to point out that which is already uppermost in your mind." Kreios leaned back in his chair. "What you choose to do with it is your own business. But I would not wait too long, Sara Wilde. Eventually, Armaeus must restore his immortality. His place in the Council depends on it, and it's a requirement for some of the magic that he taps. When he does regain his immortal state, it is quite likely that your fear will return, primal and irrational though it may seem to you."

"So this is my only chance." That seemed more of a challenge than I was willing to face. I narrowed my eyes at him. "He's never turned mortal before?"

"Of course he has," Kreios said. "I believe the last time was in the seventeen hundreds."

I stared at him. "You're making that up."

"One thing I never need to do, in point of fact. The truth is vastly more entertaining."

"Yeah? Well, tell me this, then. Why don't I, um, react to you the same way I react to Armaeus? You're both immortal. You're both on the Council. So what's up with that?"

Kreios's eyes glittered. He leaned forward again, and I steeled myself not to lean back. The man was sex on a train, but my need for information outweighed my instincts that he was way out of my league in every possible measure.

"What you want to know is how I can stoke a reaction in you with a look, a smile, a touch...yet you are not afraid?" He lifted his hand and softly traced it down the side of my face. My body immediately responded. It was very efficient like that. A thrill of awareness skittered down my skin and along my nerve endings, pooling into my belly with nervous anticipation. My breath came faster, my hands grew warm. I kept my jaw from dropping open, but it was a near thing.

Kreios had moved off his chair while I was

swimming through all my reactions. Now he was on his knees, in front of me, his body levered toward me, trapping me in the chair. But I didn't panic, and he saw that I didn't panic. This was different. He was proving his point.

Kreios dipped his head until his mouth was right at my ear. His whisper floated across the sensitized skin, and I couldn't stop my body trembling as he spoke. "And how can your body innately sense that there are oceans of pleasure for us to know, an entire cosmos of sensual experiences for us to explore that are only a whisper away—and yet you do not fear me? This is what you wish to understand?"

"Yes." I gripped the armrests of the chair, but I could no longer look at him, no longer look at anything but the softly waving leaves of the tropic fern beyond the cabana. My heart pounded, my knees shook, and a deep wellspring of need curled inside me, waiting to strike.

Kreios chuckled, moving down the length of my chin, his lips barely grazing my face as he spoke. "Because there is no fear within you, is there, Sara Wilde? Panic, yes." His gaze found mine, trapped it. "And you would do well to panic. Uncertainty. Your mind full of questions you crave the answers to." His mouth was positioned in front of mine. I couldn't help it, my lips parted. I could see the fire leap behind Kreios's indolent stare, and then he inched forward to close off the space between us. I shivered as his lips connected with mine, but he didn't press further, only spoke. "Yet you do not fear my touch, not in the way you fear Armaeus. You want to know why."

"Yes," I managed, and Kreios's magnificent body stiffened in response to the word. Laughter rumbled deep in his chest, and he edged back, his gaze heavy on me once more.

"I suspect you already know the answer to this question as well."

I stared at his lips, but the light frisson of attraction between us had suddenly taken on a darker twist. A twist that had nothing to do with Kreios, and everything to do with the Magician. "Humor me."

"It is because I cannot harm you, Sara Wilde. Our psychic abilities, magic, whatever you wish to call it — our essential natures do not conflict. Yours and the Magician's do. Not as oil and water, but flint and stone. The fire you stoke between you is impossible to resist, and it could well kill you both — if not everyone around you."

His eyes glittered, and I stared at him, unsure of what he was seeing in his mind's eye, but it wasn't me, I was fairly certain. It was something beyond me, something that filled him with an expression that almost approached awe. Awe and a hard edge of excitement that I instinctively knew in any other being would be fear. "It is a most dangerous game," he murmured, his lips curling into an appreciative smile.

"And if he's mortal, none of that bad stuff will happen?"

"Who's to say any of it is bad?" A moment later, Kreios seemed to come back to himself. He blinked at me, truly seeing me once more. "But you are correct. While Armaeus is mortal, the pieces are not all present, the game cannot be played."

He pulled back farther, and I released the breath I hadn't realized I'd been holding.

"As long as he's mortal, then you can explore the path you are meant to walk together without the deep and terrible danger that you instinctively fear looming large between you. That is not to say that there will not

264

be danger still. But it cannot destroy you, not permanently. You would do well to take advantage of the reprieve."

"Or, you know, run the other way screaming," I said, grimacing as I considered Kreios's words. "It seems like the risk of total global destruction would be a good reason to call things off."

He regarded me with amusement. "We both know that you cannot resist the fire."

I stood. "You don't know me nearly as much as you think you do, Kreios."

He inclined his head and settled back in his own chair. "A circumstance I look forward to remedying. Soon." He turned toward the open windows of the room and waved to me. "But you are needed elsewhere now. It is best that you go."

"Right." I drew in a short breath, suddenly feeling that the idyll between us was broken. It seemed too short, too rushed, but there was nothing for it. The demons had already been in Vegas for twelve hours. In another twelve, the children would be dead. "This is all going to work out, isn't it?" I asked faintly, staring at the flashing lights of the city.

Kreios's gaze was on me, and I could sense his eyes gleaming with that far-off knowing of truths better left undiscovered.

"Probably not," he said.

CHAPTER TWENTY-FOUR

No sooner had I left the Devil's domain than I was confronted with another choice. Turn left to Armaeus, which was where I really should be when I attempted the jump again, or turn right to Blue. Both options filled me with dread, and apparently, both could kill me. It was already starting out to be a great night.

I turned right.

The walk to Dixie's was longer than I expected, but the night was unexpectedly cool. Actually, that wasn't it. It was midsummer in Vegas and the evenings were balmy, yet the heat simply didn't faze me. It could be sunstroke, potentially, or it could be the side effect from having had my insides blasted out by the djinn. Either way, I didn't think I'd look at a hot sunny day the same way ever again. And when winter came...

When I finally reached Blue's studio, the OPEN sign was flashing neon again, despite the late hour. I pushed in the door, only to see Jimmy sitting behind the counter, the surface spread with tracing paper. Lines of text in beautiful calligraphy spilled across the page, and I blinked at them, then looked at the small man with renewed appreciation.

"You did that?"

"Freak-show client, but he pays well." Jimmy shrugged. "Comes in every few months to get a new section of his personal manifesto inked onto his body.

This is for the rib cage."

"That's...a lot of text for the rib cage."

He nodded. "It's going to hurt like a bitch. But, that's part of the experience of the tattoo. The pain mixed with the creation of something lasting, something true."

"What's the language?" I asked, leaning closer.

"Sumerian, he says. I had a sample sent for review when he first came in, though." He snorted. "My guy says it looks like a legit language, but it ain't Sumerian. Blue wouldn't work on the guy, so she hasn't weighed in on the matter. Sometimes, what she doesn't know won't hurt us." He stood up and admired his work, and, though no sound came from the back room, he nodded to me. "She's ready for you. Said to tell you there's not much time, that you needed to get ready."

I frowned. "Ready for what specifically? The jump?"

He bent forward again. "She'll explain it. But remember." He tapped the vellum he was working on. "The more it hurts, the truer it is."

I questioned the wisdom of trusting someone named Jimmy Shadow to provide me with the insights of the universe, but headed back to see Blue anyway. As I walked, I tried shearing off sections of my thoughts into tidy compartments. Nothing the Devil said about Armaeus mattered. Nothing about Nikki and the trauma she'd suffered with the demons mattered. Nothing about me and my hang-ups mattered. What mattered were the children stuck on the other side of the veil. Getting them back. Making them whole.

Blue was in her familiar chair in the stark room. She'd given up even the pretense of the bookshelves and simply sat there, needle gun in hand.

I frowned at her. "What's that for? I've already got the symbol for the Syx's domain."

"You do." She nodded. "And you came back almost incinerated. I'll add a way for the path to be made clearer."

"Why didn't you do that before, then?" A sudden thought struck me. "Oh, geez. Did I fail some sort of test? Did you give me the advanced jumper ink and I need the remedial version?" I didn't know why that upset me so much, but it did. "I honestly didn't realize those kids weren't actual kids. I should have, even in suspended animation; they should have looked more dead or something. But I didn't."

She smiled, and I realized how different the expression was on her than on Kreios or Armaeus. Blue's smile conveyed no humor or even affection, more a shared understanding of the way things were.

"You didn't fail any test, Sara. If anything, you succeeded beyond what you should have. Multiple possession doesn't generally go too well for the human side of the equation." She waved the needle, and I tried not to blanch. "This will simply give you more of a path to follow, should the way become difficult. A beacon in the darkness, if you will. You're jumping again awfully soon after the first time, and too soon after Atlantis as well. It's a lot."

"Jimmy said I was running out of time." I shucked my hoodie, then slid into the chair and held out my arm, angling it so the curving symbol was facing up.

"You are. Viktor can't afford for the djinn to be returned through the portal. He'll force them to take human hosts before he'll let that happen. And the magic that's currently present in the city will help him do that."

I frowned at her, then hissed as the needle bit into

my skin. "Help him how."

"The magic is idle, unfocused. The Council refuses to choose sides, and the djinn want to remain here, so the momentum is swinging in their direction."

"Viktor's part of the Council, though. He's clearly choosing a side."

"Not technically. You brought the djinn to earth. He's given them access to the magic coursing through the city, but only thanks to the efforts of Danae and her coven. Viktor may be coordinating the results, but he's not the one swinging the bat. Mortals are."

"You people can seriously sleep at night with that kind of logic driving you?"

Another smile, this one showing the glint of humor. "You have a long time to get used to it."

A searing flash of pain almost blinded me. "I thought this was supposed to get easier over time," I muttered.

"It'll never get easier. But for any creation to matter, it—"

"Yeah, yeah. I'm all about true." I gritted my teeth as she stabbed me again, and my eyes watered. By the time she finally sat back, I was breathing shallowly and my tank top was damp with sweat. I expected Blue to smirk at my reaction, but she merely gazed at me, her eyes level.

"Does it hurt for everyone you do that to?" I asked.

"I don't do it often, and certainly not so many times in the same week. But these are unusual times, and you are an unusual jumper." She turned to begin cleaning her instrument. "I'd recommend not jumping again anytime soon after this, however. You'll need to regain your strength."

"I'll be sure to clear my dance card."

Jimmy walked in then with a gauze bandage,

which he pressed over my arm. I frowned at him. "What's that for? It isn't bleeding."

"It might start." He pointed to the hoodie I'd slung over the chair. "Wear that. Keep your sleeves down. You don't want to draw attention to the ink."

I widened my eyes. "Why not?"

"Because Viktor might chop off your arm if he believes it's helping you return the djinn to their place behind the veil," Blue said bluntly. "Or he might chop it off to study the symbol at his leisure."

I stared at her. "You're not joking."

"He was only barely human before he ascended the Council." She shrugged. "His time as Emperor has not improved his restraint. Hide the ink. And this time, focus on taking weapons *with* you. They will help you when you decide to do what you will do."

"I...okay." I decided not to ask Blue for clarification. I didn't think I'd like the answer. And having a weapon on hand really did seem like a good idea, if I was going back to rescue the children.

Blue waited until I stood, then watched with keen eyes as Jimmy helped me resettle my hoodie, carefully drawing it down over the tattoo. As it had the last time, the spot had stopped hurting the moment she'd taken away the needle gun, but I remained a little woozy. Jimmy stuck by my side as we moved to the front chamber, and I blew out a long breath, gathering my energy to face what was coming next.

I squinted through the window and frowned. "Why are all the cars here?"

Blue folded her arms and leaned up against the counter. "The Council is about balance, but balance takes many forms. To some, it is negating either side's advantage, putting all players at the same base level. To others, the level is not important, as long as the sides are roughly equivalent. I tend to favor the latter."

"Which means…"

"Consider it a matter of evening the odds." She nodded to the cars outside. "They're waiting for you in the chapel. If you move quickly, Viktor won't know you've made the jump until after you get back. The weapons are waiting there too."

"Weapons?"

"Armaeus sent the rest along. He wants you to take anything you can this time."

I blew out a breath, but before I could speak, Blue continued.

"You're wrong, you know," she said. "You don't need to compartmentalize everything away to focus solely on the crisis at hand. You need to use all that's going on in your world to contribute to what you must achieve. Any pain, sorrow, joy, excitement — emotion of any kind helps your cause. Become more honest, discard your masks, and you become infinitely more powerful. Remember that."

I nodded, unsure how to respond to a pregame pep talk from Death. An infinite number of nervous quips sprang to mind and I stuffed them down. Instead, I turned and walked outside in the lit-up parking lot.

The cars lined up in front of Dixie's bore a hodgepodge of license plates. Some showed the dust of a long road trip, some were obviously rentals. One was Brody's. I crossed the wide strip of asphalt, feeling its latent heat radiate upward. I frowned that I even noticed the detail. Had Blue reset my internal thermometer as well? Probably a good thing, unless I was going to get cooked again. Being oblivious to becoming a self-contained fire pit was the only thing this next jump had going for it, and now that too seemed lost.

271

I walked into the cool chapel and was struck by…the silence. I might as well have been at a funeral home, and I strode up the hallway with increasing concern. There were people here, definitely people. I could hear their hushed voices in the main chapel. But why were they here, and what did Blue mean by evening the odds?

I wheeled around the corner, and stopped.

"What are they doing here?" I asked, or tried to ask. My voice dried up in my throat as I saw the faces in the bright chapel lights — older now, so much older, as if not ten years had passed but twenty-five. These were the parents of the children, and three sets of them I knew. Three sets I didn't. They didn't see me across the crowded room. They were talking to Dixie, who was holding court with Brody, both of them serious and achingly considerate. I blinked, trying to make sense of it, when one of the women looked over at me. Her careworn face was ineffably older, yet I would remember those eyes for the rest of my life.

She blinked, and I could see the flash of confusion and half recognition across her face. Mary's mother, so young and yet so old, her eyes rich with a pain that made my heart quail. She reached for Brody's arm, and I wheeled back, ducking my head and turning. She didn't recognize me; she couldn't recognize me. We'd seen each other once, a long time ago. And I'd been only a kid.

Then someone else moved, and I stiffened further, hesitating as a familiar figure approached me with a wide smile.

"Mademoiselle Wilde. It is such a pleasure to see you again."

I took an instinctive step back. "What are you doing here, Mercault?"

272

He stopped several feet short of me and executed a short bow. "You increase in value to me with each passing moment. What sort of business partner would I be if I did not help you in your time of need?"

I frowned at him. "Help? Since when do you help for free?"

His eyes danced. "Who says I do not gain? I have redeployed my agents in the city to serve as protectors for the Connected, as I understand we have a bit of a demon problem." He tilted his head. "I must say, working with you has already proven more invigorating than I would have expected. When this business is complete, we shall have much to discuss."

"Um, thanks?"

If by not compartmentalizing Blue intended me to be thrown into a morass of confusion, she'd accomplished that. I was relieved beyond measure to see Nikki striding across the room to me, carefully avoiding both Mercault's thugs and Brody's parent trap.

"Hey, girl," she said, taking my arm. "We thought we'd start in the same chapel. Kreios gave me the high sign that there'd be no Council onsite until the kids came through, so it's just us chickens for this."

"They decided to back Viktor?"

"Not exactly." She slanted me a look. "They decided to back you. Apparently, the house is betting on you to bring home the job on your own. They stay out of the process, balance is maintained, and Armaeus gets to see you level up. You pull this off, I think they'll throw you a friggin' parade."

"Yeah, well. Remember what happened last time." We stepped into the second chapel, and Nikki shut the door behind me. The sudden solace was a mini miracle, all the energy of the main chapel held apart. I

273

blew out a sharp breath, eyeing the gleaming Atlantean weapons piled neatly on the small platform at the front of the room. "Viktor doesn't know about this place?"

"If he does, tough tits for him," Nikki said. Her smile was hard. "Mercault showed up tonight like the Easter bunny, with the entire French Foreign Legion behind him. Viktor isn't getting anywhere close to here, demons or no demons. Though the longer I think about it, I gotta admit…those guys were smokin' hot, if you'll pardon the pun."

I stared at her, a new layer of crazy embroidered onto the insanity quilt I was pulling around myself. "You seriously *liked* them? Even though they wanted to possess you?"

"Well, not all of them—okay, all of them. Hey," she said, laying a hand against her chest. "I more than most know what it's like to be an outsized Dorothy in a world of Oompa Loompas. The fact that I made their cut did not escape me."

"You made their cut for *possession*, Nikki. Not for the prom."

"Till you walk in size-thirteen stilettos, honey, don't judge." Nikki's words were more teasing than chastising, but I remained thrown off my axis yet again. I didn't know her that well, but she seemed so strong and certain in everything she did. It hadn't occurred to me that the idea of being chosen—even chosen by a demon who wanted to dominate her, body and soul—would give her a rush. The very idea made my head spin.

I turned toward the front of the room. Once again, the carpeted stairs made the most sense for the attempt, but I had to stuff down a twinge of apprehension as I climbed the short flight. Turning, I

274

sat down on the edge and rested my elbows on my knees. My ink didn't hurt, and it was only Nikki here, so I pulled up my hoodie sleeve and peeled away the bandage covering my forearm. Nikki was sitting in the front pew, but the room was so small that that meant she was essentially in my lap. With a slight forward lean, she inspected my arm, letting out a low whistle.

"That…somehow looks really deep." She looked up at me. "And like it hurt. A lot."

"I noticed it." I smiled ruefully, looking at my arm. With the initial flare of reaction dying down, I could see the design a little more clearly. Blue had certainly upgraded my Celtic-looking symbol to something that looked, as Nikki had said, etched into my skin. The three-dimensional effect was breathtaking, but it was the clear pathing of the symbol that truly struck me. This artwork had a definite beginning, middle, and end. It was a walkway into and out of a place that seemed beyond this world.

Unaccountably, my heart began beating hard in my chest. She'd done this for me, Blue. There would be a price. There was always a price. But for the moment, I could focus solely on how much potentially easier she'd made this next jump.

I turned to Nikki, who now was spreading out the weapons I'd pulled from Atlantis. "Wow," I muttered, and she grimaced.

"Yeah, wow. These things keep getting more beautiful every time I look at them."

She was right. The arrows seemed more refined, the knife more elegant. The calligraphed symbols stood out in high relief on the blades, looking ancient and powerful at once. "You ready?"

"I've got the easy part of this assignment, babe. You're the one who goes deep undercover." She leaned forward. "But I'm here for you. You say the word, I'll do it. Whatever you need."

I gave her a smile that didn't really hold its shape, and breathed out a long sigh.

"Okay, then," I said, picking up a knife and extending my hand to grasp another blade. "Let's get me gone."

And as Nikki spoke the words, I fell into the deep trance the jump required. In the space of a single breath, I left the tiny, quiet chapel and descended...

Into madness.

CHAPTER TWENTY-FIVE

The cosmos rushed around me in a blinding blur, and I found myself once more in the plane of the Syx, but everything was different now. The oxygen seemed far too thin, for one, the very fabric of the illusion fraying away and making it impossible for me to get my bearings. I was back in the courtyard of the New England-style university, but the sky was a bright red, the grass was yellow, and the brick buildings wavered in the background, unable to hold their shape.

Another critical difference: I carried weapons with me this time — a pack of stars on my back, a large knife in my hand. I ran forward toward the nearest building, and the illusion fractured further, as it had the last time. I was once again in a cold, utilitarian room, but instead of it being lined with gurneys bearing children, there were six full-grown figures who stood bathed in light beams pouring from the ceiling.

I stumbled to a stop and took a moment to simply stare.

They were beautiful.

Tall, straight, and glowing with health, the six children had turned into the kind of people that parents proudly posted on Facebook and photographed for Christmas letters. Just as in their missing persons posters, there was no indication that they'd been stolen from their parents, their friends, their homes, their planet. They were perfect and whole. Their faces untroubled, their smiles easy in their stasis.

"Amazing, aren't they?"

I whirled, but there was no one there. Still, the voice persisted in my head. I knew that voice. Viktor Dal. I didn't know how he had found me, but it didn't really surprise me. Even if he couldn't come here himself, he had to stay in communication with the demon realm.

"Had you stopped to take more stock of the artistic record of Atlantis, you would have seen this place as well, seen the Syx, immortalized on the painted dome." The voice pounded through my head, refusing to be ignored. "They are truly remarkable creatures, born of a time when magic bowed to no rules. When all that mattered was creation and growth, learning and being. You saw them, no? The creatures they were before? Surely they remain still in the bowers of Atlantis, waiting for the hand to bring them home."

I shook my head. Viktor was talking in circles. I hadn't seen the Syx in Atlantis, I'd seen the Watchers. Angels and demons who'd rushed me like the mad creatures they were, crazed with loneliness and —

I stiffened. *Loneliness*. The Watchers hadn't truly recognized me, not in any real sense. They'd raced toward me because they'd been *alone*. Abandoned for how many centuries, how many thousands of years?

And the Syx. If these were the most powerful of the Watchers, they too had suffered long for their transgressions. Suffered more, some would say, locked in this alternate dimension, waiting an eternity for someone to notice them, someone to remember.

"And for what were they punished?" breathed Viktor, his voice twisting in my heart like a sickness. But I couldn't deny the power of his words. "For being what they innately were? For being true to their selves? There is always a price to pay for that, isn't there? You learned that price early. So early. These children would have learned it too, eventually. They would have been considered outsiders. Strangers in their own families. As you were. As you always were. Is this the life you would give to them, the life you were forced to live?"

Viktor's words riveted me to the spot. In some distant point of my mind, I realized that the veil was tearing here, the pocket of safety unraveling. In another part, I felt more than saw Nikki's strong presence, and Mercault's mischievous grin and larcenous eyes. In a farther part, I saw Brody and Dixie, and farther, the shadowy presence of the Council, safe in their immortal ivory towers.

Except not all of them were immortal. Not anymore.

Focus.

I turned back to the six figures held immobilized by the streaming light. Three girls, three boys. Featureless in the way that young people were, their lives waiting to be written on their faces in deep furrows and hard angles. Their eyes were closed, their mouths slightly open, their hands outstretched and down at their sides. They looked like nothing more than yogis in the midst of meditation.

Well, it was time to give them a whole new meaning to transcendence.

"Is it worth that much to you, to see them age and be broken over and over again by life's disappointments?" Viktor persisted. "To see them bend beneath the weight of expectations the world cannot hope to fulfill? Here they have known happiness, acceptance. Here they are not considered aberrations. They could die without pain, without heartache."

"Here they are alone." I said the words, and my heart seemed to grow too large for my chest. "No one should die without knowing those who love them."

"But no one does, don't you see? Not anymore. They love what these children *were*, what they might have become. Not what they are."

Forcing Viktor's thoughts away, I moved into the center of the six children. Not children anymore — these were teenagers in body, if not mind. They would learn, though. And they would be loved. Viktor was wrong.

Taking a deep breath, I set down my weapons and reached for the first child's hand. Mary Degnan. The girl who'd really started it all for me, without knowing it. My hand penetrated the beam of light easily, and I grasped her wrist, feeling the heartbeat thump against my fingers. Pulling her hand free of the beam, I reached for the second child, Sharon Graham. Though they could easily reach each other, their hands fell limply back to their sides when I tried to link their fingers.

Worse, there was now something wrong with the hands that I'd freed. They'd...aged. The veins larger, the skin thinner. I frowned at the beams, wondering what they were made of. If I took the children out of the light, would Viktor's prediction come true? Was that what he meant by them aging too fast, getting bent and broken by the world they were reentering?

"You're going to have to make a choice, Sara Wilde. An important choice."

Viktor again. I tried to ignore him, but his voice sounded all around me like a tolling bell. "If you damage the portal as you leave it, the demons will not...cannot return here. Their prison will be in ruins."

"Yeah? Why would I want that?"

"Because I am proposing a trade. Permanent protection for the children, if you destroy this plane."

Another voice cut across my thoughts. "Something's happening, dollface. You need to hurry."

I jerked my head up. Nikki's voice had come through far more clearly than it had the last time I'd made the jump. Another modification of Blue's? Either way, the concern in her voice was clear. Viktor had been distracting me. He could be on his way to the chapel to stop me, keep me from delivering the children—or worse, his demons could take them as they finally reached earth.

That couldn't happen. It wouldn't happen.

As if reading my thoughts, Viktor's voice pounded down again. "The demons must have hosts on earth, you know this. Who better than children groomed to the task?"

"You're lying," I snapped. "The djinn don't want them. They're not strong enough."

Racing forward, I pushed through the light beam into Mary's body, sending her toppling over onto Sharon Graham. I watched with horror as their skin darkened outside of the brilliant light, but I didn't take the time to dwell on it. I couldn't. I turned and yanked Jimmy Green and Harrison Banks out of their light, and then I noticed it. Someone was screaming.

Viktor continued as if nothing was happening. "Physically, no. They would not be permanent solutions. But temporary? Of course. Until the jump to some other human—the biggest and strongest of humans—was possible. By then, granted, the children would be...quite broken. But now there is another solution. Another choice. If you would only give it to them."

The walls of the room were starting to blacken and

curl. I pulled Hayley Adams and Corey Kuznof, and they tumbled to the ground, dropping like corpses in a boneyard. *This is dignity? This is what I brought for them?* The moment the last child was out of the light, the beams winked out and the screaming grew louder. I howled for Nikki, but I couldn't hear her voice anymore. Couldn't hear anything.

"Why wouldn't you choose to save them forever?"

I was a fool to believe Viktor, a fool to believe his lies. But he didn't give me the chance to deny him. "Destroy this realm as you leave, Sara Wilde. Without the portal, the demons can remain in their own form on the earthly plane. They are not invincible there, anymore, though they do not know that yet. They will merely be strong, new blood to feed the heart of magic. Tools to be shaped as they must be for the good of all."

"Are you insane?" Everything in me rebelled at the thought of the demons remaining on earth. It was against the Council, it was against reason.

"It's the only way you'll know—for sure—that these children will be saved. A pity to bring them all the way back home, only to lose them again. To lose them *all*. Their minds already so fragile, their bodies so—"

"No!" I dropped protectively over the children as the wind picked up and roared through the room, shattering the walls beyond me and bursting them wide.

"Do it, and I will be in your debt. I acknowledge that freely."

I pulled the children's arms and hands together, clutching them close. "I'll kill you if you hurt them!"

"But you cannot." Viktor's words beat at me, inexorably. "Think about it, Sara Wilde. You have the weapons this time. Many weapons. Who gave them to you — more than you could possibly need? Ask yourself who. Then ask yourself why."

There was no longer any time to argue. Bright white light blasted beyond those walls, infernally hot. Reshouldering my pack and gripping the knife once more, I pressed myself against the children as a wave of heat roared over us. With their bodies so close together, I could wrap my own arms around theirs, like the Ten of Wands with the worker bent over his clutch of staffs.

And still the portal held. A prison that had held creatures from a time before time. Creatures like the Watchers I had seen on Atlantis. Creatures like the children now huddled beneath me. Who was to say Viktor wouldn't try this again? Who was to say that the demons wouldn't attack the Connecteds or bring them back to study, to possess, to grow even stronger while they waited?

And another voice spoke, not Viktor's, deep in my own mind. Who was to say I shouldn't do everything I could to protect these children once and for all? To do what I couldn't all those years ago?

The wind screamed over and around me, and I tucked my head down, glaring back at the room where the children had been imprisoned. It was dwindling now, peeling away. But it wasn't broken. It was holding. A prison waiting for prisoners from a dozen worlds away.

Not anymore, I thought. Not anymore.

Flipping the knife in my hand, I flung it back toward the illusion.

The portal burst outward like a supernova.

We hurtled through space, completely off course from the force of the explosion, and I whipped my head around. Nothing looked right, nothing looked familiar. There was no Möbius strip to follow along to bring me home.

Yes, I'd destroyed the portal — but I'd destroyed my own path as well! If so, I'd never be able to get the children back. Not alone. Not at all.

As we shot forward with dizzying speed, I tried to drop myself back into the trance — but I couldn't concentrate. The wind was too strong, my own panic too great. Casting my mind out, I struggled for anything to catch hold of, anything to draw us back across the twisting path, anything —

A woman's face flashed into my mind, so fiery bright that everything else paled beyond it. Mary's mother. No, not only Mary's, but the faces of all those people in the main chapel at Dixie's, those parents, men and women, young and old, their faces turning toward me as if they'd heard a far-off cry.

"Please! Please help me!" I gasped, and Mary's mother's eyes widened with a flare of power so strong, I would have sworn she was a Connected herself. She reached out all the same, toward the huddled mass of bodies beneath me, my face up, eyes squinted against the wind, my arms tight around the limp, lost souls I carried, souls that could not fight this battle on their own, souls that needed champions to fight it for them.

Their champions raced toward us now. Arms outstretched, hands grasping, and in my mind's eye, I felt a sudden surge of parental love, the desperate, rabid force of pain and guilt and loss and terror and endless waves of grief all bursting forth, becoming a beacon in the night. A beacon that not only guided me but pulled, gripping-grasping-straining, loving not what had been or could be but what still was, what truly was, and wanting it more than life itself. The force of that light ripped through the foundation of this far dimension that held the children, shattering its edges, wrenching it wide.

There would be nothing left of this place. I built that image in my mind, powering us through. Nothing left — nothing left. Never would it hold these children again, never would it hold anything. So twelve, not six souls would be freed this night; twelve, not six souls never would return.

The way home became clear despite the thunderous wind and roaring fire, and I drove my heels into the nothingness and pushed one last time —

And we were soaring then, racing again down the path that Blue had etched so clearly in my skin and mind. All the while, the beacon in the darkness far beyond was growing brighter and stronger and true. As we neared it, something else was shifting.

The burden in my arms started moving, shuddering to life, the papery-thin skin shucking off the children's bodies like waxed paper, the skin beneath bright and warm, pink and healthy. Eyes and mouths were open now, startled and frightened and panicked and alive, so alive that I reached out again and found new tethers to hold. Nikki and Mercault, Dixie and Brody, four pillars driven into the ground to catch and bring us home.

I burst back into awareness with a rush of agony excruciatingly present and real. I surged upward, fists flying, my back seared with pain.

"Sara! Sara, relax, relax — breathe!" Nikki's voice was strident, and I heard the panic in it, her fear fueling mine.

Something seriously wrong welled up inside me, my pain too heavy and whole for this to be right. I blinked my eyes open and didn't hear the clicking noise that had accompanied the movement the last time, but my vision swam with red. I kept swinging and sensed her shift away, and my fists and face and hands were wet with a hot, steaming rain.

"Jesus, Mary, and Joseph, can you never do anything the easy way?"

Suddenly, strong arms were around me, clamping my arms to my side, rendering my punches useless. Despite the agony of the pressure on my back, I smiled, feeling the strength and certainty of it. Brody. Officer Brody Rooks ten years ago, Detective Brody Rooks now. Here to save the children. Here to win the day.

I opened my mouth to thank him, to speak, but it filled with a dark and strange fluid. Not tears, I thought. Not rain either. Something…different. I sputtered and tried to swing away, but Brody held me close.

"The parents. They cannot see her." It wasn't Brody's voice but the Magician's. His tone was clipped, hard, and a moment later, his hands were over my eyes, my face, cool through the wetness, calming my thundering heart. My brain split in confusion—Brody and the Magician, both of them here, both of them…how?

Kreios's voice sounded next. "I need but a moment."

Then I heard the sound of excited shouts, questions, pounding feet, and felt my body being turned, sheltered, barricaded away from the barrage of humanity that seemed to be racing toward this room.

The children! I started, my eyes clearing as something rough and warm was wiped over my face, my neck.

"You're all right, Sara, you'll be all right."

I couldn't understand the importance, but something seemed different. Important. Strange.

Armaeus's lips brushed over my eyes, first the left, then the right.

"When this is done, find me," he whispered, and even his voice sounded wrong, thick with emotion. "It will be all right."

Then he was gone. I blinked my eyes open, and neither Kreios nor Armaeus were there. Only Nikki, Brody, and Dixie...and the children.

Nikki was at my side. "Whoa, whoa, whoa, girl, keep that towel on your eyes, EMTs will be here shortly."

I struggled to a sitting position, held firmly by Nikki as she braced me against the chapel steps. My gaze went from the blood-soaked towel in Nikki's hands to the scene in front of me, and I shrank away from the chaos for another long moment. She turned at the look on my face and cursed.

"Hang tight, cookie, it's starting again. I'll be right back."

The children half sat, half lay in the center of the room, piled against each other, their heads covered with heavy hoods. Huge blankets were wrapped around them, a deadening weight. Was that how they had been transported to the Syx's dimension? Total sensory deprivation to ensure their minds didn't shatter?

It didn't matter. Dixie and Brody were carefully stripping off hoods as EMTs rushed through the door. They took one look at me, and I waved them toward the children, dragging myself farther back in on the platform, away from the chaos of rebirth below.

As the children emerged from their hoods and blankets, they looked exactly as they had in the beams of light—in the images Viktor had shown me. Long, glossy hair, healthy skin. They seemed drugged, dazed, but they were responding to the EMTs with semicoherent sentences, blinking around owlishly. Already I could imagine Brody's cop mind swinging into action. He'd want to protect the kids, get them evaluated, but he must know that wasn't going to be possible.

My mind seemed stretched beyond its limits as I sensed the minds of the parents, all of them huddled in the main chapel. I had no need to trance to feel their power, drawing close to their bright light. Without them, their children wouldn't be here. Without them, I wouldn't have made it either. Without them, I wouldn't have seen the miracle of a parent's love in action, to know that, at its peak, it was stronger than even the most powerful of Connected magic.

My eyes filled again with a salty mix of blood and tears, but I couldn't blank my thoughts in time. In the main chapel, Mary Degnan's mother looked up, turning away from the other parents, her eyes seeing without seeing. Perhaps there was some Connected ability in her after all?

Either way, she stood, turned. And said something to the others that had them turning as well. Their shouted voices seemed to come through the very walls of the chapel, and the teenagers' reaction was swift and profound.

They literally came to life.

Cries of "Mom!" and "Dad!" burst forth like pistol shots, and a quick glance between Dixie and Brody had them all turning, an adult to each child including the EMT's, half bracing the children, half restraining them, their voices firm, urgent, and ultimately useless.

"Mary!" The first woman into the room was the tiniest, and she raced forward into the center of the teens and nearly bowled over her much taller daughter with the ferocity of her embrace. After that it was chaos, a tangle of parents and children crying, shouting, the strident voices of the EMTs ignored as reunited families alternately collapsed against each other and to the floor. There would be time for explanations later, time for Brody to come up with something—*anything* to explain where these children had been and how they were found. Time for the doctors and the therapists and the psychologists to work through the messy experience of bringing young souls back into a world that had gone on without them for far too long.

For now, there was only parents and their children, the most human of all bonds. And that was enough.

A new wellspring of pain blossomed within me as I watched the reunion. This was what I'd wanted, all those years ago. This was why I'd fought so hard and long. This was why I'd never stopped searching for the children.

Not these souls, whom I'd believed I'd already lost. But the others, so many others. Children in every corner of Europe, Connected children, taken from their families and their homes to be used in a war they knew nothing about.

I had to find them. Keep them safe. Return them to the one thing that I knew was certain, the one thing I knew was true. The one thing I'd never had myself, in the end.

The one thing.

I felt the hand on my shoulder and smiled without turning. The flare of Connected magic was strong and ancient, but not as strong as Armaeus's touch. I glanced up at Blue...and stopped, blinking away the blood and salt from my eyes.

When I could see again, the person in front of me

289

still wasn't Blue. And when he spoke, his voice was like a distant, howling wind.

"Hello, Sara," he said.

CHAPTER TWENTY-SIX

The man who stood before me wore a long, dark, almost clerical robe, frayed at the bottom. His feet were shod in heavy boots, gray with dust, and he was lean and worn. His eyes were weathered as well, a deep and faraway blue, and they watched me with an eerie knowingness, a familiarity. Though I didn't truly recognize him…I'd seen him before. I knew this man — this being.

"You were with Llyr," I said abruptly. "The figure with it beyond the veil. I saw — you were there. That was you. You and your…lamp." My attention sharpened. "You're the Hermit, aren't you?"

The Hermit of the Tarot Major Arcana was always depicted as a lone man, usually old, usually with a staff and holding his lamp high. Some say he searched for wisdom, some for an honest man, like Diogenes. But in most readings, he was the giver of wisdom, or the gateway to the arcane.

And now he stood in a Las Vegas wedding chapel, facing me with a gentle smile. "I have guarded the dragon Llyr for centuries, since it was last blasted beyond the veil," he said. "At that time, it was decided that a creature so powerful could not be left alone. I long have questioned the choice I made. Llyr is strong. I am weak." He shrugged. "And I am not always the best of guardians."

His words struck me at odd angles, but I pushed on. "Are you here to rejoin the Council, then? Balance the power?"

He shook his head. "My position allows me to stay out of such battles," he said. "I'm only here for a moment, and then I must away. Guarding Llyr requires more vigilance than ever. He grows stronger, and we do not know why."

I nodded. "Then…why have you come?"

He shrugged, looking a little abashed. "I have long watched you from a distance, Sara, bound never to contact you, never to interfere with your growth, your life. But though I understood those rules for your protection, I couldn't follow them. Not completely." His smile wavered. "I suppose once you begin to break the rules, you lose a little bit of your awe for them. And I have broken far too many over my lifetime."

I frowned at him. "What do you mean, bound not to contact me? That doesn't make any…"

Understanding struck me so forcefully that the Hermit winced, and I didn't realize I'd stumbled back until he reached out to hold me steady. The zing of his power was there as well, but I couldn't process it. It was too fresh. Too real. Too familiar.

"No. No way. You're my…?" I broke off, unable even to say the word.

His words were quiet. "My name, before I ascended, was Willem of Galt. I have been on the Council since the era you would know as the Middle Ages. I did not realize the restrictions then. I was young."

"Young, but…" Another realization. "You're, um, not young."

He lifted his brows, his expression rueful. "There have been times in my years when I have not remained on the Council. There have been times when my work has required mortality. On occasion for years at a time." He shrugged. "During those periods, I have aged. Not noticeably, at the time, but enough that, combined with the several centuries that I have walked the planes, I show my years. Some of them more than others."

I drew in a deep breath. "But if you're on the Council — how am I..." I flapped my hand between us. "Here? I kind of thought the no-kids thing wasn't an option."

He barked a laugh. "Council membership doesn't castrate us. Neither does our immortality. It's possible to procreate, merely forbidden. In my defense, I'd been buried behind that veil for far too long. It was not unreasonable for me to go exploring. Not unreasonable for me to find what I did. What and who." My head was spinning now, but the Hermit pressed on.

"Not even the Magician knew, once I'd realized the truth of what we'd done, your...mother and me. Our silence was the only way to keep you safe, let you grow as a normal child." He grimaced. "That idea was not as well executed as it could have been. We chose your caretaker poorly."

I snapped my gaze back to him. "She died trying to take care of me."

He sighed. "She died trying to be something she was not. Which I should have foreseen, and did not. Her death is my fault, Sara. Not yours. Never yours. My role in this world is to see far, and in so doing, I forget that the details of that which is close are every bit as important."

The Hermit turned and looked out across the room, but I saw what he saw, and I stared too.

The universe spread out before us in a series of

layers, each so close to the other that their inhabitants could reach out and touch, if only they could part the veil. That veil hung thickly in some places, but shone like a gossamer wing in others, and was barely more than a web in others. Beyond the veil, the dimensions glistened and beckoned with deceptive beauty — some containing horrors, and others riches untold.

"You have to manage the veil — *all* of it?" I asked, my awe unfeigned. Awe, and a little anger. "*And* guard Llyr? That doesn't sound like such a great plan."

"I have help," he said dismissively.

"So now you're…what? Taking a coffee break?" I couldn't process him as my father. I wouldn't. This old man — from the *Middle Ages* — could not possibly be who he said he was. And yet…

His next words drove the belief home more sharply. "I am here because I grew tired watching you soar to ever higher levels in your abilities, without being able to claim your birthright. I grew weary watching you suffer. I grew angry for the secrets and the lies that I must keep."

"That's why I saw you, isn't it?" I said. "That day…I saw Llyr staring at me through the veil. But it wasn't Llyr who was searching for me. It was you. It was always you." I let out a low whistle. "Does the Magician know?"

"He suspected, once you allowed him to touch your mind. But my barriers held. Now, of course, he will know. He was here when you returned. I was here as well. He saw me."

I turned back toward the reunion in the center of the chapel. "He shouldn't have come."

"No." Willem shook his head. "But he couldn't help it. And now, in his weakened state, his powers must be dedicated solely to maintaining his façade of strength, especially with the Emperor returned. If there ever was a natural challenger for leadership of the Council, it is Viktor Dal. The Magician cannot let that happen. He will sacrifice much to ensure it does not."

I nodded, then caught myself. "Wait a minute. What do you mean 'weakened'? He drank from the Norse cup. We're done with the whole weak thing, I thought."

"No." The Hermit's words were absolute. "He stopped the bleeding, you could say, by drinking from the horn of Mim. But he did not heal."

"Well, what was the freaking point—"

"He *cannot* heal himself, Sara. It is one of the drawbacks to his magic, and there are precious few of those. But the Magician is an anomaly. He exists in isolation, he learns in isolation, he performs his many works of magic in isolation. But he cannot heal himself in isolation. It is why he so rarely leaps into the thick of battle, though war was his primary purpose of being in his mortal life. He has learned over time that the battles he would fight end up costing not only him, but those around him if he becomes injured."

I recalled what Armaeus and even Blue had hinted at. "He sacrificed something, putting Llyr behind the veil a second time." I swallowed. "A woman?"

"He was betrayed. He suffered much." The Hermit straightened. "But that isn't my tale to tell."

I snapped my gaze back to him. "You're kidding me, right? You don't actually expect *Armaeus* to tell me anything worthwhile? How else am I going to know?" I grimaced as the obvious answer occurred to me. "The Devil."

"He does have his uses." The Hermit shook his head, his gaze resting on me gently again. Almost...proudly. It was strange and awkward, and I couldn't process the emotions I was feeling. I'd never really given much thought to my father. I'd never felt any connection to him, never suspected he'd ever thought of me. Now that made sense, if he spent his life behind the veil, but...

The Hermit's weathered voice cut across my thoughts. "I think you'll find that there is not much the Magician would not give you if you asked. Whether that is information or—anything else." The last words were said with an almost gruff embarrassment. "But you should warn him that he cannot let the actions of his past guide his present. There are some battles he cannot win, some he is not meant to win. His pride does not always counsel the best course."

The Hermit's head came up suddenly, a pointer called to the hunt. "I must go," he said, and there was no sadness to his tone, no dismay.

"Wait, I wanted to—"

But he was already gone. I stood, blinking into the empty space, then turned my gaze to a different horizon, focusing on the veil between the worlds. Sure enough, in the breach where the shadow met the sun, a wildly flying cape slipped out of sight, and a lantern flared to brilliance.

The aching maw of loneliness opened wide once more, but it was different this time. It had a face. A voice. A laugh.

And a name.

I rocked back on my heels, the towel forgotten in my hand.

"You brought them back."

A small woman positioned herself in front of me, her face stained with tears. She gestured imperiously behind her at the collection of people. The chaos had slowed, and it seemed at this point the parents were mainly holding on to the children, the kids finally showing signs of shock.

"You brought them back to us. You never stopped looking."

My brain bumped back online. It was Cindy Degnan pointing her finger at me, at once accusatory and triumphant. "All this time, and you never stopped."

"Not true," I said automatically, though I realized that honesty was not really required in this instance. But the acts were the facts. I dropped the towel soaked with my own blood and kicked it behind me. "I couldn't find your daughter when I first looked. I only learned of her whereabouts recently and was able to bring her home."

Her fierce stare didn't waver, and I tried again. "I did stop looking, ma'am. Maybe I would have found her sooner if I hadn't."

"No." She pushed her finger forward, pointing me in the chest. "*Here.* You never stopped looking here. All these years, you didn't give up in here. That's what brought her back." She held my gaze for a long minute. "You brought her back."

"Mom?"

The child Mary came up to her mother's side, her father holding on to her like he might never let her go again, and her mother instantly turned to her, reflexively, the wonder of hearing her daughter's voice say that word again writ large on her face. Mary grabbed her hand, then offered me a smile. "They said our memories will come back in time, that we'll— know more of what happened. But I...I somehow don't think so."

Her expression was calm and poised, and she looked at me with young-old eyes. I glanced sharply

297

from her to the other teens milling about, seeing the same expression, the same manner. They *did* know, I realized. They knew far more than they were letting on. But Kreios had been in and among them, and had already worked his particular sort of magic. They would heal. They would be whole.

"It'll take time," I said. "You should take it easy, not push it too hard."

"No pushing needed," Mary's mother said, stroking her daughter's hair. "We have you back and you will rest. And then..." Her smile faltered. "Then you will be whatever you most want to be. You have been given that chance." She looked at me again, her eyes bright with another round of unshed tears. "We've all been given that."

They turned away then, and I rubbed my hand over my eyes. I pulled it away and let out a tight sigh. No red. Apparently, I was done bleeding from the eyes for the moment. Win.

"How're you feeling, doll?" Nikki stood a few feet away from me, peering up, and I realized I still stood at the back of the wedding platform. I stooped down to bundle up the towel and brushed my hand over my shirt. I looked like I'd been rained on by Karo syrup, and my clothes were charred in spots, but hey, this was Vegas. People didn't judge.

"Better than I look, at least." I brightened. "And you weren't kidnapped this time. I'm clearly getting better at this."

She grinned. "The kids will be shipped to the hospital for observation and more tests than anyone should reasonably endure, but it's got to be done." She nodded at the door, where more official-looking medical types were crowding into the room. "Media vans are here too."

298

I blinked at her. "The media? How did they hear about it?"

"Tip from an anonymous source." Nikki rolled her eyes. "Dixie is giving a press conference as we speak. Official story is you rolled in here with the kids after you rousted them from a meat truck heading through southern Nevada. The parents had been summoned to identify the kids, but no one knew if they would be remains, live kids, or different kids entirely. You couldn't take the chance."

"Meat truck?"

She shrugged. "We didn't have a lot of time. The parents know only that they came into the room, the kids were there, you were there, and the rest they were willing to believe." She quirked her lips. "The Council helped with that."

"Armaeus." I blinked, suddenly remembering his touch, his words. "He was here." My heart seemed too big, suddenly, emotions surging up in my throat, making it difficult to breathe and impossible to speak. Armaeus *had* been here. He shouldn't have been, I knew in my bones. He should have stayed apart, separate.

But he hadn't. He'd stood by my side until I could stand alone.

"He was, yup. But not for long," Nikki said. "I got the feeling he wasn't supposed to be either. Must have had a really good reason." She winked broadly at me. "And you did look like shit. You sure you don't need medical treatment?"

I scowled, looking at the phalanx of EMTs that surrounded the children and their family, herding them toward the hospital. "No thanks." I scanned the room. "Where's Mercault and Brody?"

"Mercault left before the cops arrived, chortling

and muttering in French. Brody coordinated the truck, the crime scene guys, the works."

I stared at her. "You guys actually found a truck?"

"Kreios sent it along with his compliments. Driver drugged and tied up in the back with a convincing story of how he was hijacked outside of Albuquerque, doesn't remember anything since then. Hot dogs and deli meats all around, and enough DNA to keep everyone busy for weeks."

"And Viktor? If Kreios and Armaeus are here, he could be too, right?" and the other shoe fell. "Oh God. Where are the djinn?"

"Up until about an hour ago, they were cruising the Strip, drunk off their asses," Nikki said. "We had tails on them from the Connected community — at a fair distance, though. Six guys that size, everyone stays clear. Viktor's dressed them like shit-kicker bikers, which tells you a little about ol' Viktor, but the look is apparently a good one."

She fished out her phone and thumbed it on, tilting the screen to me. I couldn't see all the djinn, but three of the preternaturally fierce men were leaning over a craps table, dwarfing it with their bodies. They wore jeans and various shades of T-shirts — black, gray, grayer — and tats swirled at their neck and biceps. Their hair was long, their faces were hard. I didn't remember exactly what they'd looked like before but...

"They've changed."

"Yep. They're a tiny bit shorter, and their skin's no longer tinged red. That's what's throwing you off. Whether they're acclimating to the atmosphere here or playing chameleon, they definitely look more like the home team. Still all dudes, though. I thought maybe we'd get a woman in the mix."

"It's their size. Tough enough to pull off seven foot

plus as a dude."

"True." She shrugged. "And according to Kreios, they can change form as needed, but not size so much."

"And that's what they did an hour ago? Changed form?"

"Nope. They split. They all got the internal memo at the same time and headed for the doors. Not disappearing as in poof, but they beat it."

"To go where?"

"No clue." She shook her head. "When they cleared the crowds of the casinos, they picked up pace." She scrolled forward a few images and held her phone out to me. "Check this out."

The small triangle indicated a video, and the shaky cam view of a cell phone camera blinked to life. Three men, visible above a sea of humanity, trotted down the stairs of the Bellagio. They hit the open space of the concrete sidewalk and —

I blinked. "Where'd they go?"

"They ran. The woman I had on them was babbling so incoherently, I couldn't make out much, but they split with Superman speed. Not disappearing altogether — if you replay the video, you see that — but moving quickly enough that they were a blur. The woman didn't know where to look."

"And we think they're here? In town?"

"We do," she nodded. "Blue seems to think you blew up the portal, by the way, rendering it impossible for them to return. That...changes everything, apparently."

I didn't trust myself to comment much on that. "Huh. That's strange."

"Yeah, strange." Nikki slanted me a glance. "She's not too happy that nothing is going right every time she sends you somewhere."

"Well, she should try being the one who comes back with her eyes bleeding." I pursed my lips, considering. "But if the demons were running...where were they running to? Where would they go to hide?"

Nikki closed her eyes and seemed to disappear into herself for a moment, then she came back to herself. "Where else?" she asked, showing me the screen again. "You up for a field trip?"

I grinned. "Let me get my pack."

CHAPTER TWENTY-SEVEN

Binion's Casino on Fremont Street looked pretty good, considering the explosion that had torn through its guts about a month earlier.

With the generous underwriting of the Council, the public portion of the casino had been put to rights with remarkable speed, but the closer we got to the back of the casino, closer to where the late Jerry Fitz's domain stood, the more obvious the patchwork became, at least to Connected eyes.

"They went through here," Nikki said and pushed through a door that I hadn't seen before she pointed it out. "Basement access."

I eyed her. "And you know that how? You saw it?"

She shrugged. "Not the usual way. My abilities require a person to be present unless I've known them long enough to imprint upon them. I'm not quite that chummy with the djinn, not all of them. And frankly, what I got to know of Warrick pretty much overrode my mental wiring. I was too freaked out to separate illusion from reality."

We paused in the gloom of the long staircase. It wasn't completely dark. Red incandescent lights lined the staircase at regular intervals, beckoning us downward. "Yet you saw him come in here?"

"He…" She hesitated. "He wanted to see if the possession would take. I didn't have a choice about it.

He took over my mind just like that, and I..." She scowled. "I felt him inside me. And not in any of the usual places. It was more than a little unsettling. And then he was gone, I could breathe again, all was well in the world. But it was like he left a kind of calling card. I figured he did that so he could find me, but the reverse is also true. I can see him. I can't see what he thinks, but I can see what he sees."

I looked at her. "That could get dicey in a hurry."

"Child, there are some things you don't want dancing in front of your retinas. And that's all I'll say about that. But the upshot is: I know he's here. They all are. I lost track of him at the bottom of this staircase, though. Must be warded."

"By who?" I frowned as we headed downstairs. "The only people who've been down here have been with Techzilla, Inc. onsite to salvage their electronics and take inventory. SANCTUS wasn't exactly lining up to take responsibility for the blast that leveled this place." Sudden realization dawned. "You don't think Viktor was bankrolling this operation?"

"Could be." Nikki broke off as we reached the bottom of the stairs. "This is interesting." She pointed up at a box near the ceiling. It boasted a steady incandescent glow from a bulb directly above it, but it was definitely more than a night-light. A steady digital readout streamed numbers across its surface.

"Security device?"

She nodded. "Has to be, but what are they securing?" She waved her hand in front of the unit, but nothing sounded, nothing moved. "Techzilla equipment, though, no doubt. Which puts them in a lot of interesting places where the dark practitioners are. I wouldn't have thought of them as that buddy-buddy with the human traffickers and drug-pusher types, but there's no accounting for taste these days."

We crept forward and rounded the corner. No lights went off, no alarms. As we made our way deeper into the underground lair, there was no sound at all, actually, except...bickering.

"How many times did I tell you to reread the contracts?" The first voice was harsh and guttural, and exasperated. "Of all people, Viktor Dal would have enemies he would sell us out to the first chance he gets. It's how he works. You know that."

"You weren't talking contracts when you were begging us to agree to his terms." Nikki stiffened beside me. The voice was aristocratic, haughty, but that didn't take away from its sense of menace. Warrick. "You were willing to possess those weak Connecteds to get out of that prison. That would have been far worse. Then we would have been killed."

"And this is better?" A third voice accompanied the clanging of bars that reverberated through the room. "Summoned here like dogs, to be handed off to some bastard Viktor's in hock to."

"It's a woman, if you were paying attention. I researched her." A fourth voice, supremely bored. "She won't be stupid enough to come here herself. She'll send others. We kill them, we're home free."

"From behind bars?" the third voice railed back.

A deep, resonant bass voice joined the fray. "Well, if we don't, we go from being mercenaries to indentured servants again. That appeal to you?"

Another argument erupted. Nikki and I exchanged looks, and her grin was broad. "God, I love my life," she breathed.

"Annika Soo?" I whispered.

She nodded. "Has to be. No one else has the power, and this has her MO written all over it. Sending some stooge to do her dirty work for her, and collar the djinn as her personal slaves? Could explain why she's cozying up to SANCTUS. They're sort of in the business of managing demons. Maybe she decided she needed reinforcements."

We peeked around the corner. The djinn were held in separate cages, the same cages that the previous owner of this hellhole had used to suspend dancers high above the central stage. I hadn't realized those had been magic-deadening containers. There was a lot I hadn't realized a few short weeks ago.

"So what do we do?" Nikki asked loudly after we pulled back. "Let 'em go? That seems like it'd cost someone."

We stepped into the room, and the djinn fell silent. We could only get three steps in before the magic hit us. "Wards, and strong ones," I muttered. "I can't get through that."

From far up the corridor, the sound of many footfalls flooded down the stairs, and Nikki and I both stiffened as the lights winked out.

"So we can't get in there," she said. "Which means what—we fight the bad guys ourselves?"

I shrugged, feeling the collective stare of the Syx. "We could. There'd need to be some money in it, though. Or aid down the road."

"No more deals," growled the tallest demon.

Warrick waved him down. "We will grant you six requests," he said gruffly. "Six, one for each of our souls. And no more."

I nodded. "Done."

We didn't have time to work out the finer details as the march of footsteps got closer. "Son of a bitch," Nikki murmured as the demons fell silent behind us. "How many do you figure? Ten?"

"Twelve, I'd bet. It'll take two to carry each of them after—"

The sound screeched through the air and buffeted the cages, loud enough to make our bones ache. I knew that trick, of course—a brutal tonal frequency targeted specifically to cripple psychics—but I'd built up a tolerance to it. So had Nikki. We struggled against it, and a second later, it was done.

Unfortunately, so were the djinn. Six heaps of muscle and sinew lay on the floor. They were knocked out before they'd landed their first punch. It might as well have been a UFC match.

The wards had dropped too—but we were still standing. That could only mean good things. I yanked four Atlantean stars from my pack, handing two to Nikki. "It's all I got."

"Stupid Brody and his stupid gun safety issues," she muttered, but she took the blades. She turned and brandished her weapons.

The men who flowed into the space were prepared for hauling giant hulks and maybe a spatter of gunfire. They were not prepared for Nikki Dawes armed with throwing stars. Few people were.

That said, the problem with blades intended to be thrown is that if you use them, you lose them. Surprise was our only tactical advantage.

We waited until the men pounded into the room, sticking to the shadows. The first man worked a device on his wrist, and, despite the dim light, I could see the insignia on it. SANCTUS. They were deeper in the know than I would have given them credit for. The moment he turned to his captain to indicate the wards were down, we struck.

The men turned instantly at the sound of us rushing forward, but surprise was on our side.

307

Surprise, and otherworldly weapons. Which didn't hurt.

With the amped-up energy of the Atlantean stars, my arms practically rotated out of their sockets in wild arcs as we dove into the center of the men. They didn't fire their weapons, as we had them in a tight circle — the likelihood of them hitting each other was too great. Instead, they engaged us in hand-to-hand combat, and we lost ourselves in the sound of crunching bones and splitting skin. Nikki was an accomplished fighter and I wasn't bad, but this wasn't about us, I could tell in an instant.

The edges of the world shimmered, and I felt the stare of eyes on us, the eyes of the Watchers trapped in Atlantis. If they recognized the Syx crumpled in the chambers beyond, I couldn't tell. I was moving too quickly, the blood lust on me so hard and sure that I could only pray I was incapacitating, not killing, as I punched and sliced and swung. Eventually, only Nikki and I stood there, our lungs heaving, our hands and forearms covered with blood. She poked her knife into the space before the cages. Nothing blocked us.

"We need to get these guys out of here, before Viktor comes to re-collect them," I managed. "We can't carry these guys ourselves, though."

"You're not carrying them at all." She shook her head. "I'll call Brody for this job. Surely he can find the best and biggest of the boys in blue to help a girl out. Besides," she grinned. "I want to be there when Warrick here wakes up and realizes that he owes me large. There's just something poetic about kicking a demon when he's down. So get out of here."

She grinned at me as I frowned, confused, and tapped her head. "You forget, I can see what you see, dollface. You're worried about Armaeus. Go."

I went.

CHAPTER TWENTY-EIGHT

After a brief stop at the Palazzo to wash off the evidence of my interstellar roller derby and follow-up demon defense, I kept my mind carefully shielded on the way to Prime Luxe as I tried to work out what to do when I saw the Magician again. Unfortunately, I still didn't have a clue by the time I punched the elevator button for the ride up to Armaeus's domain. Oh well.

The elevator doors opened with a soft whoosh into the Magician's office, the acre of cool carpeting flowing out before me with familiar welcome. Armaeus was sitting at his desk, but no computer blinked in front of him, no stacks of printouts detailing the state of the Connected world. The desk was empty save for the horn of Mim, and as Armaeus lifted his head to watch me enter, I realized that his hands were cupped before him. He'd been praying. Or meditating. Or holding his head in his hands.

None of those sounded very good.

He watched me approach without getting up, his enormous desk serving as a physical barrier between us. One, I realized with sudden dismay, he needed more than I did.

"Why are you here?" he asked, and his voice was rough, too rough. He seemed to notice it and paused before speaking again. "You're not hurt."

I winced. "I'm allowed to visit you without having the crap beat out of me, you know."

"True." He sat back, watching me approach. "But you don't."

"Well, maybe I want to change that." Okay, I didn't have to make a production of this. How many times had he healed me—completely? This was the same thing, only in reverse. It didn't need to be a big deal. It simply needed to happen.

I stopped at the collection of couches and chairs in front of his desk and pulled out my remaining stars. I laid them carefully on the couch. Then I pulled off my hoodie.

"Miss Wilde."

"Don't mind me." I hadn't planned for a striptease, but I could feel Armaeus's attention sharpen as I leaned over and unbuckled first one boot, then the other. I sat on the edge of the chair and worked the things off, letting my gaze lift up to meet his.

He was gripping the edge of the desk.

Okay, maybe it could be a little bit of a big deal. "You doing anything this afternoon?"

"What exactly is your intention here?"

"Oh, I don't know." I grabbed the end of my tank top and pulled it over my head. The cool air-conditioning of his suite pebbled my skin, and I shivered a little as I stood, working the clasp out of my ponytail so my hair fell down around my shoulders. All the while, I kept my gaze on Armaeus's face.

My technique wasn't going to get me fast-tracked to any Vegas stage, but it seemed to have the desired effect. Armaeus stood, shoving his chair back as I reached for my pants.

In three quick strides, he was in front of me, his hand gripping my arm to stop me. I shivered at the jolt of electricity that fired from his fingers.

"Why are you doing this?" he gritted out.

"Because I can." I lifted my left hand to his face, drifting it along the deeply bronzed skin of his cheek. He closed his eyes briefly, as if steadying himself, and a new, curious thrill danced through me. "Because I want to."

Armaeus released a tight sigh, but before he could speak, I lifted up on my toes to brush his lips with mine. He froze, and I pressed closer, twining my hand behind his neck to anchor myself against his body. His left hand slipped around me to palm my lower back. He pulled his own head up and away. His eyes glittered dangerously.

"You're doing this to heal me," he said. His words brooked no opposition. "It is a dangerous attempt."

"Not so dangerous right now," I said. I shook off his hand. "It actually feels pretty good."

And it did. All my latent fear and panic, emotions that should be there, must be there, had been replaced by an ache so strong, it seemed to erupt from my very bones—a simple, pure ache of needing. Of wanting. I lifted my hands to either side of Armaeus's face, reveling in his broken groan as I kissed him again, more firmly this time.

He felt perfect, true, and as he surrendered to the kiss, he surrounded me with a web of magic that seemed etched into the very air. My third eye opened, and once again I saw the world as I had before under his guidance, myriad streams of light overlaying each other, each vibrating with deep and primal power.

And in the center of all that power and light...was simply us.

Armaeus deepened the kiss, his tongue pressing into my lips, forcing my mouth open in a sensual assault, and then pressing further, the intrusion driving a bolt of need straight through me.

At its urgency, a hint of old panic surged up — and disappeared like smoke. There was no fear, no hesitation. I half sobbed against his mouth, and he seemed to touch everything at once, and I realized he was inside my mind again. Suddenly, there were no secrets between us, no barriers needed. He flooded my thoughts with every essence of himself — and I let him in fully. Completely. He must have realized the moment that the last of my barriers fell away, because he drew in a deep and shuddery breath. His eyes glowed with an internal fire as he drew back to look at me.

"It's begun," he said roughly, wonder in his expression. "The healing."

"See, that wasn't so hard."

Desire warred with concern in his gaze, and I shook my head. "You told me that when I wanted this, truly wanted it, you would be here for me. I do want this, Armaeus. I want it more than anything."

Without speaking, he reached to the strap of my bra, drawing it over my shoulder and watching its trajectory as if he'd never undressed a woman before. When it had slipped low enough that the bra fell away from my breast, he murmured something else, a word I didn't know.

I blinked. All my clothes were gone. So were his. "Well, that was efficient."

Armaeus pulled me against him, and I braced myself against his arms. They were trembling with exertion.

"I cannot turn back from this," he gritted out. "Not from this, Sara. I can't. The path goes but one way."

Something about his words nagged at me. They

sounded too profound, almost ritualistic. But the Magician's abilities were deeply rooted in the almost mystical power of sex, and I was inclined to cut him a break this time.

"I don't want to stop, Armaeus," I said. And I didn't. Not now. Not with his arms around me and his body heavy against mine.

He bent his head to my breasts, and I arced beneath him, willing my brain not to explode. Magic coursed and flowed over and around us as he brushed his lips over the curve of my right breast, his hand capturing the other as I gasped. My cerebral cortex lit up like the Fourth of July at the dual assault on my system. With a strength I didn't know I had, I planted my hands on his chest and pushed him back.

Whether out of surprise or because he was simply humoring me, Armaeus fell away easily, and I pursued him as he toppled to the floor. I sprawled over his thick chest, which was scored with scars, and slid over his knotted abs. My gaze dropped farther, and I couldn't stop, didn't want to stop. I reached down and took his shaft in my hand, reveling in a surge of primal power as he hissed. The kinetic energy between us was almost electric, and I had no interest in how perfect or powerful or pure the act of making love with the Magician was supposed to be. I just wanted to be in the middle of it already.

"No. you should—" Ignoring whatever warning he was going to sling at me, I levered my body up and sank down on top of him.

I couldn't hear the rest of his sentence because my brain was blowing apart.

A sense of completion so strong it nearly consumed me roared into my consciousness, the feeling that *this* was what I was made for, *this* was the answer I sought.

With that realization came a wave of such unexpectedly knee-knocking fear that I was caught up short. *What am I doing, what am I thinking?* Why was Armaeus here, with me, and why had I feared him so much? There had been a reason — what was it?

Directly on that surge of panic came another need, one more primal and, if possible, yet more desperate, made up purely of Armaeus and me, and the connection we were forming. A bridge of a million jolts of energy that were so much greater than anything I could have imagined. It was as if my body was no longer mine but a conduit between the ancient magic of the rioting ley lines beneath us and the magic of every Connected on earth around us, to the latent magic that was hidden in the stars above us, dimension on dimension, layer upon layer, bone upon skin upon breath upon soul.

"Sara," Armaeus cried out, and I held on as he surged up, burying himself in me more deeply, my body bucking as it stretched and writhed in reaction to the unexpected pressure, the pleasure-pain of an act that had no connection to anything that had come before it, nor to anything that would come after. I pitched forward, bracing myself on his chest, and was mesmerized by his face as his hands came up to anchor themselves on my shoulders, the two of us moving in perfect synchrony, as the pressure within us built to a raging crescendo. I saw Armaeus's awareness of how close he was to the brink hit him, and as he tried to shift away, I pursued him, pressing down over him as my mouth found his again.

"Kiss me, Armaeus," I said, my lips an inch from his. "I want to feel your mouth on me till the end."

With a guttural growl, he moved his hand from my shoulder to cup it around my head and pulled me close, his mouth trapping mine as he pinned me against his body. I felt my own climax build inside me at the simple touch of his kiss, felt his palm splayed on my backside as if he thought I could escape, as if he thought I could do anything but ride through this storm of electricity and emotion and need.

With white-hot chaos, the wave crested, and Armaeus bucked beneath me, his head falling back as his entire body seemed to explode from the inside out, every molecule separating and snapping back in the same moment, the human equivalent of the Big Bang. Except an entire universe hadn't shattered — only mine.

I collapsed forward, lungs heaving as he slowly brought his gaze back to mine. The naked vulnerability in his eyes caught me up short, and in those eyes there was so much pain and emotion and loss that I couldn't help but stare, couldn't help but bring my hand to his face, to comfort when I had no idea what I was comforting for.

The touch of my hand seemed to recall him, and he shifted his body to lie beside mine on the plushly carpeted floor. He sighed, pulling away from me to rest his forehead against mine. What would normally be a simple gesture, almost a respite, had the opposite effect for me.

Because my third eye was open.

And I *saw* him.

A fiery cataclysm opened up before me, screams of terror in the night, and Armaeus was there, running, searching, screaming for someone who would not answer, could not answer. They were dead, he knew they were dead, there was nothing he could do about it, and —

Armaeus chose that second to pull away, and I shifted my gaze off to the side so he couldn't see the well of reflected sorrow that had opened within me. I didn't know when or where he'd experienced that pain. He'd looked the same age as he did now. But the fire had been everywhere, and everywhere had been death, destruction...and madness. Utter madness.

How much did I truly know about the Magician and the decisions he'd made? The lives he'd touched...or taken? And those who'd been taken from him? Further, I realized that, though I knew I'd dropped my own barriers, Armaeus didn't realize I'd glimpsed into his past. He didn't know I'd sampled a portion of his pain.

For now, I needed to keep it that way.

I closed my eyes and steadied myself. "You have to return to your immortal self, Armaeus. You're healed."

"I am definitely that." He sighed in contentment, and I felt a surge of protectiveness for this impossibly strong being who...for the moment...was a man. Simply a man. Lying here on the floor, a cocoon of safety surrounding us. As I watched him, though, he shrugged. "There is yet time."

I looked from him to the Nordic cup still prominently displayed on his desk. "But why wait? You are stronger as an immortal, and a full member of the Council. You need that strength." I thought of what the Hermit had said, his patent concern for Armaeus. "You need it now more than ever."

"Yet as an immortal, I cannot do this." He reached out one arm and gathered me close, the immense strength of him seeming to block out all other considerations. "I cannot do this." He drifted a kiss on my hair, and I felt the stirrings of want again, of need.

"Not true. You kissed me plenty before today," I managed, trying to block out the torrent of loss, of pain that I'd seen trapped within him. All this time, he had been determined to learn more about me, and I'd not given any thought to learning about him. Arguably, I'd been busy. But what were the secrets that Armaeus Bertrand was hiding from me? What paths had he walked that he didn't want me to know about, let alone share? What decisions had he made?

And was the *real* reason of my fear of him truly that he was immortal...or was it something different? Something that being immortal allowed him to do, that he couldn't do when he was mortal? Kreios had said as much, but he'd explained without explaining, leaving me wanting more.

A small measure of the fear I'd come to dread crept back into my heart. Armaeus was dangerous to me, but not in the way I'd thought he was. As a mortal, he was safe...as a full Council member, rich in his immortality, he could do things that could harm me, could transform me, could destroy me.

Why did I want that suddenly, so badly? When I knew that I would blank with fear once he returned to his immortal state?

"I'll be leaving soon," he said, interrupting my racing thoughts. He was watching me, and I carefully shuttered my mind again. His brows lifted. "You don't need to hide your reactions from me."

I gave him a winning smile. *Oh, yes I do.* "Where are you going?"

"With Viktor returned to the fold, I am reminded of the need to reclaim *all* the members of the Council. Especially those who do not wish to be reclaimed. Viktor is dark, and there is light that is needed on the Council. Light that has been sorely missed for too long."

I frowned at him. "Who's left?" I ran through the Council members in my mind. Of the twenty-one

Arcana, not all were directly translatable to human forms, I was certain. The Star and the Moon, for instance, didn't have a clear mortal incarnation.

So I started with the obvious choices. "Temperance, Justice—maybe. The Hierophant, Lovers..." I stared at him. "You're getting the Lovers? Because that'd be two for the price of one, right?"

Laughter rumbled in Armaeus's chest. "I do not seek the Lovers. Theirs is a twisted path." He fell silent again, and I poked him in the chest. He opened one eye.

"So, who?"

"It can wait, Miss Wilde." He turned over onto his back, pulling me close, so close I couldn't hear his words too well. When I lifted my head, he grumbled. I pounded his arm. "Who?" I demanded again.

"The Hierophant," he said, pulling me close again.

I considered that. "The Hierophant. As in the pope. But not actually the pope, pope, right? Because he's seriously old. And sort of busy."

Armaeus propped one arm behind his head, impossibly gorgeous, impossibly content. "Not the pope, no. The being I seek is far older than that."

My eyes went wide. "Who?" I searched my internal Google for Connected: Ancient History Division. "Old, religious, orthodoxy, tradition, not a pope..." My eyes bugged. "Don't tell me you're going after Solomon."

He smiled, and it was a thing of beauty. I'd never seen the Magician so relaxed, and something shifted in my chest. *This.* I wanted *this.* Someone to talk to, someone to hold me. Someone to share the day's conversation with, when all the bluster and fury had passed.

Someone to stop playing twenty questions.

"Not Solomon." Armaeus shook his head. "But

you're getting closer, in a manner of speaking."

"You really suck at this." I propped my elbows on his chest and stared at him, hard. He gazed back at me, completely unfazed. "Okay, so he's biblical. Moses."

"No."

"Isaac. Abraham."

"No and no."

"God."

He narrowed his eyes at me, and I waved off his censure. "Kidding." I shook my head. "I give. Who?"

"If I tell you, will you give in to your body's demand for sleep?"

"I'm not—" As I said the words, the wave of drowsiness spilled over me, an overfilled cup of sleepy. I shoved at his arm. "I can tell you're doing that, you know. You're not sneaky."

He sighed expressively. "One can but live in hope."

"Fine. Tell me who it is, and I'll let you sleep."

"Good." He laid his head back and closed his eyes. The darkness encroached further, a comforting hug, and I gave up trying to fight it. I was tired, and tomorrow was another day. The Magician would be leaving soon, he said, and the way he talked, he was going alone.

I'd almost fallen completely under when I realized I still didn't have the information I'd asked for. "Who, Armaeus?" I prodded.

He grumbled in his sleep, then almost sighed the words. "He is most commonly known as Michael."

His words hit me square in the face. I popped up like a cork in the ocean and stared at him, goggle-eyed. "Um…as in the *archangel* Michael? You're serious? He's really a *thing*?"

"Yes, Miss Wilde, he's really a thing," the Magician said. His eyes flickered open, fixing me once more with

320

their gold-and-black gaze, glittering with a twist of grim amusement. His lips quirked into an enigmatic smile. "But it's going to be Hell to find him."

— Available May, 2016 —

WICKED AND WILDE

Hell hath no fury...

Tarot reader Sara Wilde has spent her whole life finding
the lost with the use of her trusty cards — from missing
kids to shifty criminals to ancient, arcane artifacts. But
when her newest assignment sends her straight to Hell,
she discovers more than she bargained for.

The journey through Dante's playground forces Sara to
endure a client's bitter loss, fall victim to a vicious
betrayal by her own kind, and come face-to-face with
the woman she might have been--a soul capable of
heartless brutality. Not even Sara's blossoming love for
the darkly sensual Magician is safe in the underworld.
She's tested in ways she never fathomed, ways that
could drive her mad or utterly destroy her.

But time waits for no artifact hunter. Back in Vegas, the
war on magic takes a fatal turn, with the worst of the
dark practitioners focusing on all Sara holds dear. If she
doesn't escape the bonds of the underworld, scores of
psychics will die. To flee Hell for good, however, the final
sacrifice Sara must make may be more than she can bear.

Nothing's ever easy when you're *Wicked And Wilde*.

A NOTE FROM JENN

The cards that appear at the opening of Born To Be Wilde help Sara navigate her first assignment of the book. Their general interpretations are below – but if you find yourself in a castle looking for treasure, be sure to consider the symbols of the cards themselves, not just their more abstract meanings. Sometimes a cup…really is a cup!

The Star

As Trump 17 of the Major Arcana, the Star is one of the most hopeful cards in the deck. Symbolizing balance, harmony and all things associated with Aquarius, it's both the card of peace, compassion and of having your dreams come true. New opportunities abound for you and you attain your highest potential. In matters of romance, you follow your heart and your intuition and will not be led astray. In matters of creativity, you are on the right track to receive the inspiration you need to lead to profound success.

The Seven of Swords

The Seven of Swords can mean different things in different situations, but is always a card to note - particularly if you are in the midst of a difficult conversation or a negotiation. As the nimble, sly trickster scoops of swords and steals away in the night, we are reminded of the dual-edged nature of the card. It can mean trickery, deceit or wrongful actions (either on the part of the querent or against the querent) - but it can also mean quick thinking, new strategies, or brash thinking to save the day.

324

The Ace of Cups

The Ace of Cups is a card of joy and abundance overflowing the heart. It could mean the onset of a new love affair – or, if you are already committed, the renewal of your relationship. Everything is fresh and new (as with all access) and the card recalls the Holy Grail – symbolizing the great quest of your heart or your life. By going with the flow and following your heart, you reach the greatest level of success, and both your work and your creative pursuits are fulfilling.

ACKNOWLEDGMENTS

Born To Be Wilde would not have been possible without amazing readers, who asked for another book in the series by sharing the story of Immortal Vegas with their friends and encouraging sales and reviews. Thank you for letting me continue to tell these stories! My gratitude as well goes to Elizabeth Bemis for your unwavering friendship, as well as for your mad book formatting and web design skills. Sincere thanks also to Gene Mollica for the photography and cover design/illustration for Born To Be Wilde, and to Linda Ingmanson and Toni Lee for both detailed and intensely valuable editing skills. Any mistakes in the manuscript are, of course, my own. Kristine Krantz, your extraordinary critiquing skills helped improve the story dramatically, and Rachel Grant, your early read and enthusiasm helped me believe this book might become what I hoped it would. Thank you as well to Dana, Jen and Nell. You will never, ever know how wonderful you are (but you are!) Finally, as always, to Geoffrey — thank you for your vision, insight and guidance, every step of the way. It's been a *Wilde* ride.

ABOUT JENN STARK

Jenn Stark is an award-winning author of paranormal romance and urban fantasy. She lives and writes in Ohio. . . and she definitely loves to write. In addition to her new "Immortal Vegas" urban fantasy series, she is also author Jennifer McGowan, whose Maids of Honor series of Young Adult Elizabethan spy romances are published by Simon & Schuster, and author Jennifer Chance, whose Rule Breakers series of New Adult contemporary romances are published by Random House/LoveSwept and whose new modern royals series, Gowns & Crowns, is now available.

You can find her online at **www.jennstark.com,** follow her on Twitter @jennstark, and visit her on Facebook at **www.facebook.com/authorjennstark**.

ALSO BY JENN STARK

One Wilde Night (Novella)

Getting Wilde

Wilde Card

Made in the USA
Monee, IL
06 July 2020

35884952R00184